BELOW THE LINE

ALSO BY HOWARD MICHAEL GOULD

Last Looks

BELOW THE LINE

A Charlie Waldo Novel

Howard Michael Gould

DUTTON

DUTTON

An imprint of Penguin Random House LLC
penguinrandomhouse.com

Copyright © 2019 by Howard Michael Gould

LIBRARY OF CONGRESS CATALOGING-IN-PUBLICATION DATA
Names: Gould, Howard Michael, author.
Title: Below the line: a Charlie Waldo novel / Howard Michael Gould.
Description: New York: Dutton, [2019] | Series: A Charlie Waldo novel; 2
Identifiers: LCCN 2018036617 (print) | LCCN 2018037673 (ebook) |
ISBN 9781524744885 (ebook) | ISBN 9781524744861 (hc)
Subjects: | GSAFD: Mystery fiction.
Classification: LCC PS3607.O8847 (ebook) | LCC PS3607.O8847 B45 2019 (print)
| DDC 813/.6—dc23
LC record available at https://lccn.loc.gov/2018036617

Printed in the United States of America
1   3   5   7   9   10   8   6   4   2

For Mom and Laurie,
with an appreciation that grows every year

BELOW THE LINE

ONE

It was a lone pearly strand in a rich ocean of sable, one in a hundred thousand, dazzling in the early gleam and his favorite the instant he saw it. It was a bounty, this white hair; it was dimension; it was the new her, the new *them*, a token of the hell they'd been through and the hell they'd put each other through and, most of all, the unexpected glory of having somehow found their way back.

She'd hate it, of course, if she knew it was there. She'd have plucked it by now, and no doubt have started a conversation with her stylist about whether it was time to start coloring. So it must have kept itself a secret, this singleton, hiding behind the ones sprouting closer to the crown, betrayed this morning only by the random splay of her thick mane on the pillow, and only to Waldo. Which would make her hate it even more: she'd rather die than show weakness, to him or to anyone. In fact, but a month ago he had believed she'd made that very choice, only to learn that she'd faked her death by propping a finagled corpse behind the wheel of her sort of husband's sort of borrowed Porsche under a Santa

Clarita overpass, then dousing car and cadaver in gasoline and setting them both ablaze—and doing it all, Waldo was willing to bet, in the usual killer stilettos.

She'd also hate his knowing because, while she treated unabridged knowledge of everything about Waldo as something like a prerogative, she herself was furtive in countless ways and expected him to accept that. Which he did. But here the first late-spring daylight was peeking through the slats of her plantation shutters and revealing a secret about her very body, a bulletin that he'd read and she hadn't, which he cherished and she wouldn't. All of that made Lorena Nascimento's first white hair in this moment the sexiest thing about her, and, Lord Almighty, that was saying something.

He pressed against her backside, testing how deeply she slept. Not deeply enough, he was pleased to find; she reached back for him and shifted to make herself available, liking it this way early in the morning, and raised her head just enough to let him slip an arm under her neck. As he crushed his lips to the locks against her nape she let out a sleepy purr, all the more fetching in her unawareness of what it was he was worshipping so.

His natural inclination to rise early reinforced by the habits of three years in the woods, Waldo knew he wouldn't fall back asleep. He listened to Lorena's breathing slow and deepen, one more little pleasure he hadn't realized how much he'd missed. Goddamn, he thought, it was good to be back with her, but goddamn, it was complicated, navigating the orthodoxies he'd adopted since the last time.

The past month, in fact, seemed like nothing but sex and

negotiation. It was hard even to find a place to spend a night to-gether; uncomfortable as he felt at her house, it was still, when she had it to herself, their least bad option. In his tiny cabin there'd be no sleeping space for her unless she took his loft, leaving him to curl up on the floor between the sink and the desk. One time they tried a hotel in Idyllwild but its shower alone overwhelmed his zero-footprint sensibility with its casual outrages, from the non-low-flow head to the tiny plastic bottles of shampoo and condi-tioner and body wash and lotion; the very thought of the megajoules required to manufacture each, just to give some tourist a single partial use before a chambermaid tossed the bottle and remaining contents into a garbage can on the way to a landfill where the left-overs would seep into the groundwater and the container could take centuries to degrade, led Waldo to dry quickly and scurry from the bathroom. He threw on his clothes while Lorena watched from the downy bed in a gauzy postcoital torpor, nonplussed but indulgent, almost amused. He biked to his cabin to sleep, then rode the few miles back to see her in the morning.

Trying to blend their lives, even a little, presented bottomless challenges. One day, flush in physical love, Lorena had presented him with a light purple Hugo Boss dress shirt made of Italian cot-ton. She didn't mean it as a challenge to his Hundred Things—she'd figured he could replace one of his two work shirts, or maybe choose another possession to shed when he got back to his cabin—but it threw him into a spin nonetheless; the whole point was that the Hundred were painstakingly selected, that nothing *was* easy to discard, that there'd never be *room* for a possession so frivolous, and they'd quarreled.

They'd also quarreled over frying pans. Waldo had set out to scramble some eggs on his first morning in her house, only to discover that, oddly, there wasn't a single skillet in the otherwise fully appointed kitchen. When Lorena brought home a two-piece Calphalon set from Williams-Sonoma that afternoon, Waldo felt she should get rid of a Thing—or, better, two—to offset the purchase. She argued that the Things were *his* rule, not hers, and that she could have as many possessions as she cared to. But this Thing was for *his* use, he countered, and therefore a de facto cheat of his Hundred. She must have found something appealing underneath his scolding, because she reached into his pants, tabling the debate.

Now Waldo remembered one Thing Lorena *did* have, which predated him and was thus devoid of moral complication: a top-of-the-line Omega masticating juicer, which sat waiting in the kitchen for him and for the oranges he'd bought at the L.A. Farmers Market the evening before. He sat up, poked a toe under the bed and found his boxers. Sliding them on, he watched the gentle rise and fall of the sheet atop Lorena and marveled for the thousandth time at how everything had turned out. There was no woman like her, and they were each other's again.

He slipped out of the bedroom and headed toward the kitchen. Yes, there were squabbles over shirts and kitchenware, but these were a lot less taxing than the bloodier skirmishes of the old days, over things like fidelity and jealousy and commitment. So while you couldn't quite call it easy, this Lorena & Waldo 2.0, it was definitely easi*er.*

These cheery thoughts were interrupted by the appearance of an unexpected penis.

It was attached to Willem Vander Janssen, Lorena's beauteous husband. He had been working overseas and wasn't due back until the next day—but here he was, standing at the center island of the kitchen with an array of fruits and vegetables and a knife and carving board and the masticating Omega before him, juicing in the nude. "Hey," he said, casually, as if he and Waldo, near strangers, had on more than one pair of boxers between them.

"Hey," said Waldo.

Willem and Lorena were theoretically separated but had decided to share their house until they could figure out the best way to dispose of their joint ownership. They were cordial enough cohabitants, notwithstanding Lorena's torching of Willem's ninety-thousand-dollar car, about which he apparently remained oblivious.

But his nakedness—what did it mean? It could simply be that Willem was preternaturally comfortable with his body. After all, he was nude on a billboard on Sunset, not two miles from here—in a slightly abridged view, perhaps, but that was just a matter of logo placement. Or was he marking his territory? Had he come out here knowing Waldo was in the house, wanting to remind the interloper padding about in his underwear that he was still Lorena's husband, and that during Waldo's three years as a hermit, he had laid a claim on her so physically intoxicating that she'd actually married him, whereas she and Waldo had never so much as lived together?

More troubling was the notion that Willem would have been just as nude had it been *Lorena* walking into the kitchen. Shouldn't their "estrangement" have triggered some sort of modesty? Just how cordial *were* they? Lorena and Waldo had established no "rules" to this reunion. Was she screwing her husband on the sly, while her lover was out of town?

Willem said, "The last day of the shoot got rained out. Ever been to the Azores?"

"No."

"Beautiful," he said, turning to face Waldo full on, nothing but friendly. "You should totally go." There didn't seem to be a hair on his body below his jaw. How did these male models get that way? Shave? Wax? Felicitous disease? Willem poured himself a glass of thick green extract and downed half of it in a gulp. To any hygienic concerns about preparing food without clothing, his perfection stood as its own rebuke; he was Michelangelo's *David*, fortifying himself for another day under the world's gaze with a healthful dose of enzymes and antioxidants. Still and all, Waldo resolved to find something other than juicing to do with his oranges.

He returned to Lorena's bedroom and found her sitting up and checking her phone. "I thought I heard voices," she said.

"Mm," said Waldo. "Daddy's home." He crawled back in beside her, looking around the meager bedroom. Willem had somehow managed to appropriate the master. "How long you think you'll live here?"

"Why?" she said with a chuckle. "Think we should get a place together? You can't even get through a night in a hotel, for fuck's sake."

He wondered what had made him court trouble with a chancy question like that. Actually, he knew full well: it was the penis in the kitchen. "I'm not saying that."

She continued as if he hadn't answered. "You'd probably want us to share Two Hundred Things. I couldn't get down to two hundred *blouses*." She slid down and rolled on top of him. "I love you. And I love that we're together."

"Me, too."

"How about we have an understanding?"

"Uh-oh." They were careening into the badlands. With one flash of insecurity he'd jeopardized everything.

"Doesn't have to be 'uh-oh.' How about until we figure out where this is going, we just agree not to see other people?"

"Easy for me. I didn't see *any* people for three years." She giggled. They locked eyes, sealing the deal without needing to say it.

"Now," she said, crossing her hands on his chest and resting her chin on them, "can we talk about something *really* important? The reporter still wants to sit down with you." Of course he did. Waldo was a big story—again—since coming out of his self-imposed exile to solve a spectacular Hollywood murder case, that of Monica Pinch, found beaten to death and locked in a house with her TV star husband, a violent blackout drunk who claimed not to remember what happened. For legal purposes, Waldo worked the Pinch case as a nominal employee of Lorena's agency. Afterward, trying to capitalize on the notoriety, Lorena hired a publicist, who persuaded the *L.A. Times* to do a feature on her.

But she wasn't actually talking about the *Times* article, which they both knew was merely a conversational gateway to the proposal she'd refrained from reviving for the whole week: that Waldo return to detective work full-time, as her partner. She was sure his name on the door would be a Golconda, that all the celebrity work in town would come their way. For Waldo, though, it was all too much to contemplate, starting with the very idea of moving back to the city.

Now, though, she had a new pitch. "You wouldn't even have to do much. Live in Idyllwild if you want. Come into town when you're in the mood." She tilted her head and flashed her eyebrows. "Or once in a while for a meeting when we need you to show your face. Only work a case if something comes along you actually care about."

The variation gave him something to consider, but he gave her his usual wordless *no, for now,* by screwing up his face and smiling with his eyes. She responded with her usual sigh and pushed herself off of him and the bed.

"Wait—where you going?" He raised a hand, an invitation.

"Can't, Marathon Man. I've got to drive down to Newport Beach. Some of us *do* have to work."

"Newport Beach?"

"New business."

"Peep show?" Marital investigations, which he disdained, made up the bulk of her practice. She continued into the bathroom without contradicting it.

"I guess I'll head back," he said, meaning his cabin.

She came right out. "No." Waldo tipped his head toward the door: *we're not alone anymore.* "Don't go," she said. "Please?" Such a direct entreaty was unlike her. "Hang around one more day," she offered. "I'll meet you tonight in Santa Monica"—she was alluding to a very green restaurant they'd been frequenting—"and then I'll blow some of my Newport Beach money on a hotel." Waldo started to object but she cut him off. "I did some research. Sustainable stay." She didn't care a whit about any of this, naturally; it was all for him. "The bedding is made from recycled plastic bottles, and they've got a waterless urinal in every room. We'll be ballin' out of control."

She had him and she knew it. She turned back into the bathroom, her hair whipping too fast for him to catch one more glimpse of the resplendent thread.

TWO

A month earlier, Lorena resurfaced after her gasoline stunt and offered Waldo a lift back to his cabin in Idyllwild. Waldo got into her Mercedes. They weren't even out of Burbank when she mentioned that Willem had left that morning for a fragrance shoot in Miami Beach; they turned the car around and headed straight for her bedroom, which they barely left for the next four days.

Then her husband returned and jerked Waldo out of their private euphoria. He was instantly abashed by the debauchery of those four days—not the sex, but the ethical blight. It had started with that first accepted ride, a brazen flout of the iron rules that had once redeemed him. Worse, floating on a half-week-long endorphin buzz, he had let her keep ordering in food from a pernicious enterprise, new to Waldo, called Grubhub. The meals were varied and delicious and Lorena cannily accepted the deliveries and plated the food out of his vision, allowing him a blind eye to the extraneous bags and plastic utensils she must have been discarding, not to mention the surely less-than-green practices of the originating restaurants, let alone the wanton atmospheric brutality of twice-a-day automobile deliveries.

He'd defiled himself. He'd completely fallen off the eco-wagon, to no end but personal indulgence; he had lost connection to all that had restored sense to his life.

And it terrified him.

If he allowed those slips to harden and perdure, he knew he'd lose his soul all over again. He didn't need to end things with Lorena, but he did need to renew the foundational precepts that had saved him from his crippling guilt, and he needed to do it immediately.

So he bought a new Brompton folding bicycle to replace the one damaged (and discarded all too cavalierly) at the end of the Pinch case, rode a bus from L.A. to Banning and struggled the rest of the way uphill on the bike. There'd be no more travel by anything but public or self-propelled transportation, with rides in private cars only when at least one other passenger would have made that particular trip without him. There'd be no more food that had any kind of packaging. And certainly there would be no compromising of the centerpiece of his personal covenant, the Hundred Things.

The sun was beginning to set as Waldo bypassed Idyllwild, the eccentric little mountain town in which he'd barely set foot, and headed straight for his property on its outskirts. As soon as he veered off the asphalt and started bumping along his private dirt road, he began to feel like himself again, the man who'd lived for three years virtually without human contact.

He checked on his chickens first, saw that they looked healthy and were still well fixed for food and water. Then he went into his cabin, the prefab that became his home when he entered self-imposed exile over a tragedy for which he blamed himself. It was tiny, a mere 128 square feet, but he never felt cramped by it, especially with his acres of woods and his pond right outside. Indeed, it was something of a cocoon. And the features most extreme in their compactness—the bare-bones kitchenette, the combination shower and composting toilet—weren't just environmentally sound but reassuring in their efficiency.

It was too late in the evening to do much else, but, as Waldo always did at his cabin to drain the last of his mental energy, he played four games of computer chess against a level powerful enough that he could be sure in the end it would pick him apart. Then he climbed into his tiny, prism-shaped sleeping loft, that cocoon within the cocoon. But this time, when he settled into his sleeping bag, he did something he hadn't done in years: he recited aloud the canon he'd composed at the time of the original move.

"Don't want," Waldo said to himself, "don't acquire, don't require.

"Don't affect.

"Don't hurt."

In those first days, he'd spoken those words last thing every night and first thing every morning, until he'd perfected his design for living, until actual articulation was superfluous because the whole thing had become self-sustaining and automatic.

The next morning he resumed his daily mountain routine—tending to the chickens, drawing water from the well, picking meals from his garden and doing the gardening itself, and then the repairs and the daily hike and the reading atop the floating chair on his pond.

There was one new element now: a couple of daily phone calls with Lorena. To make room for those, he pared not his hour-long ration of soothingly insipid TV, his treasured *Hoarders* and *Kardashians*, which he watched through his MacBook, but rather his consumption of news. That was all too dismal and tedious now anyway, with this chaotic new president himself fresh off a reality show, and one of Waldo's least favored at that (excepting, of course, the nonpareil seasons with Gary Busey).

Those calls of Lorena's, though, and her half-dirty texts, unsettled his routine more profoundly than he could have imagined, making his mountain existence distinctly less hermitical yet somehow also more so. He had never felt lonely in his first three years up there, but now the desolation was palpable: at unexpected moments his body literally ached for her, not just in the obvious zones but in random innocent spots—a shoulder, a leg, a finger— that recalled her touch.

His cabin and his woods had restored enough of his equilibrium that he knew he couldn't give in to her appeals to abandon them and move back to L.A. So Lorena drove up to Idyllwild instead, a brief visit of only moderate success, the moments of delight offset by Waldo's freak-out in the hotel shower. By the time she left, there were more new questions than answers.

Not long afterward, though, Lorena learned her husband would be leaving town again—for a fashion shoot in the Azores— and invited Waldo down for a visit of his own. This time they managed to solve the food problem, at least, with a little planning; the L.A. Farmers Market wasn't all that far from Lorena's place, offering culinary variety far greater than he had in his woods, and nearly as sustainable. Minor disputes about the nature of Things aside, on this visit, it was working—*they* were working—as well as they ever had. That, coupled with her earnest plea, made his decision to spend an extra day in town an easy one.

With Lorena off to work in Newport Beach and her husband flopping about in the kitchen, Waldo couldn't hang around the house, so he showered quickly and slipped out. His daily ablutions didn't take long, as he hadn't cut his hair in three years and had decided to let his beard, shorn by a different woman the last time he'd been in L.A., grow out again. It felt of a piece with the rest of his design for living and made him feel more like the self he'd grown comfortable with.

As soon as he rolled out onto St. Andrews Place on his Brompton, carrying the backpack with all of his traveling Things, he began to regret the extra day in town. Early in his time in the woods he'd devised a routine to give shape to his unfettered hours, attending, in strict sequence, to his property, his body and his mind, and the days passed in their simple, fruitful way. Back in L.A., though, time seemed shapeless and unhealthy. Except when he was with Lorena, he never quite knew what to do with himself.

He rode down to Melrose and headed east, away from its funky-chic stretch, to an indie coffee joint called Shauna's, which he'd stumbled onto a few days earlier when he noticed its mismatched, salvaged-looking furniture and a sign in the window that read, WE COMPOST, not exactly the savviest or most appetizing come-on for most, but catnip for Waldo. Indeed the place was empty when he first visited, and its eponymous owner, a flower child born at the wrong time, had too few customers, leaving her free to chat. Shauna was committed to bringing a new level of sustainability to the L.A. coffee business, doing the roasting right there in her shop and buying beans not only organic and Fair Trade Certified but shade-grown, thus preserving habitats for migratory birds, and shipped exclusively in reusable bags. She offered a fifty-cent discount if you brought your own cup, and if you didn't, you had to drink from one of her ceramic mugs; disposables were unthinkable here, even the greenish ones. Waldo wanted to kiss her. Shauna knew the business would be tough going, that a price point of five-fifty for a medium would scare off a lot of people. When Waldo said, "Not me," she grinned and told him that if he could go eight bucks, she could hook him up with a surprisingly flavorsome cup made with beans grown, believe it or not, right up the 101 in Santa Barbara.

Today he took a table by the window and sipped that tasty local from a BPA-free travel mug he'd recently bought, after donating his cabin drinking cup to Goodwill. He browsed the day's news on his phone, then took out his Kindle and dove into a history of Winston Churchill's tragic attack on the Dardanelles in World War I, a blunder that led to the slaughter of forty-six thousand Allied troops, more men than the US lost in the entire Korean War. Churchill never shook the specter of that disaster: it became part of him, played a role in forging the man who'd save the free world a generation later. Maybe there was something hopeful in the story.

A limping passerby caught a glimpse of Waldo and doubled back. He rattled the glass with both hands until Waldo looked up at him and, when he did, came inside. "I know you. You're Charlie Waldo."

But Waldo didn't know him. The man was pudgy and middle-aged with salt-and-pepper hair shagging out from under a pink fishing hat at irregular lengths, like he'd cut it himself. Waldo was accustomed to being recognized by strangers, to the occasional

gaze lasting way too long, but actually being accosted was unusual. The first time he was semifamous, after Lydell Lipps, it was
as a fire-breathing madman; even the people who thought he was
a kind of hero steered clear. And since this second time, he simply
hadn't been out in public much.

"It's you, right?"

"Do we know each other?"

The pudgy man dragged his bad leg closer to Waldo, too
close, and now looked straight down at him. "I've been wanting to
talk to you." His thick-lensed red plastic glasses were askew and
he sniffled. Waldo wondered what he was on. "Monica Pinch—it's
bullshit, right? I've been following it all on the internet." Waldo
had seen the conspiracies online and knew what was coming.
"Those guys who bought the network just wanted to keep Alastair
Pinch out of jail, so they had that other guy murdered so he
couldn't defend himself. You weren't anywhere *near* there when the
guy got shot, but they're blackmailing you not to say anything,
right? With more information about the black guy."

Waldo was actually able to follow every twist of the pronoun-
laden gibberish, familiar as he was with this fun-house mirror per
version of his two famous cases, a conspiracy theory launched in
the wilds of cyberspace that had spread so quickly on social media
that it had become a story in itself, reported as a curiosity by
mainstream outlets and then joked about in late-night mono-
logues, irresistible given Pinch's celebrity. All that amplification
had somehow given the ludicrous proposition a weird sheen of
half-facetious credibility, so that now, according to CNN's polling
on the subject, this nonsense was believed by twenty-three percent
of the American public, or about three times the number who believed the US government faked the moon landing.

"What the cops are saying isn't true, right? You can tell me, I won't repeat it. I just have to know." He sniffled again. Maybe it was just allergies and the guy just a wack job.

Waldo said, "If there were a trial, you'd see it was the truth."

The guy squinted through his thick glasses, then seemed to decide that Waldo was confiding in him in code. "I hear you," he said with another sniffle. "Thank you. I won't tell anyone." The guy started out, then paused in the doorway. "Thank God we have the internet, right? The legal system just wants to *fuck* us." Limping back out to the street, he smacked the doorframe with his palm, taking out on Shauna's shop his rage at the soulless cabal out there working day and night to bamboozle us all.

Waldo was used to a long daily hike when he was on his mountain, five miles or more, but today he replaced it with a bike ride, Melrose into Santa Monica and all the way to the ocean, then south past the pier, along the Pacific to Venice Beach. He found a bench on the boardwalk and killed the rest of the afternoon people watching and reading more about Gallipoli. Then it was back to Santa Monica and the restaurant on Main Street, where he was to meet Lorena at six. Arriving a few minutes early, he peeked inside and saw she wasn't there yet, so he sat at a bus stop and disassembled and bagged his bike before going in.

The place was called Caffe Ecco, the extra *f* and *c* a little pretentious for his taste, but otherwise all he could ask a restaurant to be: run entirely on solar, carbon neutral, all dishes prepared with local-sourced ingredients, deliveries made only by foot or bicycle and in plant-based compostable boxes. They even recycled their cooking oil to power their owner's modified Jetta. Lorena, more the gastronome, gave the cuisine a C-minus, but, as even she said, you didn't really eat at Caffe Ecco for the food.

The hostess seated Waldo at a rectangular four-top in the corner. He browsed the menu, decided on the pasta with crab, Broccolini and cherry tomatoes, and had just pulled his Kindle from his backpack when he realized a young blonde with a pale pink braided streak was hovering at his table, fingers drumming the chair opposite his. "Are you Mr. Waldo?" She was very thin, seventeen, he'd guess, but dressed older, a halter top under an open diaphanous shirt that showed a lot of midriff and a belly-button ring, a short skirt and oversize sunglasses. If she were his daughter, he'd tell her to go back to her room and change. He nodded and she sat down without being invited. Apparently she wasn't a waitress.

She propped the sunglasses on her head, revealing smoky eye makeup with copper glitter. "I'm Stevie Rose. Ms. Nascimento said to meet you guys here." Waldo waited for more. "She didn't tell you about me?" Waldo shook his head, disconcerted. She said, "Don't be scared," with a flirty, pursed smile so immodest that he recalculated: maybe she *was* much older. "I need to hire a detective. Ms. Nascimento said you work with her sometimes."

Waldo half shrugged; it wasn't really true, not in any practical way, and anyhow Lorena shouldn't have ambushed him like this.

"She said I should come here and meet both of you." She put her sunglasses on the table and peeled off the top shirt, showing even more skin as she stretched, then laid it over the empty seat beside her and, all golden hair and bare, slender shoulders, leaned across the table toward him. "Can I call you by your first name?"

"People call me Waldo. Like a first name."

"Waldo. Waldo." With that coquettish smile again she tried it out a couple of more times, like she was testing how his name felt in her mouth.

"Why don't you tell me why you need a detective."

"Before Ms. Nascimento gets here? We don't want to start having our own private secrets, do we . . . *Waldo*?" That pursed smile again.

"How old are you?"

"Fifteen."

Waldo started to raise his hand and ask for the check, then remembered he hadn't ordered yet. He said, "You go to school?"

"Stoddard. In the Valley. You know it?"

In fact, he knew it well. It was where Alastair and Monica Pinch's daughter went to kindergarten. It was her teacher, Jayne White, who'd given him that shave, though Jayne White was long gone. "Yeah. You live in the Valley?"

"Sherman Oaks." That would be an hour trip in rush-hour traffic. "I took an Uber. So are you and Ms. Nascimento like a couple, or do you just work together?"

"Why don't we talk about why you need her help."

"Yours, too. Do you have a cigarette?"

"L.A. County—can't smoke in a restaurant."

"It's for later."

"You're fifteen."

She leaned in again. "I won't tell anyone. Promise." She knew he wouldn't give her a cigarette; now she was just screwing with him. "If you order a glass of wine for yourself, can I share it with you?" The way she held his eye suggested she'd be up for raising the stakes beyond that.

He was tiring quickly of her challenges. He held a flat look until her boldness wilted and her self-possession cracked. She started drumming again with her left hand and looked away. Sounding more like a scared fifteen-year-old, she said, "I don't know where my brother is."

"How long has he been missing?"

"Like a week? Sometimes he stays late in the library, or I thought maybe he had a date or something, so I didn't take it too seriously at first?" Now that she was back to being a teenager, she slipped into the verbal tic of making most of her sentences sound like questions.

"Where are your parents?"

She shook her head. "They died. Car crash, like two years ago? Terrence became my guardian."

"How old is he?"

"Twenty-three now. He's always been like super-responsible, honor student at UCLA, prelaw, the whole thing."

"Still, I'm surprised the court went with that, if he was only twenty-one."

"My parents had it in their will. They wanted to make sure we didn't get split up."

"So, what—you've been staying home by yourself all this time?"

Now it was her turn to half shrug. "My friend Dionne's mom drives me to school. People, like, always want to do stuff for me, since . . ." She trailed off and looked at the silverware. *Since her parents got killed.* He was getting it now: she was an orphan, playing grown-up because she had no choice, because she *had* to keep selling the world on her maturity. With nobody to tell her to go back to her room and change.

Waldo asked, "Other relatives?" She shook her head. He felt the urge to fix it all for this kid, though he knew it was probably better left to the authorities. "How did you get Lorena's name?" he said, then clarified: "Ms. Nascimento."

"Yelp."

Lorena was at the front door, scanning the restaurant. She saw him and headed to the table. She seemed unsurprised to see the girl with him, which reminded him of his annoyance that she'd bushwhacked him with a client.

Waldo had Stevie repeat her story. He angled his chair so that he could watch Lorena listening. She seemed thrown by Stevie's appearance; he could tell this tarted-up teen wasn't the foundling she'd been expecting. When Stevie got to the end, he asked her why she'd called Lorena instead of the police.

"My brother's into drugs a little? I don't think anything serious, but especially with the whole legal-guardian thing, I didn't want to end up getting taken away and put in, like, a foster home?" The ice she was drawing them onto was looking thinner and thinner. He tried to catch Lorena's eye but she didn't look away from Stevie.

Lorena asked for grilled swordfish and Waldo got that crab pasta. Stevie, despite Lorena's entreaties to order something more substantial, would accept only an appetizer salad. Her dressing on the side went unused and she mostly picked at her lettuce. Waldo noticed that Lorena left half her fish uneaten, too.

Stevie took out an envelope and said that it had five hundred dollars in it. She told them that she and her brother both had access to a checking account, that their father had arranged things so that there would always be money for them on the first of the month and that they were fine. Lorena told Stevie that her agency's fee was one hundred dollars per man-hour plus expenses and that she usually began with a one-thousand-dollar retainer but would accept Stevie's five hundred in this case. Waldo's instinct was not to take the money, but he kept that to himself. Lorena took a small ledger from her bag and wrote out a receipt.

Waldo asked what else Stevie could tell them about her brother. Not much, it turned out: she didn't know many of his college friends very well, and those she did were gone from Los Angeles, having graduated and moved on while Terrence took his time off.

"What about girls?"

"I know he has hookups. Once in a while some girl spends the night—we've got, like, a hot tub and everything? But I kind of try to stay out of the way?"

Lorena said, "Tell us more about the drugs."

Stevie pushed her salad around the plate. She said, "I don't want him to get hassled over it, okay?" Out of the corner of his eye he could see Lorena nodding. The cop in him knew that was a tough promise to make. "He smokes a lot of weed. Especially since our parents? But he definitely does too much Adderall, you know? He says it's for school, but he takes more than he can get with a prescription." Lorena kept nodding.

Waldo said, "Enough that you think he might get in trouble for it?"

Stevie said, "It's really more the guy Terrence *buys* from—I think he might sell more than that? They've been hanging out a lot."

"Who's the guy?"

Stevie put down her fork and shook her head.

Gently, Lorena said, "Stevie, we can't help you if you don't help us."

The girl took a deep breath, looked at Lorena and said, "It's this guy, Mr. Ouelette? He's a history teacher at our school? We both had him—Terrence in ninth grade, and then me last year."

Waldo said, "At Stoddard?" Stevie nodded. "And he still works there?"

"He's, like, the cool teacher, you know? But maybe, like . . . a little *too* cool?"

THREE

'll split the five with you. It probably won't go any further than that."

He'd barely shut the passenger-side door of her Mercedes and she was already talking money. "I was surprised you took it at all."

"This ain't a charity, Waldo. It's how I make my living. How my ops make *their* livings, too."

He didn't answer.

"Hey, if you want me to keep all of it—"

"What we *should* be doing is calling child services."

"Oh, yeah, that'll help. Put a girl looks like that in a foster home, even temporarily?" She was right; it was a tragedy waiting to happen. "Let her stay in her house by herself a few more days. It's not like it's hurting anybody. She's going to school."

They stopped for a light. Waldo watched a cluster of well-dressed diners compete for a valet's attention outside one of the tonier restaurants on Main, then watched them scatter as a white-haired wild man staggered down their sidewalk shouting something about fascism. Santa Monica.

Waldo's silence made Lorena defensive. "We could find this kid, you know. Could be in a hospital. Could be he got tired of being twenty-three and having to play dad, so he's with a girl somewhere blowing off a little steam. There are a dozen explanations that could end with these kids getting to stay in their house." When Waldo still didn't answer, she said, "Really, you want to fuck up this girl's life even more? God, she looks terrible."

She'd looked a lot of things to Waldo, but terrible wasn't one of them. "What do you mean?"

"Did you see her arms? They're like twigs."

"She's fifteen. Give her time, she'll put some meat on her bones."

"She's *anorexic*, Waldo. She's putting *lettuce* on her bones. She didn't even eat the fucking tomatoes."

Chastened, he decided this wasn't the time to bring up the way Lorena had sprung Stevie on him in the first place. But that's what bothered him all the way to the Malachite, the supposedly ultra-green hotel Lorena had found overlooking the beach in Santa Monica, in among the expensive joints on Ocean Avenue.

Lorena checked them in. The Malachite's self-satisfied vibe made him dubious and he perused the hotel brochure. The very fact of its glossy finish was a tell that the eco-friendliness was more sales job than substance. Some of the gestures—vegan beer at the lobby bar and headboards made of recycled barn wood— were almost laughable.

Nonetheless, they *were* gestures, and meant Lorena was trying. So what if they stayed one night at a hotel whose commitment to the Earth was less substantial than it pretended? He was going to have to start compromising, start making exactly this kind of tiny bend, if he was going to try to build something with her.

So he gritted his teeth and said nothing as they rode the

elevator—an *elevator?* to go up *two floors?*—Waldo with his backpack, Lorena rolling an overnight bag. He opened the door to their room. The barn headboard looked ridiculous. He peeked into the bathroom, which indeed featured a waterless urinal, but the toilet paper was far too snowy to be recycled. Jesus, these people.

"What?" said Lorena, annoyed, his moral judgment apparently cutting through his silence.

He deflected by turning to the withheld grievance about Stevie. "You shouldn't have dropped her on me like that."

"It wasn't deliberate. She called this afternoon and said she needed to see me right away. I didn't want to cancel our dinner after you'd hung around town all day. And it sounded like the kind of thing you might work with me on—Gary Cooper stuff, right? No motel windows. Come on, it's good for us. Trial run."

If he were going to bail, this was the moment. But he said, "If we're dry after a couple days, we bring in CFS. We shouldn't be leaving her on her own for weeks without telling anybody."

"Deal." She grinned, triumphant.

He couldn't abandon an orphan, and the case had found Lorena, not the other way around. Still, he couldn't help feeling like he'd been played. Fucking Lorena.

She said, "I'm the one who *knows* you, Waldo," and took the collar of his jacket between her thumb and forefinger. "Relax into it. Trust me. You'll see: we can make all of it work." She gave him a quick peck on the lips, took a few things out of her overnight luggage and disappeared into the bathroom, closing the door. "Oh," she said from the other side, "I didn't have a chance to tell you—I crushed it in the O.C."

"Yeah?"

"Rich asshole from Newport Beach—first day on the job,

caught him having a nooner at the Best Western right next to Disneyland. Gets a room you can see the Matterhorn out the window, probably even the dwarfs walking around. You think that gets some people hot?" He understood why she was buzzed on the day—a quick win in an enclave like Newport Beach could mean word of mouth with a big upside—but he always found this sort of Lorena war story vaguely distasteful. "Could you imagine if I got it rocking down on that Gold Coast, had a second set of ops? Anyway," she said, "I was feeling so good about myself, I bought something for you."

That pushed him past the edge. The whole night was already feeling wrong—the unexpected case, the eco-bullshit hotel—and now she'd done it again: another Thing? "I told you," he said, "I don't *want* anything else. It's too hard for me to find something to get rid of. Why can't you listen to what I'm—"

The bathroom door opened and she cut him off. "Stop being a fuckhead." The fixture over the sink backlit her but he could hear the smile in her voice. When she stepped deeper into the room, she had on a pink scoop-neck bodysuit he'd never seen before. His breath stopped; his huff dissipated. She said, "*This* is what I bought for you," and did a turn, modeling the hardly there back. "Guess what else? You know that old Dodgers sweatshirt I keep in my trunk?" He nodded. "I stopped on Ocean Park and gave it to a homeless woman. So *my* Things? I'm still at an even Ten Thousand."

Waldo laughed, at himself and with her, enchanted in every way.

They luxuriated in the ocean breeze and in each other well into the morning and barely made the noon checkout. Waldo had little to do until late afternoon, anyway: they'd agreed that Lorena would dig around UCLA to see what she could learn about Terrence Rose, while Waldo would brace the teacher Victor Ouelette after he came home from work.

But first he had chickens to deal with.

He kept a coop up on the mountain, five hens and two roosters, their output a principal source of his nutrition but a ceaseless responsibility. When he came down from the mountain the first time, almost two months ago, he'd left them water and a full feeder, but the whole time he was away he was nagged by the fear that something could go wrong. Abandoning them again, possibly regularly, required a sturdier solution, complicated by the fact that he'd lived his years up there without meeting a soul other than his letter carrier.

His first thought had been to find a local vet who might recommend an enthusiastic high schooler whom Waldo could hire to check on the coop every couple of days. But he learned there were no vets atop the mountain; he'd have to look to Banning or maybe even Palm Desert, and there wasn't much chance of finding a kid willing or able to make the long haul up 243. There was no choice but to do something that would have been unthinkable just months earlier, before his experiences with Alastair Pinch and Jayne White: hike down his long dirt drive and out onto the public road and attempt to meet his neighbors.

All the properties nearby were large—Waldo himself owned a dozen acres—so the entrances were set pretty far apart. The nearest driveway, well down the road from his, on the opposite side, turned out to be composed of perfectly laid brick and lined with flowers. He walked its length, finding, around a bend to the right, a wooden chalet, big enough to support at least four bedrooms.

The grounds were impeccably tended. He rang the doorbell but no one answered. He peeked in the windows and was stunned by the opulence, a plush set of sofas arranged around a large stone fireplace and an open floor plan revealing an eight-chair dining table beyond. It was probably some big shot's weekend spot, a million-dollar home, maybe multimillion, in shouting distance of his austere cabin. Waldo had lived across the street for three years with no idea. He circled the manse, scoped the black-bottomed pool and spa behind, then hiked back out into the road.

In sharp contrast, the second driveway hardly merited the name; it was more like a pair of tire indentations through over-grown weeds, the path leading not even to a mini-cabin like Wal-do's but to a rusty Airstream with a single cheap folding lawn chair beside it. A family of raccoons watched Waldo from beyond the trailer, which surprised him, because he'd never seen any on his own land, and unnerved him, because raccoons had always held the spot just above bats and just below opossums on his private list of the world's creepiest animals. He also knew that, despite his careful system of fencing and locks, raccoons were clever and persistent enough to pose a danger to his chickens and even to his cabin itself if they took up residence on his land while he was away.

The door to the trailer flung open and a seventyish woman came out brandishing a broom in Waldo's direction, though he was a good twenty yards away. Amazingly, the raccoons didn't flinch. She wore a tattered housedress and was in all ways a good physical match for her driveway.

Waldo introduced himself as her neighbor and she engaged in tentative conversation from a safe distance. As her paranoia sub-sided she told him that her name was Hilda Flitt, that she'd lived here for decades, and that the raccoons clustered on her property because she fed them regularly. She'd come to treat them almost like pets, not only naming them but becoming surprisingly involved with their physical and even emotional lives. She called the mother Grace Slick and believed she was suffering from a urinary infection. The older child, Rascal Face, wasn't much interested in cleaning himself, and the little girl, Julie Nixon Eisenhower, wasn't growing as fast as she should. Hilda told him that the father, Egg McMuffin, was prone to anxiety attacks.

Waldo figured that so devoted an animal lover, however nutty, might be as good a match for his needs as he was likely to find. He suggested that she look after his coop when he was out of town, in return for which she could take the eggs, plus he'd compensate her in chicken feed to pass on to the McMuffin brood too. Hilda agreed and also suggested a neighborly exchange of keys to each other's homes, for safety reasons. Beyond the premature intimacy, that would also mean, of course, a problematic additional Thing. Waldo demurred on the latter grounds, explaining to her his minimalism and the Hundred.

Hilda Flitt screwed up her face and said, "Holy moly, man. That's freakin' bonkers."

After checking out of the Malachite, Waldo tried calling Hilda several times and, when she finally answered, told her that he'd be down in Los Angeles for at least a couple of more days and asked her to keep tending the chickens until he let her know he was back on the mountain.

Then he looked up Victor Ouelette on his phone. It was an unusual enough name and when he found one with an apartment in Valley Village, not far from the Stoddard School, he figured he had his man. Just to be sure, he called the school posing as a prospective landlord doing a routine check, gave the secretary Ouelette's name and address and got confirmation of employment.

He decided to bike all the way from the beach, up through the Sepulveda Pass, and reached the address around four thirty. It was an unspecial stucco building on Whitsett, north of the 101, each unit accessible via one of several stair-and-catwalk arrangements, each of those secured by a locked iron gate with a set of door buzzers. He chained his bike to a parking sign and rang the buzzer for Ouelette.

A neighbor stood on a third-floor catwalk and watched him. It made him self-conscious about announcing himself through the intercom by his real name, especially after the conspiracy theorist at Shauna's, but there wasn't much choice; he was too well known to pretend he was anyone else; any detective work from now on would have to be as *that* Charlie Waldo.

This time, at least, the name worked, drawing the teacher out of his apartment immediately. Ouelette trotted down the stairs, saying, "Oh my God!" He was in his midthirties, smallish, with dark hair, a neatly trimmed beard and clear plastic aviator glasses that were either ironic or just out of date. "I can't believe it! You're my biggest fan!" Waldo had no idea what that meant. "I mean, I'm *your* biggest fan! I *teach* you—did you hear about that? Is that why you're here?"

"No, I'm actually— What do you mean, you *teach* me?"

"At Stoddard. I teach a sociology course, and we do a whole section on Lydell Lipps. Come in, come in."

Waldo followed Ouelette up the cement steps and into his apartment, a crappy one-bedroom that smelled of tuna. There were a lot of books, personal photos mostly of a younger Ouelette and an older woman who was probably his mother, a lava lamp and framed posters of Pearl Jam and Weezer concerts. He wondered if Stevie would still describe Ouelette as cool if she saw where he lived. Then again, to a fifteen-year-old this might seem cool in the way of a really good dorm room. Actually, that's what the place looked like to Waldo: the home of a guy who didn't get enough college *in* college, still trying to live what he missed.

"Look!" said Ouelette, thrusting an overstuffed manila envelope at him. "Boy, if there were ever a way you could come in and talk to the students . . ." Waldo slid out the top item, three typed and stapled sheets, and gave it a quick look. It was a homework paper with "B+" at the top in red; Waldo's name appeared five or six times on the first page. "You're a hero. The kids love you, the way you stuck it to the Man."

What *was* this? Years back, Waldo had devastated the life of an innocent man: Lydell Lipps, sent on the strength of Waldo's policing error to Pelican Bay, where he languished for more than a decade. When Waldo realized he'd gotten the case wrong, he spent months battling with his own supervisors and the legal bureaucracy, pissing into the wind to no avail, until tragedy struck again and Waldo went off the rails.

Anyway, he sure didn't feel like someone who'd stuck anything to anyone. This new brand of attention was too much to deal with, so he didn't. He said, "What can you tell me about Terrence Rose?"

The teacher blinked a couple of times. "I don't know a Terrence Rose."

The straight denial surprised Waldo; he'd expected something more artful. "He was in one of your history classes at Stoddard? About nine years ago?"

Ouelette said, "I've had a lot of students since then."

Waldo's phone buzzed in his pocket. He reached in and pushed a button, forwarding the caller to voicemail. "How about his sister? Stevie Rose? I think her real name's Stephanie."

"Stevie, sure—Stevie Rose was in one of my ninth-grade sections last year." Ouelette shifted his weight, angling away from him.

"How much do you know about their family situation?"

Ouelette shrugged ignorance, but his eyes were all caution. He *had* to know about the Roses' tragedy: a school that small, a kid's parents get killed in a car crash, everybody knows. Just like they all knew about Monica Pinch. He was hiding something, and he wasn't good at it.

"Victor—can I call you Victor?"

"Sure."

"Ever sell any pills, Victor?"

"No," he said, acting offended. "What kind of pills?"

"Adderall? Anything like that?"

"What's this about?"

"Relax, Victor, I'm not looking to bust you. I'm just trying to talk to Terrence Rose." He didn't want to reveal that Terrence was missing; if Ouelette had nothing to do with that, Waldo didn't want the teacher tipping the school that Stevie was unsupervised and setting the child services wheels in motion, not before he and Lorena decided it was time. "Tell you what," Waldo said, "if you should happen to 'remember' anything about Terrence Rose, or if his name should even come up in conversation, give me a call." He borrowed a pen and wrote his cell number on a corner of the envelope full of Waldo homework.

Ouelette shut the door quickly behind him. Waldo walked down the steps and out the gate to the street and checked his cell:

the incoming call had been from Lorena. He unchained his bike and pedaled a couple of blocks away from Ouelette's place before phoning back.

He told Lorena, "Teacher claims he's never even heard of Terrence Rose."

"I got you beat," she said. "Neither has UCLA."

"What do you mean?"

"No Terrence Rose enrolled, grad or undergrad. Last time UCLA had *any* Terrence Rose was in 1968 at the School of Dentistry, and that one died in Wisconsin eleven years ago."

"Huh," he said.

"What the fuck, Waldo? Why'd a fifteen-year-old girl give us five hundred dollars to look for a brother who doesn't exist?"

"Guess we should ask her. Meet you at her house?"

"Her house, fine. I sure ain't buying her another salad."

FOUR

It was five miles from Ouelette's apartment to the home address the girl had given them the night before, off Longridge on the Valley-side hills above Sherman Oaks. Stevie's street—if indeed it *was* her street—was steep and Waldo had worked up a sweat by the time he found Lorena waiting outside the gate. "You try it yet?" he said.

"Waited for you."

"Think she even lives here?"

"We'll find out." Lorena pressed the intercom button.

The girl's voice squawked through the box. *"Hello?"*

"It's Lorena and Waldo. Let us in." The twin gates opened outward with a mechanical hum and they trudged up the sharply inclined driveway. Waldo walked his bike and leaned it against an oleander hedge. Stevie opened the door for them, in a top that showed a lot of skin again, bare shoulders and belly, tight cutoff denims, nothing on her legs or feet.

Waldo said, "Can we talk to you?"

Lorena added, "Inside."

The girl led them down the steps into the living room. The back of her blouse consisted of two thin cross-strings to hold the measly front in place.

The house was California tasteful-ostentatious. A glass wall offered a lordly view of the Valley to the northeast, and large glass sliding doors opposite led to a gardened pool area and a guest-house beyond. The modern paintings on the walls made Waldo feel ignorant.

Stevie plopped onto a white sectional and drew her legs up under her. Waldo and Lorena sat more formally on a matching sofa opposite. The big square onyx coffee table between them was adorned with two stacks of oversize books and an abstract stone sculpture in the middle, plus two Atkins Bar wrappers and a can of Diet Mountain Dew.

Waldo said, "Mr. Ouelette doesn't remember your brother."

Stevie snorted. "Of *course* he's going to say that. He doesn't want to get busted for selling him drugs."

Lorena said, "UCLA doesn't have any record of your brother, either."

Stevie said, "Really?" She took a sip of soda. "What name did you use?"

"Terrence Rose."

"Terrence is his middle name. It's *Michael* Terrence. That's why."

"I can go back and check again—"

"You'll find him."

"—but it'll cost you. You've already used up almost all of your retainer."

"I gave you five hundred dollars!"

"Hundred an hour, two of us—it goes fast."

That made Stevie hesitate. Waldo said, "We're going to have to call Children and Family Services."

"No! That's why I need you to find my brother!" The desperation seemed real enough.

Lorena asked if she could use a bathroom. Stevie pointed around a corner and Lorena left the two of them alone.

Stevie looked Waldo square in the eye. "Would you really call child services on me, Waldo?" Discomfited by the knowledge of what that would actually mean for the girl, he looked away. "Seriously," she said, nudging the soda can with her toe, "do I look like a child?" She'd slid back into flirting mode and he hadn't seen it coming. He felt like he shouldn't be there. She said, "What would they do, anyway? Like, put me in some foster home or something?"

"Are you sure there aren't any relatives? Aunts, uncles . . ."

"Aren't those foster parents all, like, pervs? That's what I heard. They just want the government to bring them kids they can molest."

There was nothing to do but shuffle. "Probably not so bad. There's a screening process—"

But she'd moved on anyway. "What did you think of Mr. Ouelette?"

"Hmm?"

"Did you think he was cute?" The question threw him. "Guys never say they think other guys are cute, because it makes them sound gay? But you can be honest with me. I won't think you're gay. I can tell you're not." It felt like half an invitation. Waldo tried to will Lorena back from the bathroom.

He said, "How do you know Mr. Ouelette sells your brother drugs? Assuming you do have this brother—"

"Are you and Lorena, like, a couple? You at least hook up sometimes, I can tell. What are you, like, private eyes with benefits?" She giggled at her own joke.

"Do you know other people who buy drugs from Mr. Ouelette?"

"*I* think Lorena's cute. I don't care if it makes me sound gay. I'm not. I mean, I made out with girls a couple of times, trying it? But I'm, like, *so* not gay."

"I'd rather talk about Mr. Ouelette."

"Sure."

"Good."

"He's not very tall, but he has a great body. Did you notice that?"

Waldo sighed. "No."

"He's really freaky too. In a *good* way. *Mostly* a good way."

"What do you mean, freaky?"

"What do you *think* I mean, Waldo? So, like, what did he say to you? Did he get all nervous because there was a detective there?"

Lorena returned. She said to Waldo, "Can I talk to you? Privately?"

Waldo said, "Please," and all but leapt off the sofa. He told Stevie to stay where she was.

Lorena led him down a hallway and started to open a door. Waldo leaned close and said, "I think she may have had sex with that teacher. She was starting to talk about it."

Lorena was more interested in her own discovery. "Check this out," she said, opening a door and leading him into a three-bay garage, filled by a silver two-seat Jaguar XF, a white Lincoln Navigator, and a deep blue BMW 5 Series that clung stubbornly to an I'M WITH HER bumper sticker. Lorena said, "Why would two kids—one who can't drive—have three cars? And which one is the Hillary fan?"

They went back into the house proper, detouring through the kitchen on their way to Stevie. Lorena went straight for the refrigerator. Waldo noted that it was fully stocked; Lorena noted a Mount Eden Vineyards chardonnay. "That's a sixty-dollar bottle," she whispered. "Little fucker." Waldo followed Lorena as she stomped back toward the living room, her heels clicking on the Roses' marble flooring.

Lorena said, "Where are your parents?"

"How can you ask me that?! I told you, they're dead! You're *so mean*!"

"How did they die again?"

"In a car crash! On the way to Montecito!"

Waldo said, "The mail come yet today?" Stevie didn't answer. "It should be in the mailbox; I'll go get it for you."

Lorena said to Stevie, "And I'm going to check out your parents' bedroom. I bet all their clothes are still there, right? Two years later?" She headed back toward the hallway, Waldo toward the front door.

Stevie stood up and shouted, "Okay, *okay*! You guys are such *assholes*!"

Lorena said, "Sit down," and Stevie did. Waldo and Lorena took their previous places on the opposite sofa. "Where are your parents?"

"Hawaii. They have a house there?"

"And this 'brother'? Do you even have one?"

"*Yes*," Stevie said, with all the obnoxiousness she could muster. They both glared at her. They'd had enough of Stevie Rose.

Finally the girl sighed and confessed. "I do have a brother, but not like I said. He's a *half* brother, and he's old. He lives in Chicago."

Lorena said, "How old?"

Stevie said to her, "Old—you know, *old*. Like *your* age."

Waldo looked at his feet.

Stevie started crying. Waldo didn't trust the tears but treated the girl like they were real. "Okay," he said gently, "what's this all about? Mr. Ouelette?"

Stevie cried a little harder and nodded. "I wanted him to know I could make trouble for him."

Lorena said, "Tell us about it."

"I used to have sex with him."

"Start from the beginning."

"I had him last year for ninth-grade history, and he was way cooler than the other teachers. He knew good TV shows and all, and he was into anime? And then over the summer we started texting? He treated me like a grown-up and stuff, and *nobody* else did that, definitely not Paula and Joel."

Waldo said, "Who are Paula and Joel?"

"My so-called *parents*?"

Lorena said, "Tell us about how it got physical with Mr. Ouelette."

"My parents went on vacation? I didn't want to go because the school year was starting soon, and I talked them into letting me stay by myself? I mean, I obviously can."

Waldo said, "Obviously."

"I know, right?" said Stevie, the sarcasm going over her head.

Lorena shot Waldo a quick look and prompted the girl: "So your parents went to Hawaii . . ."

"And Mr. Ouelette came over here to go swimming? And he kissed me in the pool and we ended up doing it in the guesthouse."

Lorena said, "Had you ever had sex before that?"

Stevie shook her head.

"You said you 'used to have sex.' So there were other times with him?"

"Like, four more."

"Here?"

"No, at his apartment. On Whitsett? Then, like, I hooked up a couple of times with other guys, like, closer to my age—and I wanted to cool it with Mr. Ouelette?"

Waldo said, "You call him Mr. Ouelette?"

"When I was actually with him, like doing stuff, I was allowed to call him Vic? But like other times he still wanted me to say Mr. Ouelette."

Coaxing, Lorena said, "So you ended it with him . . ."

"Well, I told him I wanted to, but he kept texting me and stuff. He wouldn't leave me alone."

"Did you tell anyone about it?"

"Yes! And no one would do *shit*! Mr. Ouelette denied, like, *everything*." Waldo assumed the primary "nobody" she was referring to would be the headmaster of her school, with whom he had a history. "Everyone thinks I'm lying. Including Paula and Joel."

"But you had the texts, right? You could show them."

This was clearly, to Stevie, crazy talk. "I don't want people looking at my *phone*." They both frowned, not understanding. "I have stuff on there! *Personal* stuff." She got impatient with how dense they were. "Like stuff you send to boys? Pictures. You know, *pictures*?" She pushed back on the sofa and crossed her arms. "If everybody just believed me, there wouldn't be any problem."

Lorena said, "Okay, so why did you call me? Why this whole act about your 'brother'?"

"I don't know. I thought if I got detectives to go over there and ask him questions about something else, it might scare him or whatever and get him to back off." She picked at a fingernail. "Hopefully it worked."

Waldo studied Stevie, then Lorena. Five hundred spent, five hundred earned. Fucked-up situation, fucked-up world, but maybe this was exactly the kind of transaction private eyes were useful for, every day. Better than peeping in windows, but still not his calling.

Stevie looked up at him. "You don't have to tell my parents about this, right?"

"That's the first time I wished I was still a cop." They were in Lorena's car, heading up Coldwater, back to the Hollywood side.

"Why?"

"Guy should be in jail."

"If it even happened. There hasn't been a straight line out of that girl's mouth since we met her."

"The guy's a creep. I knew something was off." Lorena hiked a shoulder, not buying it. Waldo said, "Why would Stevie lie?"

"Why would she lie? Jesus! To get your attention!"

"*My* attention? Not yours?"

"Oh, please!" She was taking the sinuous canyon road too fast. Waldo gripped his door handle and hoped she wouldn't notice. Lorena said, "Bouncing around for you with her perfect little titties and her belly ring." Just then she came up on the back of a Honda taking the hairpin curves at about ten and had to slam on the brakes. Waldo hadn't seen this coming at all, though given their history, maybe he should have. He stayed quiet, not even wanting to ask Lorena where she was taking them.

She drove back to her house. Willem wasn't home. Lorena banged cookware around the kitchen toward a stir-fry made of vegetables they'd bought together but also some tofu she or Willem must have bought at a chain supermarket. The passive-aggressiveness of the soy was impossible to miss; she knew Waldo never ate anything from its kind of plastic container and was daring him to object. He took a strategic bite to let her have a small victory, then said, "Whatever you think about that girl . . . I didn't do anything."

She dipped her head a fraction of an inch, an acknowledgment.

"This isn't going to work if we start getting jealous again. That was the point of this 'understanding' you suggested, right? So we wouldn't go through that shit anymore. In either direction."

"What's an understanding?" she said. "It's something that lasts, until it doesn't."

That was the entirety of the dinner conversation. He ate around the rest of the transgressive tofu.

Later, he read more of the Churchill book while she took an unusually long time in the bathroom. When she came to bed he wondered if he should reach for her, but she preemptively said, "My period's starting." He knew it was a lie: it was only two weeks since she'd told him, on the phone to Idyllwild, how convenient it was that it had come while he was away. He wondered if she remembered that and was goading him again. Probably.

She turned on her side, away from him. In the old days, they'd rarely spent a night together without any kind of sex. He gently ran his fingers through her luxuriant tresses. She didn't respond, but she didn't stop him or shift away, either. That gave him a minute or two to study carefully, and by the time she reached over to switch off her night lamp, he was pretty sure that the white hair had been discovered and expunged.

FIVE

She fell asleep quickly, or pretended to, but Waldo lay awake for hours. He logged onto the chess website on his phone, something he'd never done with Lorena beside him. He played the usual set of four losing games, then tried again to sleep; no luck. He didn't drift off until well past three, and when he woke up, she was already gone.

Willem was in the kitchen—covered, barely but mercifully, and about to go for a run. He pointed out a note Lorena had left for Waldo on the island.

Went back to O.C.—L

She'd known he was planning to return to his woods today, and she hadn't even left him a good-bye.

Waldo had one bit of business before going back. He took the Metro to the Valley, then biked Chandler all the way to the

Stoddard School. Stoddard had been more or less the epicenter of the Monica Pinch murder case, and the coincidence of Stevie being a student there nagged at him. He didn't believe in accidents.

He couldn't imagine, though, how this new situation could relate to the knotty transactions he'd had in the past with the man he was going to visit, the headmaster, Sebastian Hexter. Waldo had kept a secret of Hexter's but had then demanded a highly problematic favor in return. The headmaster was no doubt certain he'd seen the last of Waldo, and glad of it.

A superannuated security man on a stool waved ineffectually as Waldo glided past and through the gates. Waldo left his bike in the familiar rack and continued to the main office. The receptionist's face fell when she saw him, and Hexter's assistant let out a tiny but audible gasp.

Waldo said, "Tell him I'm here." The assistant went in to see Hexter, then returned and tipped her head toward the inner office.

Waldo closed the door behind him. Hexter looked like a man about to have his prostate checked. Waldo skipped the greeting and said, "Let's talk about Victor Ouelette."

Hexter shut his eyes briefly. "What about Victor Ouelette?"

"Victor Ouelette, and Stevie Rose."

"How are you involved in this?"

"So you're aware. And you're not doing anything."

"The school can't take action based on unsubstantiated claims."

"She's fifteen. Someone needs to do something about this guy. He can't be left in place to prey on more girls."

"We don't know that he's done anything. A man's career is at stake, and his reputation. He's entitled to due process. Without it, the school's exposed to all kinds of lawsuits."

"So give him due process."

Hexter just looked at him.

"You don't believe her."

"I don't *know* whether I believe her. What I do know is that I've had a lot of experience with teenagers. How much do you know about their brain chemistry?" Waldo shook his head. "The adolescent brain develops as rapidly and violently as the adolescent body. While it's in flux, it pretty well resembles, physiologically, the brain of an insane adult. That's why so many teens pass through a troubled phase at some point. Some girls become fabulists; some develop an agenda. And some discover their sexual power, perhaps before developing the maturity to wield it responsibly. Do you understand what I'm saying?"

"Yeah."

Hexter nodded, relieved.

Waldo said, "You're blaming the victim."

At the North Hollywood Greyhound station, he called Lorena before paying for his ticket, but it went right to voicemail and he hung up without leaving a message. He hated leaving town with their relationship suddenly precarious and decided to stick around another day. He biked down the street to the Red Line and took it back over the hill.

It was a beautiful late spring day—not Idyllwild beautiful, but as good as it got in L.A.—so he thought he'd hit one of the parks, Echo or maybe Pan Pacific, and spend a couple of hours reading. But somewhere after Universal City, lack of sleep, the narcotizing prospect of more undirected hours in the city and the motion of the train rocked him into a doze. When the train slowed for the Hollywood/Highland station he woke with a start, panicked and checked to make sure his bike was still leaning beside him on the wall of the car; it was, and the loop of his backpack was still safely wrapped around one of his arms. Nonetheless, the thought of falling asleep on a park bench and finding himself mugged or arrested for vagrancy made him change his plans: he'd make for Shauna's instead and let a cup of her overpriced Santa Barbara jolt him awake.

Carrying his bike out of the subway, though, he was hit by another warm wave of fatigue and knew that he needed more sleep, and soon. These jagged Los Angeles days were wrecking him. Maybe if Willem was in the house, he'd let Waldo in. The thought of Lorena's bed magnetized him and he started down Western. He told himself that missing her had nothing to do with it.

Breathing the scent of her shampoo on her pillow, he dialed her cell, got her voicemail and hung up again. He decided to message her instead, saying that he was still in L.A. and asking if she wanted to meet at six thirty at a new place downtown Shauna had told him about, figuring it would be freeway-convenient after Lorena drove back up from Orange County, and sending her a link to the restaurant's website. He didn't mention where he was, thinking it might sound creepy in a text.

The first time he'd spent a night in this bed, it had been in Lorena's studio apartment near Echo Park, after their first date. All through dinner Waldo had found Lorena intimidating, not only in her profound allure but in her confidence, and worried that he wasn't measuring up. His remarkable career at the LAPD, his prodigious climb to detective III—it was like none of that ever happened; it was like he was back in high school, picking up his date for his junior prom and trying to pin the boutonniere on her chiffon dress, fumbling for sweaty, agonizing minutes before the girl's mother mercifully stepped in and showed him that it belonged on his own lapel. He was asking Lorena all the wrong questions, giving all the wrong answers, slipping into all the wrong silences. But when he asked if she'd like dessert, her answer was "Where do you live?" and when he told her the Valley, she said, "I'm closer," and that was that.

Their sexual alchemy, even that first night, was so staggering that in the morning he did something completely out of character, calling in to division and arranging to trade a shift. That, plus a scheduled weekend off and a slow patch in Lorena's own work, let them stretch their first date across the better part of a week. They'd break for a walk or a meal and tell each other stories about their lives until one would find something about the other a fresh aphrodisiac and in no time they'd be back in one of their beds and at it again.

One afternoon when he was on top of her, she suddenly put her palms under both his shoulders and pushed up hard. (The strength in her arms and small hands continually surprised him, even now.) He didn't know what was wrong but then he understood that she wanted to be looking into his eyes, and for him to be looking into hers. Whatever it was that happened then, and in the long minutes afterward, soundless but for their breathing, scared him. He almost lied and said he had to get home, but he told himself to let go and let himself fall, that maybe this was what the real thing felt like, the thing the songs were about.

The next day, Lorena's boss called—she was an op in those days for a small agency on the Eastside—and put her on a case. Waldo had to go back to work anyway, so they said a slow goodbye and set a date for the following Friday afternoon. They texted a bit in the interim but, their jobs being what they were, answered each other irregularly.

Come the day, Waldo took her to one of his favorite spots in town, the Petersen Auto Museum, a three-story celebration of L.A.'s car culture, which Lorena had never seen. Then he took her to an Italian place that took pride in importing every last ingredient and element of the meal—pasta, cheese, olive oil and, of course, wine—shipping it all from Tuscany, six thousand miles away. At the time, all of that seemed pretty cool.

Later that night, after they'd made love, Lorena said, "Just so I know the ground rules—we're not boyfriend and girlfriend, right?"

The question surprised him. "Meaning . . . ?"

"Exclusive."

It had all been so overwhelming that he'd made assumptions. But none of it had been articulated, and he realized there was no reason to expect that she'd have done the same. He said, "We *can* be."

"Oh," she said, "okay. I didn't think we were jumping to that." She was quiet, then said, "It doesn't usually work. That's been *my* experience. People say they're going to be exclusive, but somebody ends up cheating, almost always the guy, and then you're sorry you didn't do it first."

"I guess so," he said. He hadn't been in many committed relationships, certainly not enough to support or refute her take, and he was starting to feel at sea. He did have a glimmer, though, the first of his life, that being with this person and only this person from here on might be okay. Might be more than okay. He knew that was something one oughtn't say at this point, but he wasn't sure what one *did* say, and he started feeling boutonniere-ish all over again. Maybe he should suggest they *try* being exclusive, "boyfriend and girlfriend," to use her middle schooly language, and see where it went. Anyway, he knew he needed to step carefully with his next sentence.

But she spoke first. She said, "Because I slept with somebody."

He said, "When?," feeling stupid even as the syllable came out.

"Last night. A guy I've been sort of seeing. Not even seeing. More like a fuck buddy."

Reeling, he found himself quickly seconding her assessment that monogamy is problematic, especially with such a new thing as theirs, and that they should "keep taking it slow," even though, for Waldo, it felt slow like a plane plowing into a mountain at six hundred miles an hour.

He never got past it. He sought sex with others, much as she had, as a form of self-protection, and told himself that that was a good thing, that it helped him keep his feelings for Lorena in perspective and was thus in fact a boon to the health of their fledgling relationship.

Which, of course, it wasn't.

Because while he took care not to flaunt his other dalliances, Lorena was, after all, Lorena, and when they began to quarrel he learned just how closely she was tracking his non-Lorena life. He couldn't get it right: he'd try to treat their affair as casually as she claimed to want, but then he'd draw fire from her over anything, from a white lie he'd told so as not to stoke her jealousy to the utter moral failing of his longest-running distraction, a series of afternoon trysts at the Sheraton Universal with a married casting director.

And dazzling as Lorena was, she'd always have a potential paramour ready and willing to help her reaffirm her independence with a fling of her own.

The whole thing torqued Waldo so completely that it took him half a year to understand the obvious, that Lorena was every bit as obsessive about him as he was about her. When he finally got it, he suggested they try to overcome suspicion and habit and take a stab at fidelity.

Thus they entered their next cycle: they'd succeed for a while; someone would get insecure and backslide; they'd fight; they'd try again. Slowly they found their way, becoming a couple, damaged by their past but not shattered by it, and just beginning to feel safe in each other's faith.

Then Waldo's life exploded, and he committed the ultimate betrayal, disappearing from her life—and everyone's—without a word.

His midday sleep was fathomless. When the first threads of consciousness drifted past, if felt like he was crawling out of a coma. He slowly pieced the day back together, then the week. He reached for his phone. Lorena had texted back but one letter:

K

It was already five. He'd have enough time to bike to the restaurant, but not by much.

Shauna's recommendation was called the Greene, one more eatery gussying up its eco-theme with an extra letter. Set atop one of the tallest buildings on Fifth, this one was more extravagant than he'd expected, lavish to the point of dissonance with its original noble mission, the restaurant equivalent of a Tesla. Stunning cityscapes out its high windows were complemented by the illumination of hundreds and hundreds of soy candles. He felt hopelessly out of place with his jeans and windbreaker and backpack. At least there was a chance Lorena would like the food better here.

The hostess seated him in a booth and an auburn-haired wait-ress around Waldo's age brought him a water and asked if he was waiting for someone. He said yes, then commented on the ice in his glass. The waitress said, "Did you not want ice?"

"I'm a little surprised, that's all, place like this. You know, with all the halocarbons, when you dispose of a refrigerator it's like driving a car ten thousand miles." She studied him for a second, then chortled; he'd inadvertently won her over.

Waldo waited. And waited. At six forty-five he texted Lorena to make sure she was on her way, but she didn't answer. He started to think maybe she wasn't going to show, that her "K" was a mis-understanding or perhaps some kind of poorly executed brush-off. He wondered if he should order dinner for himself or simply leave. Then again, where would he go? He'd locked Lorena's house be-hind him, Willem apparently having gone out himself while Waldo was sleeping. The Greyhounds to Banning had stopped running hours ago. This visit to L.A., which had begun with such hope, had somehow set him tumbling into a strange helplessness.

She was almost an hour late when she slid into the booth op-posite him, looking flushed and flustered and barely apologizing. Something was off.

He asked how her work went.

"*My* work? A breeze. Wrapped up really quickly. Very success-ful case. I sat with the wife and her lawyer—she's going to clean up in this divorce. I'm *sure* it's going to lead to more business. I'm definitely buying tonight."

She was talking too much and too quickly.

The waitress took their orders. When she left, Waldo said, "You were out of touch all day."

"Was I? Sorry. My phone died. And I got really tired for some reason, so I went home and took a nap."

"In your bed."

Lorena forced a laugh. "Well, I wasn't going to drive to where *you* live and take a nap in *your* bed."

The worst part of knowing that she was lying to him was that he understood. Old ghosts were haunting them. Stevie Rose had stirred her insecurities and she was inoculating herself against the very notion of Waldo's infidelity by acting out first. It was like that first wallop when she'd told him about her fuck buddy. Only worse, because this time she wasn't even being straight about it.

She said, "And what did *you* do all day?"

He wouldn't tell her the truth and expose her lie, not yet. But he didn't have a lie of his own at the ready and found himself tongue-tied, stuck for an answer. He saw suspicion flicker behind her eyes and he knew exactly how she was filling in the blanks.

It felt like the beginning of the end.

As he tortured his imagination for a passable story, a massive figure in a dirt-brown suit dropped onto the bench beside Lorena, his big rump squeezing her into the corner of the booth. "So *this* is where the liberal fuckfaces get their thirty-dollar kale."

It was Waldo's nemesis, Big Jim Cuppy, LAPD.

SIX

W hat—surprised I found you?" Cuppy was an extortionate cop; the aftermath of Waldo's seismic blowout when he left the LAPD had somehow left Cuppy untouched but taken down his even dirtier partner, and he'd been carrying beef since. When Waldo didn't answer, Cuppy said, "Everybody on the force knows your face, asshole. Put out an APB, Revenant's in town? Had you in ten minutes."

"Why do you have an APB on me?"

Instead of answering, Cuppy turned to Lorena. "How's business, sugar?"

"I had an excellent day, matter of fact."

"Yeah, what's that look like? Somebody leave the shades up?" Back to Waldo: "Tell me about Victor Ouelette."

"Don't know the name."

"No? Then who was it dropped by his apartment on a bike— Lance Armstrong? You're not a cop anymore, scum breath. Not permitted to interrogate the citizenry."

"He's a private investigator," said Lorena. "Operating under my license."

He turned to her. "Start piling up harassment complaints, someone's gonna *pull* that ticket."

"*That's* what you're here for?" Waldo said. "That piece of shit filed a complaint—about *me*?"

"No, I'm here because someone decided to wait in the garage under his building with a hammer and X out that—what'd you just call him?—'piece of shit'?" Waldo and Lorena exchanged a glance. They knew enough to let Cuppy do the next bit of talking. "And it wasn't a robbery—wallet, keys, phone, all right on the ground next to him. Neighbor upstairs said she saw a guy looked just like Charlie Waldo hassling him on the street. Anything you want to tell me?"

Waldo squinted at him. "That haircut isn't working for you."

Cuppy clucked. "So where were you last night, about eight?" Resentment ran deep at LAPD and a month earlier Waldo had been locked up for a murder the investigators probably knew he didn't commit. Cuppy had come by the jailhouse to gloat and then some; no doubt he'd drag Waldo through all that again and worse if he could. But now he turned back to Lorena. "Let me guess. You're each other's alibis."

Lorena was even more vulnerable to harassment: her livelihood was at stake. Waldo said, "What does *she* need an alibi for?"

Cuppy said, "Let's talk Stevie Rose."

Waldo shrugged. *Don't know her.*

"Going to play that again? Rack your brain: poor little rich girl, dresses like a hooker? Probably throws up after every meal, even when she isn't eating garden waste or whatever the fuck they serve in this joint." Waldo and Lorena held stone faces. "Nothing?

How about Ouelette's boss at her school—Principal Fancypants, remember him? He says you had a bug up your ass about Ouelette." Lorena threw Waldo a glance at the news of his Stoddard drop-in. "Not just a bug, either," Cuppy continued. "Sounded more like a great big mutant cockroach." He took a pad from inside his jacket and read, for effect: "According to the principal, you said, 'Somebody needs to do something about him.'"

Now Lorena looked straight at Waldo, her eyes widening. Waldo checked her with a quick look.

Cuppy said to Lorena, "Might want to keep your boyfriend on a leash and out of the news. Bodies have a way of piling up around him. Can't be healthy for that little business you're trying to build."

Lorena didn't flinch but Waldo knew Cuppy had landed a shot to the solar plexus.

Cuppy grabbed a menu from a stand behind Lorena and put it in front of Waldo with a pen. "Cell numbers. Both of you."

Waldo wrote his down and slid the menu to Lorena. He said to Cuppy, "So you've talked to the girl?"

"What girl, the one you don't know? Not yet, only seen pictures. She's next."

"I want to be there when you do." That pissed Cuppy off and pissed Lorena off even more. Waldo felt the heat rising from her corner of the table but stayed focused on the detective, who waved a dismissive paw. "Come on," Waldo said, "at least let me bring her in."

Cuppy said sharply, "Fuck. That." Other diners turned to watch.

"Come on. The kid's home by herself. Parents out of town."

Cuppy thought about it.

Waldo said, "She's fifteen years old. Can't even drive yet."

"Give you till noon," said Cuppy, sliding out of the booth. He looked down at an older couple studying their menus. He leaned over the wife's shoulder, said, "Try the mulch," and sauntered out.

When Waldo turned back to Lorena she was all daggers, chewing on her tongue. Whatever she was thinking, he didn't want to hear it, not with her furtive afternoon still hanging out there.

Lorena said, "Go ahead. Call her."

"I don't have her number."

"Right," she said, in a tone just on the edge of suggesting she didn't believe him. She took her phone from her purse, found Stevie's info and hit the call button. After a few moments she said, "Stevie, it's Lorena Nascimento. Call me as soon as you can."

The waitress arrived with their food. They ate in a silence that gave him room to ruminate on all of it. Well, Lorena had what she wanted now, to a point. No client or income, maybe, but nonetheless a case they'd be working together, and one he cared about, even if it was just to clear himself.

He thought about the final months with her in the old days, the best of times, before the catastrophe of realizing that in his ambition and hubris he'd robbed a man of his entire adult life.

Waldo had left L.A. and found peace in his woods. Lorena would scoff at the notion that it had been peace, but it was.

He thought now about how she had upended all that by dragging him into Alastair Pinch's murder case and her own mess. He'd made it through, had maybe even grown. But this comfort he was able now to take in Lorena—physical comfort, emotional comfort—*was* that growth? Or only compromise *masquerading* as growth?

Was it even possible to sustain a connection to another person and still honor his private canon, or did coupling one's life to another's axiomatically create damage? At bottom, wasn't that the question this moment was about?

If, instead of surrendering to the pleasures of Lorena's bed, he had kept the vows he made to himself and stayed on his mountain, would Victor Ouelette be dead? Would Stevie Rose's life be at least a little less troubled?

Indeed, wasn't the very point of reclusion to avoid even having to *ask* himself questions like that ever again?

Plus, apart from those elemental questions, the toxic mystery still hung over their table, the one he *really* didn't want to face: *whose bed had Lorena been in all afternoon, while he had been sleeping in hers?*

He played with his mushroom confit while he worked through all that, to nothing like a resolution.

Lorena said, "What are you thinking?"

Waldo said, "Nothing."

SEVEN

S he didn't ask again. Lorena beat him to the check and they went down to the garage and all the way to her house without a word. Willem was watching television in the living room when they arrived, beach volleyball. Lorena clomped past without acknowledging him. Waldo half raised a hand, fractional apology for his girlfriend's hostility. Another turn he'd never have predicted.

Lorena rummaged through her bureau, then went into her bathroom and closed the door. Waldo took his toiletry kit from his backpack and waited. The bed, which he'd rushed from in the hustle to meet her at the restaurant, was still unmade.

The bed. From that first week, sex had been their essential expression of every emotion: after success, it was celebration; after grief, comfort; after jealousy, reclamation and reassurance. Even the night he heard about Lydell Lipps, they'd made love twice. They'd never discussed it afterward and it astonished him to recall, but at the time it made all the sense in the world. Now the possibility of a second sexless night loomed like a second night without language.

Lorena emerged from the bathroom in a stoplight of a nightgown he'd never seen, plaid blue flannel with a schoolmarmish white fringe at the collar. She grabbed the comforter by two corners and flapped it to straighten it, then crawled in underneath. She took her phone and checked her email or pretended to, ignoring him. He'd always been mystified by her ability to hold on to anger over nothing—a trait that, in calmer moments, she'd acknowledge with a self-joshing snicker as her Latina prerogative—but this took it to a new level. Which one of them had lied, for God's sake, about where she'd spent the afternoon? Waldo took his toiletry kit into the bathroom, peed, washed, and brushed his teeth. When he returned, the lights were off and she had the comforter clutched around her. Waldo lay down in his clothes atop the bare sheet.

He couldn't imagine staying here after tonight. But where else could he park himself in town, until he cleared himself of Ouelette's murder? That silly hotel in Santa Monica? Probably not: it's faux-eco offenses aside, his modest investment income needed to be carefully husbanded. And what would the *days* even look like? Could he imagine getting on well enough with Lorena to keep working together? They'd slipped back into the old place, the bad place, and this time he didn't feel like working to fix it.

"She did it."

It took him a few moments to find his way onto her page, to realize she was saying that Stevie Rose had killed Ouelette.

"She steered us to him, to set us up. Then she killed him."

He knew he shouldn't respond, that if he let that line of conversation continue, she'd end up provoking him into calling her on her lie and then the fight would be on. He didn't want it. He just wanted to leave quietly in the morning and figure out the rest later. But he couldn't help himself; the obvious illogic was too much: neither Waldo nor Lorena had motive to kill Ouelette, and any suspicion Stevie drew toward them would just lead straight back to her. "Why would she do that?"

"Because she's fifteen."

Waldo frowned in the dark but he held his tongue; he could feel her stumbling toward his detonator and he didn't want to help her find it.

"Remember that," said Lorena. "She's fifteen."

She'd found it. He said, stonily, "Where were you today?"

"Newport Beach. I told you."

"After that."

"Here. In bed."

"How long did you sleep? This 'nap'?"

"Fuck are you interrogating me for?"

"I'm just wondering when you got here. Two o'clock? Four o'clock? You were late to the restaurant—"

"I finished in Newport Beach around one thirty," she snipped. "I stopped at In-N-Out and had a Double-Double and a shake. You going to give me the lecture again about the cows and the methane?"

"Just answer my question."

"I got here about three thirty. I'll take a polygraph, if you want."

"Bet you'd pass, too."

"Fucking A, I'd pass, because it's true. *What the hell is your problem?*"

"*I* was here."

"You were where?"

"*Here,*" he said. "*In this bed.* I couldn't sleep last night, so when I decided to stay in town, I came back here for a nap. Willem let me in." She was quiet, caught. He said, "You've been seeing someone else, right? This whole time." When she still didn't answer, he said, "I knew it."

"No—"

"Somebody you were already involved with before you came up to see me the first time, right? Another fuck buddy." It was *exactly* the same old, bad place. "I was thinking maybe it was your husband, but—"

"Waldo, *stop. I* was the one who suggested the understanding, remember?"

"Yeah, I remember. Understandings—which last until they don't."

Neither of them spoke. Did he even need to hang around L.A.? Let someone else figure out Ouelette. The cops didn't have anything real on Waldo. It would get solved or it wouldn't. Wasn't his problem. Fuck it. L.A. was over; *this* was over. Time to get back to his woods and get back his balance. His peace.

Finally, Lorena said, "I got pantsed."

"What?"

"This isn't what you think. There isn't anybody else. It was my case in Newport Beach. I got totally pantsed." She turned on the light and sat up. "I got an email from this woman, had some questions about marital surveillance. Rates, confidentiality, wanted to know everything before she gave me her information. Sometimes it's like that, and you never hear from them again."

He listened, jealousy abating, as Lorena told him the rest of the story. After a few days of emailing, her prospective client had agreed to a phone call, placing it from a blocked number. The woman was distraught, frightened of her rich, powerful, abusive husband. She was sure he was spying on her—thus all her secrecy—and particularly terrified of what he'd do to her if he found out she was hiring a PI. In fact, she was afraid even to call from California; she waited until she was in the Berkshires, where she was visiting family.

Late in that first conversation the woman identified herself to Lorena as Brenda Wax. Her husband, Roy, she said, had founded a toy company and made a small fortune. Brenda was sure that Roy, who'd stayed home in Newport Beach, was cheating on her while she was away. If she could get proof positive, she'd pull the trigger on a divorce. Without that, she feared Roy's attorneys would clobber her in the settlement. Lorena told Waldo that that was a common fear among wealthy women who came to her, especially ones who grew up without family money of their own.

Lorena had asked Brenda for a thousand-dollar retainer. Brenda's response was that time was of the essence and that if Lorena would put it at the top of her pile she'd make it *five* thousand up front—and that if her divorce lawyer determined that Lorena found sufficient evidence against Roy, she could keep the whole retainer even if she hadn't used it up.

Waldo said, "So, what—you nail him and she stiffs you?"

"I'm not *that* stupid. I'm not going to start until the money clears, not with all that out-of-town stuff. High bullshit potential, right? But while I'm waiting, I *do* check out the rest of what she gave me and it's all good: Roy, the company, everything. Then two days ago the money drops, PayPal. So yesterday I start tailing the guy. Morning, he goes from his house to the office, and at lunchtime he's riding the Matterhorn.

"First I'm thinking, maybe the whole Disneyland thing is smart: second-rate tourist hotel, no chance he's running into anyone from the country club. Anyway, jackpot: blonde, slightly washed-up, a little too much dress for the middle of the day. On camera, clear shot, dwarf-fucker's checking in with his hand on her ass."

"And you're already shopping for O.C. office space."

"Don't rub it in."

Next, Lorena emailed Brenda Wax in the Berkshires and Brenda emailed back that she was coming right home, taking a six A.M. flight out of Logan, and could Lorena meet her at their house at two o'clock? "All good, right? I go to the FedEx store, make some beautiful prints, head on down to Brenda Wax's in Newport Beach, finally meet her in person, hand her the envelope, she looks at the pictures . . . and asks me who the hell I am. Turns out, the woman who hired me to catch Brenda Wax's husband? Wasn't Brenda Wax." Before Waldo could react, she said, "You laugh and I'll tear your nuts off." He didn't. "Anyway, *this* Brenda Wax swears she never heard of me, swears she never emailed me, swears we never talked on the phone. Though, of course, she wants to keep the pictures."

"And the other Brenda's email—"

"Dead before I get back to the car. Naturally. So then I go to the bank I got PayPal'd from, some pissant S and L in fucking Tustin. I tell them what happened, all they'll tell me is the account's empty."

"How'd you even get *that* out of them?"

Lorena shrugged like it hadn't been a problem. Some assistant manager was hoping to get lucky, was how. Lorena had a way of pulling those out of the air.

She said, "I've never been pantsed before. Now this *and* Stevie, twice in a couple days? Fucked me up, Waldo, I couldn't even call you back. I *did* go to In-N-Out—and by the way, I *am* trying to stop eating that shit. Had fries, too. And a second shake, to have in the car. I don't know what I was thinking—two sips, I had to throw it out the window." Waldo blanched at the image. "And then I took the wrong exit on the freeway, got halfway to City of Industry before I realized. That's why I was late." She stood and paced, reliving the stress. "*You're* the one who's always saying there are no accidents. How the fuck does this happen to me twice? Is someone trying to screw with *me*?"

"Through Stevie Rose? I doubt it. This one probably is a coincidence."

"But explain *Wax*, even. If somebody wants to screw with *him*, why pick *me*? An L.A. detective for an O.C. case?"

"Name of your company, maybe? Very Private Eyes? I told you: says you're a specialist."

"Yeah, maybe I should change it. Maybe I'll *have* to. And now I've got Cuppy threatening my whole business? Shit, Waldo, I've been trying so hard to get this thing going." She plopped onto the bed and covered her eyes.

Waldo said, "Hey. We'll figure them out. Both of them."

"'*We*'?" Her voice dripped skepticism. "'*We're*' going back to the woods." She didn't take her face from her hands. Lorena distraught was as rare a sight as Lorena in flannel jammies.

He said, "I'll stay. Till we've got them both. Okay?"

She turned, still scowling, and regarded him. Maybe he spoke too fast. What was he committing himself to? Okay, she hadn't been with someone else, but it's not like things were going smoothly even before O.C. blew up in her hands.

Then again, maybe she'd turn down his offer anyway. The distress on her face—he'd never seen her like this. Could be she wouldn't even want him around.

She ran her eyes down his body and back up. She said, "Why are your clothes still on?"

EIGHT

Her voice woke him up and she was starting the day pissed. "Fucking voicemail's full. Can't even leave her a message." It was a rarity for her to get up first, but here she was, ready for the world in a silk floral blouse and skinny jeans. The two misfires and Cuppy's threats had shaken her hard.

Waldo indicated the phone with bleary eyes. "Stevie?"

"She's dodging us. Can't help the girl if she doesn't want help."

"Could be she doesn't know she's in trouble." Lorena snorted and kept doing something on her phone. He sat up. "Where you want to start on Wax?"

"I've been thinking about that. I don't even know if the wife's going to confront him. If she doesn't, and we put it on his radar, we could make everything worse."

Waldo suggested that she call Wax's office and, if he took the call, that she ask if he knew who she was and why she was calling. If Wax said he did, Lorena should ask to go down there and see him, then offer to work the case for free until she figured out who was looking to burn him.

"But what if it's *me* they were trying to burn?"

"Deal with that then."

Lorena glanced at her bedside clock. "What time you think I can try him? Quarter to nine?"

"Sure." Waldo's phone vibrated and he looked at it. "What did you send me?"

"My shots from the hotel and the background links I found on the Waxes. Check them out while I do my makeup."

He pulled up her Disneyland photos first. Roy Wax had the look of a former high school pulling guard who'd started soaking in martinis back when that meant gin. Lorena had been a little uncharitable about his lunch-hour blonde, but then again, she was used to peeping north of the L.A. County line, where the bar was higher. Plus this rough run was making her harsh on everybody. At first Waldo thought there was something familiar about the woman in the photos but on second look decided she was just a common SoCal type, the kind of bland beauty who'd come to Hollywood and maybe topped out with a short run on a soap. Or could be that her mother had. Anyway, the photos Lorena managed were impressive stuff for the purpose: she'd gotten close enough to Wax to catch him squeezing a platinum card with one hand and a spongy cheek with the other.

The first background link took Waldo to a three-year-old edition of tony *Orange Coast* magazine. The photo-filled feature ostensibly celebrated Brenda Wax in her role as co-chairwoman of a group called LiteracyOC but in fact devoted most of its real estate to real estate, specifically the Waxes' recently renovated, Tuscany-inspired, fifty-five-hundred-square-foot beachfront home. Most of the photos featured Brenda posed before ocean vistas from its various rooms, but most striking was a sunset shot of Roy standing behind Brenda at the end of their private dock, his arms around her waist, both with eyes closed and smiling. Infidelities notwithstanding, the Waxes' life was good.

The next link, a *Fox & Friends* human interest feature via YouTube, laid out where the money came from: Roy Wax, it turned out, was a plushy tycoon. Though most stuffed animals were made on the cheap in third world factories, Wax had found a way to manufacture his in America—and quite profitably—by draping the enterprise in red, white and blue.

Taking note of the massive audiences for children's books by the likes of Rush Limbaugh and Bill O'Reilly and seeing an opportunity to expand the patriotism market all the way down to the crib, Roy Wax had lit on the notion of Born in America Babies, cuddly stuffed likenesses of various presidents and other national icons as infants. He started with Baby Georgie Washington and Baby Marty Luther King and, most lucrative of all, irresistible Baby Abey, the must-have toy of one glorious Christmas, complete with beard, mole and stovepipe bonnet. Later came Baby Liberty, Baby Benjie Franklin, Baby Ronnie and even a surprisingly fast-selling set of Baby Bush Twins (any resulting misconceptions to be corrected, presumably, by history teachers down the line).

The last link, a piece in the *Orange County Register*, identified Roy Wax as a prominent supporter of two of Southern California's red-district congressmen, noting that he and his wife regularly opened those fifty-five hundred square feet for their fund-raisers. Waldo recognized both the legislators as fervid hawks on immigration issues and couldn't help wondering how many of the workers in Wax's Born in America factory had been born in America themselves.

But did any of this suggest anything about Lorena's imposter? In the singular world of Orange County, as Waldo understood it from up the freeway, Roy Wax didn't seem an outlier, just one of the many SoCal success stories who'd turned the Orange coast gold and built a conservative citadel luxuriously out of step with the rest of the state. Anyway, politicians were scandal bait, but donors generally not. So the animus against him was probably personal—maybe some friend of Brenda Wax's who didn't like how Brenda's husband mistreated her, or even some other hale fellow at the club who didn't like the way Roy took mulligans and decided to get a couple of strokes back by hiring an actress to pose on the phone calls to Lorena. Or maybe the lunch-hour blonde came with a husband.

Or, possibly, Lorena's paranoia was well-founded, and she was the target.

When she came out of the bathroom, he asked, "What have you been working on? What's the last month been like? Any unhappy clients?"

"Not that I know."

"Walk me through your last few cases."

"Working backward?" She ticked them off on her fingers. "Cheating husband, cheating husband, cheating wife, *not*-cheating wife . . ."

"All marital."

"Well, before that, there was this TV actor on a murder rap—can I count him?"

Waldo smiled. "How about the targets? Any chance someone you caught was pissed enough to burn you back?"

She shrugged. "Always. Occupational hazard."

"How about your company? You got three ops?"

"Not a problem."

"You pay them well?"

More firmly: "Not a problem."

"Tell me about them. There's a Willie Williams—"

"Wait, wait," she said. "How do you know that? You been spying on me?"

"*Me?* Spy on *you?*" She smirked and conceded the unlikelihood by dipping her head. He said, "When you were missing, your husband gave me the names. I was going to follow up but I heard from you before I got a chance. Williams, he told me, and a Lucian Reddix, and was it a Dave Goldberg?"

"Why are you focusing on this? I'm telling you—"

"Why are you holding back?"

She hesitated before deciding to say, "It's not Dave Goldberg. It's Dave Greenberg."

It took a few seconds for the name to land. "*Fat* Dave Greenberg? From Foothill?" Greenberg was a plainclothes notorious through the Valley Bureau both for his girth and for his general douchebaggery, which came together infamously on a robbery-homicide at a liquor store in Pacoima. Greenberg had spotted what no one else seemed to, a reddish-brown smear on the door and a similar one near the cash register. When he noted the forensic crew overlooking it, he not only snapped at the incompetents to run a swab but roasted them with a five-minute, curse-laden torrent. They let his choler burn down before pointing out a fact of which he was apparently the only cop on the scene unaware: that a matching reddish-brown glob sat on Greenberg's own elbow, Korean barbecue sauce courtesy of the all-you-can-eat joint where he'd just spent a quarter of his shift. He'd rubbed it against the two surfaces he'd noticed and three more he hadn't, and nobody had wanted to say anything. Within hours the story had made Dave Greenberg a full-on legend.

"Damn," said Waldo now.

"He's mellowed."

Waldo raised a dubious eyebrow and said, "Yeah? Who's Williams?"

"You probably overlapped with him. He had some problems then."

"What Williams did I know who had—? Not *Dexter* Williams." Lorena nodded. Waldo said, "*Dumpster* Williams?"

"He goes by Willie now." In stakeouts back in the day, Sergeant Williams was known to bring along fellow officer Captain Morgan to keep him company. One night, looking for a spot to take an unnoticed piss alfresco, he staggered across Coldwater and thus across the division line, unfortunate because, when he was found by a shopkeeper the next morning, passed out behind a dumpster, the young Van Nuys team who took the call didn't know him and he woke up in a cell on a D and D. A couple of compassionate rehab cycles followed, but then, already saddled with the nickname, he blew a 0.12 after crashing a squad car into, fittingly, a big green trash receptacle and was finally drummed out of the department.

"Dave Greenberg *and* Dumpster Williams? You pay those clowns actual currency? I don't even want to know who Reddix is."

"He's a kid. He's going to be really good. Hungry, very loyal—"

"Kid, meaning . . ."

Lorena bobbed her shoulders before admitting, "Nineteen."

She had been claiming to have three ops full-time plus three more freelance. "None of them are full-time, are they?"

"I guarantee them twenty hours a week. The older guys."

He was sure she didn't have any freelancers, either. Paying her bills with PI work, starting to build any kind of agency at all—even with second-rate, part-time ops—was nothing to be embarrassed about, certainly not for a thirty-year-old woman in a hard city like L.A. But Lorena was falling short of her own lofty ambitions, so short that when she re-encountered Waldo after all the years, she felt the need to pose, and now she'd gotten caught at it. He realized how thoroughly he'd humiliated her and changed the subject. "I bet you can call Wax now."

She dialed and put her phone on speaker.

"Roy Wax's office," said a woman's voice.

"Lorena Nascimento for Mr. Wax."

"I'll see if he's in."

Lorena and Waldo eyed each other through the hold.

"This is Roy Wax."

Waldo nodded encouragement. Lorena said, "Mr. Wax, this is Lorena Nascimento. Do you know why I'm calling?"

"I do."

"I'd like to come talk to you." When he didn't say anything, she added, "Mr. Wax, somebody set the two of us up. I believe it's in both our interests to figure out who that was." They waited for a response. Finally she said, "Are you still there?"

Wax said, "My office, one o'clock," and hung up.

Lorena said to Waldo, "You're coming with me."

"Don't you think your charms'll play better solo?"

"I think my charms'll play better with the most famous detective in California for a wingman."

"Then I'm in. You feeling better?"

"Starting to," she said, and stretched on the bed. The top of her blouse slipped open, unveiling a fringe of red lace. "One o'clock. That leaves us hours. Any ideas what we should do?"

"Uh-huh," said Waldo. "Start checking bus schedules."

Lorena howled the whole time he was figuring it out, but Waldo dug in. They'd been nonchalantly sullying the planet far too much, tooling about L.A. in her sports car, and if she wanted to work cases together, especially cases forty-five miles down the coast, she was going to have to start getting around Waldo-style. Of course, that was going to be much harder à deux; alone, he could simply bike to Union Station and catch the MetroLink, but Lorena was nobody's cyclist, so they were looking at a two-block walk (she in stilettos), a ten-minute bus ride, a few more blocks on foot to Wilshire and Western, then thirteen minutes on the Purple Line—all just to get to Union Station, where the trip to Orange County would actually begin.

Even the first brief leg made her tetchy. Waldo saw the 207 a block ahead, about to reach the stop before they did, and made the mistake of saying, "Let's make it!" and breaking into a trot. He managed to catch the driver's eye, and when he caught up kept one foot on the step and one on the curb, forcing the driver to wait, grumbling, while Lorena took her pointed time strolling the last half block, scowling at Waldo all the way.

On the bus, there were empty seats but none together. Lorena, sore and bossy, said, "Sit here," and Waldo took the spot she indicated, next to an octogenarian black woman. Lorena continued back a couple of rows and plopped down beside a twentysomething with a handlebar mustache, thick-framed rectangular glasses and a porkpie hat. If the guy was smart, he wouldn't try to talk to her.

Waldo studied the rest of the itinerary that Google Maps served up. There was a hitch he hadn't noticed coming up in Anaheim, a half-mile stretch from train station to bus stop that they'd have to take on foot. He decided to break the news when they got off this bus so she could have some time to get used to the idea.

The next thing he knew, Lorena was standing behind him. "Trade with me."

He gave her his spot and stepped back to where she'd been sitting. Her erstwhile seatmate, glasses pressed high on his forehead,
was holding the middle of his face and moaning. Red droplets fell
freely onto his khakis. Waldo watched the back of Lorena's head
and hoped the elderly lady next to her now would fare better.

When they got off at Wilshire the first thing Lorena said was,
"I don't want to talk about it." But she did. "Goddamn perv put his
hand on my leg. How the hell do you ride with these people?" She
was walking faster now, agitated. She definitely had a higher gear
when she wanted it, even in heels. "Look at the back of my jacket,"
she said. It was ivory quilted leather. "Did that hipster fuck get
blood on me?"

He decided not to tell her about the walk in Anaheim quite yet.

South Coast Plaza was the biggest and ritziest shopping center in
California, everything you'd find on Rodeo Drive collected, air-
conditioned, and set down closer to the Gold Coast money.

Independence Infants, Inc., was headquartered in a tower beside the mall, in a suite all glass and paneling, hushed like a law
office. A young blond receptionist with fake pearls quickly shut her
Facebook, and Lorena introduced herself and then Waldo. While
the girl made a call to the back, Lorena checked a mirror from her
purse. Waldo knew to leave her alone; that half-mile traipse had
made her sweaty and even more peevish and she was trying to do
something quickly about both. Wax's assistant, a shade younger
than the receptionist and two shades blonder, appeared and led
them back to his capacious corner suite.

Wax was more tan in person than Waldo had expected from
the Disneyland photo. His glass desk faced the door, a view that

stretched to the Pacific behind him. The room reeked of ciga-
rettes. Wax lit a Marlboro as they entered, not something you
often saw indoors in California. There was a meeting area off to
one side but no chairs in front of Wax's desk, so Waldo and Lorena
stood.

"I'm Lorena Nascimento. This is Charlie Waldo. You may have
read about him in the news recently—he solved the Monica Pinch
case."

Wax smiled and said, "I know who you are." Maybe this was a
moment when Waldo's celebrity would help them. Wax added,
"The Judas cop." Maybe not. Wax drew a deep drag and blew
smoke in Waldo's direction.

Waldo knew Lorena would have rehearsed her speech in her
head, but Wax's raw antipathy had her back on her heels. "I want
to, um . . . *apologize*," she stammered, "for any difficulty this may
have caused you." Wax tilted his head and peered down his nose
while she tried to find her footing. "Whoever hired me obviously
wanted to damage you, Mr. Wax, and exploited me to do it. I don't
like looking bad, and I'm going to find out who it was." Wax's cool
was unsettling her; she was selling too hard. "However you feel
about the way Detective Waldo resigned from the LAPD, he was
their very best for a long time—"

Waldo couldn't watch her spin any more for this asshat and
cut in. He said to Wax, "California doesn't allow smoking in office
buildings. Newport Beach hasn't broken off from California yet,
has it?" Lorena turned to him, fretful, but Waldo pretended not to
notice.

Wax said, "We're in Costa Mesa. And California allows smoking in designated break rooms. This"—he spread his arms to take in
his showy office—"is a designated break room." He took another

draw, exhaled extravagantly and turned to Lorena. "So what's the hustle? Take some pictures, harass my wife, then start milking me?"

"Milking you?"

"Getting me to pay you to try to find the person who did this to me. Who may never have existed in the first place."

"Mr. Wax, I'm not asking you for any money. I'm here to offer to work pro bono. When we find out who set us up, I'm sure you have grounds for a lawsuit—"

"Oh, I've already talked to my attorneys; I *know* I have grounds for a lawsuit. Against *you*, for invasion of privacy and emotional distress." Lorena swallowed. Wax took another drag. "Here's what's going to happen. I am going to try to repair the damage you've done to my marriage. But if I so much as hear your name after today, I'm going to make one phone call and have your license revoked. Am I clear?"

"Yes, sir." She hesitated, then glanced at Waldo and started for the door.

But Waldo didn't. He said to Wax, "You learned something today."

"What do you mean?"

"You had Ms. Nascimento come all the way down here; when you talked to her this morning, you at least wanted to hear what she had to say. Now you don't. What happened in the meantime?"

Wax blew another stream of smoke in Waldo's direction. "I guess that famous mind of yours has taken you pretty far."

"I get by."

"Then how come I'm the one who's rich?"

Waldo said, "There are larger things."

"There sure are. And I'm the one with money to buy them."

Lorena plucked Waldo's sleeve and he followed her out.

They rode down the elevator and walked out into the pounding sun and toward the bus stop, Lorena clomping half a step behind Waldo. He told her she should just try to forget this ever happened, but the words sounded hollow even to him. He felt so bad for her that he actually suggested they go next door to South Coast Plaza to window-shop and to see if they could find a dinner he could live with.

"I'm getting my ass kicked, Waldo. Today isn't the day to buy fucking Louboutins."

"I said, *window*-shop."

"Find a bus to Costco. Time to start window-shopping there."

They waited on a metal bench. After a few minutes his phone rang, an unfamiliar number. "Hello?"

"You owe me a girl, Waldo." It was Cuppy.

"We're trying. I'm sure we'll get hold of her soon."

"We got hair looks like her color in his apartment, and phone calls to and from, right up to the day of. I'll give you till tonight. Tomorrow morning I'm perp-walking her out of prep school." The line went dead.

He repeated Cuppy's threat to Lorena, who shook her head, her mood steaming off her. Then he started working out a route to Stevie's house on his phone while Lorena took care of some business on hers, tapping so hard he thought she might crack her screen.

There were MetroLink options and Amtrak options for the main leg from Anaheim to Union Station. He tried to figure out whether one left a darker carbon footprint than the other but could find only a press release saying that the two companies had partially merged. He abandoned that research and looked instead for a two-bus route to the Anaheim train station on this end, which might at least spare Lorena a repeat of that long hike.

A white Honda Accord pulled to the curb in front of them. Lorena got up off the bench and opened the back door. "Let's go," she said. "It's an Uber." Waldo recoiled. "You don't get in, the only footprint's going to be the one I put on your skinny ass." It wasn't the day to argue.

NINE

At the foot of the driveway, Waldo hit the intercom button while Lorena held the Uber in case Stevie Rose wasn't at home.

"Hello?" It didn't sound like Stevie. Waldo signaled to Lorena, who got out of the Honda. She walked over to Waldo as the car turned around and headed down the hill.

"Hi, is this Ms. Rose?" he said into the intercom.

"Yes?"

He noticed a tiny camera atop one of the gate stanchions, tilted down toward the intercom, and turned to show himself. "Hi, my name is Charlie Waldo, and this is Lorena Nascimento."

"Yes?"

"We're private investigators."

"Could you leave your information in the mailbox? This isn't a good time for us."

Waldo and Lorena looked at each other. He said, "We've been working with your daughter."

"With my daughter?"

"Stevie?"

Lorena added, "She hired us?"

"Do you have any identification?" Lorena took an ID card from her purse and held it to the camera. The double gates parted for them.

They walked up the Roses' private hill. A woman in her early forties waited at the open door. The tan might have been natural but the tousled and highlighted amber hair hadn't come cheap. She wore an opal pendant on a thick gold chain, and knee-length khaki shorts and a sleeveless blouse showing off calves and arms that had taken some investment, too. "We just got back."

Lorena said, "Are you Stevie's mom?"

"Paula Rose." She held out her hand and shook each of their hands with a firm grip. "What did you say your names were again?"

Could any parent at Alastair Pinch's daughter's school not know who Waldo was? What did that say about Stevie Rose's mother? "Charlie Waldo. This is Lorena Nascimento."

A man appeared behind her, twenty years older but not quite her height, in shorts, sandals and a Hawaiian shirt buttoned tight over a thick chest. He had bountiful hair for his age, curly and dark, graying at the temples. "Charlie Waldo? Jesus, come in, come in. I'm Joel." He gestured down the steps toward the sofas where they'd sat with Stevie and elucidated for his wife as they followed. "Honey, this is the guy who figured out Monica Pinch." He turned to Waldo. "I'm a huge fan. Huge. And that other thing? The way you ripped the LAPD a new one? You're a rock star." He must have been talking about Lydell Lipps and everything after. The adulation made Waldo queasy. "Can I get you something to drink? I'm not sure what's in the fridge. We just got back from

Hawaii." Waldo and Lorena both declined. "We just bought a pineapple farm. Well, not *just*—about a year ago."

Paula sat beside her husband. "It gives us a reason to spend more time there. We love Hawaii."

"Plus we're doing good, you know?" Joel lowered his voice conspiratorially, though there was no one around to listen in. "We outbid Dole for it. They just brutalize their unions. We can give them better wages, better medical . . ."

"*Well*," said Paula.

"Well, not *crazy* better, but *you* know."

Paula said to Waldo and Lorena, "They see a private owner come in, especially when they see 'rich, *Hollywood* private owner,' these union people think they can walk all over you."

"We're not going to let them walk all over us," Joel said to his wife.

Paula kept explaining to Waldo and Lorena. "They start demanding all these things you can't give them. *Paternity* leave? *Really?* I mean, okay, if people are gay and they adopt, I get it, but how do you decide *which parent* should get the leave? I mean, why should that fall on *us?* Like if one works on our farm, and the other works on a golf course or something."

"We're not going to give them paternity leave."

"But if they strike . . ."

"They're not going to strike."

"How do you *know* that?"

"Because if they strike, we'll just sell to Dole." He turned back to Waldo and lowered his voice again. "We *won't*—not really— but we'll make them *think* that."

"Fuckers," said Paula.

"*They're not going to strike.*"

"Fuckers," she said again. Then, realizing the fuss she was making in front of strangers, she said to Lorena, "I'm sorry. But this one guy Kekepania we met with when we were out there? He is not a good person."

"Um," said Lorena, "is Stevie here?"

"I don't know," said Paula. "We haven't checked."

"We just got home," said Joel, telling them again.

Paula looked at a wall clock, said, "She's usually back from school by now. I'll go up and look," and left the room.

"So," said Joel, "did I hear you say you were doing something with Stevie?"

Lorena said, "Yes, but let's see if she's—"

"I don't want you to have to tell it twice. Let's wait until Paula comes back." He turned to Waldo. "Can I ask you a question? Has anyone contacted you about TV rights? To your story—the Pinch case, I mean. *And* the other stuff, as background. Is it true that you live in a tree house or something?"

"No, I haven't talked to anybody about TV rights."

Joel perked up. "Really?"

"I wouldn't be interested." He'd taken some money for the rights to the original Lipps case; it had become one more thing to regret.

"Are you sure? You could give the money to charity. You know, some of it." He actually winked. "I'm a TV producer. Well, you already know that; I mean, you're *here*." He dropped into the conspiratorial voice again. "By the way, we got picked up for two more seasons. That's not for public consumption yet, but you'll see it in the trades this week."

Waldo said, "I'll look for it."

Lorena said, "What's the name of the show again?"

Joel Rose's face froze for a fraction of a second. She had quietly wrecked him. *"Malibu Malice."*

"Oh yeah," she said, putting on enthusiasm, though all three of them knew she'd never seen it.

Paula returned. "She's not here."

Waldo said, "Any idea where she is?"

"I checked my phone—she didn't leave a message or anything. But she usually doesn't. She might just be running a little late. Her friend's mom drives her when we're away."

Lorena said, "Mr. and Mrs. Rose—"

"Paula and Joel. Please."

"We should tell you what's going on. Your daughter called me while you were out of town and hired us to look for her brother—"

"Her *brother*?"

Joel said, "I talked to her brother this morning. He's in Chicago."

Lorena said, "She made up a whole story—that you two had died in a car crash, and that her brother was only a little older, and lived here, and went to UCLA, and was Stevie's legal guardian. And that he was missing."

Paula said, "Why would she . . . ?"

Joel said, "And she paid you?" He looked at Paula. "With what?"

Paula said, "I always leave her some money for emergencies."

Waldo said, "What she really wanted was for us to go talk to Victor Ouelette. She was frustrated because your conversations with Sebastian Hexter didn't go anywhere."

The Roses squinted at him in matching confusion.

"Do either of those names mean anything to you?"

Joel said, "Say them again?"

"Victor Ouelette, Sebastian Hexter."

"Wait!" Paula said, pleased with herself like she was about to nail the Daily Double on *Jeopardy!* "Sebastian Hexter—he's the headmaster at Stoddard."

"Have you ever gone to talk with him about a problem Stevie was having with a teacher?"

Joel said, "Never. She's a great student. She's made honor roll."

Paula snickered. "*Honor* roll? Like in fifth grade."

Joel said, "Not fifth grade. Junior high."

Paula said, "Fine," and rolled her eyes.

Waldo said, "So, Victor Ouelette—that name doesn't ring a bell?" They both shook their heads. "She had him for history last year."

Joel said, "Oh, then I'm sure we met him. We always go to back-to-school night." He asked Paula, "Was he the African American fellow? I liked him."

"No, that was Mr. Bynoe. Algebra." She said to Waldo and Lorena, "There are so many teachers every year, you meet each one for ten minutes."

So Stevie had gone to the headmaster about Ouelette but hadn't mentioned him to her parents. Even the story under her story was springing fresh holes by the second. Lorena said, "You left Stevie alone while you went to Hawaii?"

Paula said, "We've always tried to nurture her independence."

Waldo said, "How's that working out?"

"I beg your pardon?"

"Is it possible she's a little *too* independent?"

"There's no such thing."

"There's a lot out there that kids get exposed to . . ."

"Sex and drugs are part of kids' lives. Parents who think they can hide all that from them are just fooling themselves."

"All of them are doing everything," said Joel. "The trick is to get them to be responsible about it. That's truly all you can ask."

Paula added, "You need to be open; that's the key. If your child feels they can do anything at home that they'd want to do any-where else, then they don't have to keep secrets. And they're less likely to get into some situation that they can't handle."

Lorena said, "Listen, Stevie's in some trouble. She wanted us to talk to that teacher, Victor Ouelette, and shortly after Waldo went to see him, he was murdered."

Paula said, *"Murdered?"*

"The police want to talk to Stevie."

Joel said, "How was he killed?"

"He was shot."

Joel said, "Oh," and the Roses looked at each other, relieved. Joel said to Waldo and Lorena, "Our family is totally anti-gun."

Paula said, "I'm on the board of the Center for Sensible Hand-gun Policy. I got Lady Gaga to sing at our benefit at the Beverly Hilton—I know her manager." Waldo began to wonder how close the bathroom was and whether it had a big enough plunger to pull this lady's head out of her ass. She said, "That poor teacher, though. The police really have no idea who did it?"

Joel, who was starting to understand, snapped at his wife. "They think *Stevie* may have done it." He turned to Lorena. "That's what you're saying, isn't it?"

"They want to talk to her."

Joel was getting more agitated and turned on Paula. "God-dammit. We should have insisted that boy stay here."

Waldo said, "What boy?"

Paula ignored Waldo, answered Joel. "We didn't have a choice. His parents said no."

"We should have called and talked them into it."

"Stevie didn't want us to."

Joel shifted in his seat, distressed. "This is our fault."

Paula got short with him, too. "She didn't shoot anybody. This'll get straightened out."

Lorena asked the question again. "Who's the boy?"

Joel said, "This new boyfriend Stevie's got. I wanted him to stay here while we were in Hawaii. Truth is, I don't like leaving her all by herself." He shook his head and added, "But apparently his parents wouldn't go for it," sneering bewilderment in his voice.

Lorena said, "What's this boy's name?"

"Koy."

Joel said, "I thought it was Ky."

"No, Koy. I *think* Koy."

Lorena said, "Last name?"

"Ling. Or maybe Lee. Ling or Lee."

Lorena wrote down all four names. "I take it you never met him."

"No, I met him," said Paula, with tone, clearly irked by the implication of irresponsibility. "I wouldn't ask a high school boy to stay alone with our daughter in our house if I hadn't met him."

"Of course not," said Waldo. He didn't give them time to decode *his* tone. "Look, the police have given us a window to keep a little control of this thing. If we don't, they're going to find Stevie and bring her in without us. She won't return our calls; could I ask you both to try her, and text her, and let her know it's critical that she come back here right away?"

The Roses nodded and sat there looking at him, earnest.

Waldo said, "I mean, now."

"Oh," said Joel, and they took out their phones and dialed.

Paula said, "She never answers."

Joel said, "And her voicemail is full half the time."

Lorena said, "That's why you should text, too." She and Waldo waited while Joel and Paula simultaneously listened to Stevie's outgoing message, then watched them both text. Waldo said, "Why don't you try calling the school, too? Maybe she's still there."

Paula dialed and walked into the other room to talk. Joel said to Waldo and Lorena, "She'll probably be home from school soon. You could wait if you want. I think Naomi Shapiro's been driving her."

"Who's that?"

"Her husband's a feature lit agent." They looked at him patiently until he understood that that description wasn't pertinent. "Her daughter's a friend of Stevie's. They live on Dixie Canyon." He said, "How serious is this? I mean, do you think Stevie's actually involved?"

Waldo didn't have an answer for him.

Paula returned, worried. "Stevie didn't go to school today, or yesterday."

Joel asked Waldo, "When was the teacher killed?"

Waldo said, "The night before that."

TEN

Girl's fucking poison," said Lorena under her breath. The two of them were alone in the living room, Joel and Paula having gone upstairs to talk privately. "I'll be lucky to come out of this without losing my ticket." Waldo didn't see how any of this would actually jeopardize her PI license, but both Cuppy and Wax had threatened it in the last twenty-four hours and by now everything about Stevie Rose set Lorena's teeth on edge. "Soon as they come back," she said, "we're out of here and we're calling Cuppy. Tell him everything we know, and then cut this whole fucking family loose."

Waldo didn't like the idea of Stevie in the wind. But Lorena was right: the girl was as unstable as a homemade nitrogen bomb, PETN with a belly ring. And in the end, she wasn't their responsibility. She had these parents, and they had her. Good luck to them all.

Joel and Paula swept back into the living room like the power couple they were, Joel saying, "The truth is, it isn't that unusual for Stevie to drop off the radar. Sometimes she'll just go off to a friend's for a day or two without telling us." Good luck to them indeed.

Lorena, already starting for the door, said, "Yeah, I'm sure she's fine—"

Joel wasn't finished, though. "Still, we're thinking we should treat this more seriously. Given the situation with the teacher."

Paula said, "We want to hire you to find her."

Waldo should have seen it coming, but it wasn't in him to think like a hustling PI, with an eye for the next gig. And Lorena hadn't seen it coming because she didn't want it to come.

Waldo said to the Roses, "Given everything, you should probably talk to the police and report her missing."

Joel said, "No—dead teacher and Stevie disappears? That's a bad look. Better to find her before they know she's gone. I assume you do missing persons."

Lorena turned to Waldo for help, but he wouldn't give it; he wanted the job. Lorena said to the Roses, "Could the two of *us* have a minute now?"

Paula said, "Sure. You can use one of the guest bedrooms."

She led them to it, smallish for a house this size, dominated by a four-poster queen bed laden with lacy pillows. But *one of*—how many guests bedrooms did these people have?

Lorena waited for Paula's footsteps to recede down the hall, then spoke in a harsh whisper. "We are *not* doing this."

"Because . . . ?"

"Because she killed him."

"They're asking us to find their daughter. Not to prove she's innocent."

"That's next. And you know she did it."

"I don't know that," said Waldo. "I don't lead with conclusions."

"What happened to all that high-minded cop bullshit from when you were turning me down on Pinch? 'Catch the bad guy.'"

"Wait, look at *you*: you don't want this one because you think she did it, but Pinch was a dead lock for guilty and all you saw was a business opportunity."

"I'm a businesswoman. And this case doesn't even have that going for it."

"No? Keeping a fifteen-year-old from getting pinned with a murder she didn't commit? *L.A. Times*'ll like *that* story."

"'A murder she didn't commit.' Sure *sounds* like we're leading with a conclusion."

"You said I can pick the cases I want to work on. You want to team up, here's where we start."

She chewed on that, giving Waldo enough time to ask himself just what was compelling him to stay involved with this girl, but not enough time to answer.

Lorena said, "Did you really get two thousand a day on Pinch?"

He nodded. "But I gave the money to charity."

"Yeah, well. We're not doing that."

"We'll see."

"How'd you get them to give you that much?"

"I told them that's what it would take."

"That's it? And they just said yes?" He nodded.

Lorena turned and left the bedroom. Waldo followed. He assumed this meant he'd won, though it didn't feel like it.

They followed the Roses' voices to the kitchen, where Paula was opening a bottle of Cabernet. Lorena cut right to it. "We get three thousand dollars a day, plus expenses. For that you get Waldo full-time, me part-time, plus all other resources my agency provides, as needed. We want one week's fee as a retainer, the unused balance to be returned if we find her sooner."

Joel said, "Credit card okay?"

Lorena said, "Sure." Waldo knew she was kicking herself for not asking for four.

Paula, pouring, said, "Red all right?"

Lorena and Waldo declined, so Paula poured a third of the bottle each for herself and Joel.

Then they all went to the living room and Waldo and Lorena began their work, collecting background on the family. They learned that Joel was sixty-five, Paula forty-three, and that they'd been together for seventeen years.

Joel said of their courtship, "It was your classic Hollywood location affair, with all the usual drama." It was hard to tell whether the irony in his voice was self-awareness or theater. "I was running this procedural I created called *Sea Legs*. It was about this disgraced FBI agent, total hard-ass, nobody'll hire him, so he goes to work as the head of security on the biggest cruise ship in the world—sort of *Love Boat* meets *The Shield*." War stories about a long-dead series weren't going to help anyone find his daughter, but somehow he couldn't resist sharing. "The network never got behind it. You know who we had as the guy—?"

Lorena steered him back toward port. "So that's where you two met? On that show?"

Paula said, "Yes. He was the boss, and I was as far below the line as you can get." Waldo didn't know what that meant. Paula explained: "'Below the line'—it comes from budgeting on shows. The producers, the actors, the director, we're all 'above the line.' 'Below the line' is the rest of the crew."

"So you weren't a producer then."

Paula said, "Hardly. I was a PA—I brought Joel his latte every morning."

Joel said, "But you could tell she was a Ferrari going ten miles an hour."

"I was totally smitten. But he was totally married."

"Not *totally* married. It was all but over."

"Of course, he didn't tell *me* that when we started. He was telling me that they were happy. I think it was his way of keeping himself 'emotionally unavailable.'" She said it with affectionate indulgence and ruffled his hair. They'd obviously told their origin story together before and seemed to think it was adorable.

Joel said, "Next thing you knew, the show was canceled, but we were living together."

Paula said, "I was his midlife crisis."

"You still are." They both chuckled. Yeah, thought Waldo, many times before.

Lorena said, "And you had Stevie . . ."

"Two years later. You should see our wedding pictures. I was in this white dress, out to here." She held her hands out in front of her, fingertips together.

Joel explained, "We had to wait for the divorce to finalize."

"But we wanted Stevie to be 'legitimate.'" Paula turned to her husband. "How old-fashioned were *we*?"

Joel said, "That's us."

Waldo said, "Has Stevie been going to Stoddard all the way through?"

"Mm-hmm," said Paula.

"Thirteen tuitions," said Joel, another practiced witticism.

"She's loved it. She was a really good student in elementary. Always one of the smartest girls. Straight As."

Lorena said, "And when did the issues start?"

Her dislike of Stevie had made her a little careless, a little presumptuous; the Roses stiffened. Joel said, "Issues?"

Waldo covered quickly: "Have there *been* any issues?"

"I wouldn't call them 'issues,'" said Paula, giving it some thought. "No, I wouldn't use that word. But her grades in high school haven't been what they were in junior high."

"And . . . no drugs, alcohol . . . ?"

Lorena added, "Promiscuity? Eating disorders?"

Paula said, "Not especially. You know, she *diets* more than she needs to, but all the girls do that. And compared to . . . *well*. Let me just say, I hear *some* of the kids at that school have *real* problems."

Joel erupted. "Paula! Christ Almighty! She's missing, and the police think she might have killed somebody! What the fuck do you think 'real problems' *look* like?" He'd finally gotten out of his own head long enough to recognize the gravity of the situation.

Waldo and Lorena held neutral faces in the residuum of the outburst. Paula finished her wine.

When, at length, Joel spoke again, he sounded penitent, albeit for older transgressions. "Maybe I shouldn't have been having another baby at fifty. Maybe I was too old, and maybe we were too busy with our career to pay attention to Stevie like we should have." Waldo was struck by his use of the singular; this model of self-involvement came with room enough for two.

Paula reached for his hand. "There's always been someone around for her. A nanny . . ."

"Yeah, yeah," said Joel, "and a fancy school. Spending isn't parenting."

His wife withdrew, wounded. "I think you're being hard on us."

He reached for her now, but she pulled away and poured herself the rest of the bottle.

Waldo said, "Let's find your daughter. Okay?"

Neither parent knew Stevie's password, so they couldn't use the Find iPhone feature. Lorena asked which social media Stevie used. Paula said she thought Stevie mostly was on Instagram but she hadn't been looking at what Stevie was doing there or on Facebook because she knew Stevie didn't like it. Lorena asked her to log on and see if Stevie had posted anything in the last couple of days. It appeared that Stevie had in fact blocked Paula from both sites, probably some time ago. Joel tried also and found the same.

Lorena asked for a photo of Stevie. Paula had some extra wallet-size prints of Stevie's latest school portrait and cut one off the sheet for each of them.

Together they browsed the Stoddard School directory. The Roses figured out that Paula was right, that the name of their daughter's boyfriend was indeed Koy, though not Lee or Ling but Lem. Lorena took a picture of the boy's info with her phone, and also that of Stevie's two closest friends, Dionne Shapiro and Kristal Whiting.

Lorena said that they were going to start following up these leads and that the Roses could assist in the meantime by going online and printing out a log of all of Stevie's incoming and outgoing calls and texts for the last month. They'd probably only be listed by phone number, Lorena said, so they should go through and identify any ones they knew. Lorena jotted Waldo's cell number on two of her own business cards and gave one to each Rose, saying they should call if anything at all occurred to them, and that they'd be in touch soon.

By the time Waldo and Lorena started down the driveway, Paula and Joel were holding hands again.

When the front door closed behind them, Lorena said, "We split fifty-fifty. You want to piss away your half saving the hippopotamus, up to you."

"The hippos are in trouble, no joke."

"No? Because it sounds like one." Then she said, "How about we leave the school for tomorrow and hit the kids tonight? It's close to dinnertime; they'll probably be home."

"That's what I was thinking."

At the bottom of the driveway the gates opened for them. "Shit," said Lorena, remembering. "My car's not here."

"We'll get you a bike in the morning. I'm buying."

"Comedian." Lorena took out her phone to order another Uber. "Tomorrow, we ain't doing this shit."

ELEVEN

Waldo was a different flavor of carsick, nauseated by the awareness of the hydrocarbons this colossal Kia Sedona kept coughing into the atmosphere, not only during their first swing through the hills—a trip that could have been perfectly walkable, by the way, at least in normal shoes—but also before and after their ride, while the Sedona's driver trawled aimless miles up and down Ventura Boulevard waiting for a fare. Still, if the Shapiros weren't home, discharging the Uber too soon and having to call for another to climb the hill to fetch them would be even worse, so Waldo stayed behind in the back seat, pinning down the beast, while Lorena rang the Shapiros' doorbell. When no one answered, she got back in and they started the eleven miles to Woodland Hills, where Koy Lem lived, far for a Stoddard student.

The westbound 101 was already strangled with rush-hour traffic, further agitating him. He bought the pilot episode of *Malibu Malice* on iTunes, waited through the slow download without Wi-Fi, and popped in his earbuds. Having spent time with the artists, he was eager to assay their famous canvas.

The show opened with a nighttime beach party, teens around a bonfire—dancing, beer, weed, sex, coke, sex, pills, sex, and, just before the opening credits, the body of the new girl at school found naked and dead in the surf, triggering the vertiginous plot: the Malibu Police Department calls it an accidental overdose, but Sandy Walker, nerdy freshman reporter on the *Malibu High Daily Eagle*, won't let it rest, as the dead girl, whose name was Laura Roberts, in a moment of kindness to less-than-popular Sandy, had mentioned that she didn't drink or do drugs either, but suddenly inquisitive Sandy, who, by the way, just had her braces removed, gets her first-ever boy attention from, of all people, Jesse Butler, football star and campus man-whore, or maybe campus date-rapist, who, Sandy learns, went out one time with the dead girl, Laura, and perhaps something happened that night that drove Laura to suicide and perhaps that's also why Jesse is paying attention to Sandy in the first place, to cover it up, but then again Jesse does seem really interested and he's *sooo* cute, though his attention to Sandy also draws some decidedly less desirable attention from Jesse's putative, much-cheated-on girlfriend, Eden Conner, head cheerleader, blond and bitchier than the bitchy brunette girl who in turn is bitchier than the bitchy black girl but even *that* girl is pretty bitchy, and the three of them invite Sandy to Eden's house, where they roofie Sandy and take pictures of her with her shirt off and then post them on Sandy's Instagram with Sandy's own phone, and next thing you know, Sandy's in trouble with the principal, Mr. Story, who would come down harder on Sandy except that Mr. Story is having an affair with Sandy's mother, Kelly, herself once upon a time—quite unlike her daughter—the blondest and bitchiest cheerleader at this very school and now, by evidence, the bitchiest mom in the PTA and a closet alcoholic. The hour was garish, depraved and unapologetic. It was no mystery how this had become the Roses' golden goose.

All of them are doing everything. The trick is to get them to be re-
sponsible about it.

The Lem house was off De Soto, a distant and less tony portion of
the Valley. Waldo wondered if the boyfriend would be walled off
from them by the protective parents Paula had mentioned, but
when they rang the bell they got lucky: a high schooler opened the
door, a big-shouldered kid with a floppy undercut, in cargo shorts
and a tank top that showed off ropy arms. Lorena asked if he was
Koy and when he said yes, they signaled that the driver could
leave. Waldo watched the Sedona accelerate into its next stopgap
voyage to nowhere and held down a fresh wave of nausea.

Lorena explained to the boy that they were detectives working
for Stevie Rose's parents. Koy said, "Why?" and looked nervous.
Lorena asked if they could come inside and talk and he said, "No,"
very quickly.

They heard voices from in the house. The teen turned and
called, "It's for me, Ma," then stepped outside and shut the door
behind him. He confirmed that he went to Stoddard with Stevie
and told them he was a senior, headed to Santa Clara in the fall.

The door opened. Koy's mother took a quick glance at Lorena,
then inspected Waldo head to toe. Koy said, "It's okay—they're in
my class," and almost winced at the clumsiness of his own lie. The
mother did a second pass on Waldo, toe to head, harrumphed and
went back inside.

Waldo asked Koy if he'd seen Stevie around the last couple
of days. The kid shrugged. Waldo said, "You're her boyfriend,
aren't you?"

"No! Damn! Who told you that?"

"Her parents."

"Damn," he said again. "We hooked up, like, one time." The kid felt their disbelief. "*Two* times," he conceded. "But one was just a blow job."

It still didn't compute. Curtains in the window parted: Koy's mother making her presence felt.

Lorena said, "Why do Stevie's parents think you guys are more?"

The kid, overwhelmed and annoyed, led them away from the house. He spoke in a loud whisper. "The first time was at a party, okay? The second time was, like, three months later in this, like, extra, like . . . *building.*"

"What kind of building?"

"Like, at her parents'. By the pool."

"You mean the guesthouse?"

"I guess, yeah. And after, we went in the regular house and her mom was all, like, *suggestive.* I think she was shit-faced."

"What do you mean, 'suggestive'?"

"Like, coming on, practically."

"In front of Stevie?"

Koy shook his head. "Stevie was getting me a Red Bull. Her mom kept talking about my gams. I looked at my shorts, to see if they were hanging out, but they weren't."

Lorena said, "Do you know what 'gams' are?"

Koy giggled. "Yeah—they're your boys. Your frankenberries."

Waldo said, "They're your legs. Gams are legs."

Koy knew better. "You're thinking of nads."

"Like gonads?"

"Exactly."

Waldo said, "Gonads are frankenberries. Gams are legs."

Koy looked to Lorena to break the tie. She nodded.

Koy said, "*Oh.* She said I had water polo nads."

Waldo puzzled, then offered a correction: "Water polo *gams*?"

"Yeah, maybe. Probably. I guess she knows I play." That filled in a gap: this kid wasn't riding to Santa Clara on his SATs. "And then her husband came in—like, Stevie's *dad*? He was, like, all in the next room and shit! And Stevie's mom goes, 'This is Stevie's boyfriend,' and suddenly he's all, like, 'Why don't you stay here with Stevie when we go to Hawaii?' Like my parents would ever let me do *that*—stay all week at some girl's house when her parents are away."

Lorena said, "And that was it? You never hooked up with her again?"

"Nah. That shit with her parents weirded me out. And she's, you know, *Stevie*." He seesawed his head back and forth, a gesture that he must have thought communicated something. "We haven't even talked at school since then."

"How long ago was that?"

Koy thought. "Two weeks?"

Lorena said to Waldo, "You got anything else?" and Waldo said no. He knew she was prompting to see if he wanted to tell the kid Stevie was missing, but Waldo didn't see where that would help. Instead he suggested that Lorena give Koy her card and asked the boy to please let them know right away if Stevie happened to contact him. They turned and headed toward the street.

"Hey," said Koy, after them, keeping his voice down so his mother wouldn't hear. "Stevie's bananas—but I like her, you know? Somebody should tell her to slow down."

This next Uber was an SUV too, a Hyundai Santa Fe. They decided to try Stevie's friend Dionne again in Sherman Oaks before continuing on to the other girl's house in Studio City. This time

Naomi Shapiro, the mom who'd been driving Stevie to school, answered the door. She embraced her age more than Paula Rose and it was working for her, with thick, smartly cut hair gone fully gray. She was trepidatious at first but unwound on hearing that they were working for Paula and Joel, and when they told her that Stevie was missing she invited them inside.

Naomi apologized, saying that she'd been on edge since hearing about her daughter's former teacher getting murdered, and asked if they knew anything more about that. Waldo and Lorena played dumb. They asked her when she last saw Stevie. Naomi said she drove Stevie home two afternoons ago—in other words, just before Waldo and Lorena had last seen her themselves.

Naomi described her friendship with Paula Rose as long and convenient, Dionne and Stevie having gravitated toward each other in nursery school and the families living so close. They'd been carpooling to one school or activity or another for a decade. She said she hadn't picked Stevie up the previous morning because Dionne told her that Stevie had texted that she had a bad cold and wasn't up to going to school.

That gave them the opening to ask to talk to Dionne. Naomi at first insisted on being in the room with them, but Lorena, referencing her own teenage girlfriends and asking Naomi to think back to hers, said that if Stevie was in trouble, Dionne would be more likely than anyone to have some bit of information that could make the difference, and that it might be something she didn't want her mother to hear. Lorena was gentle but determined and Naomi finally agreed to stay a couple of rooms away watching *Dancing with the Stars,* on standby should Dionne want her to intervene. Waldo was grateful Lorena was there; he never could have negotiated that himself.

Dionne Shapiro, who'd herself been lounging in front of the

TV, wore heels and complicated eye makeup, no doubt new to her at fifteen and essential at all hours. Lorena began by saying they knew Stevie hadn't been at school the last few days. "Any idea where she is?"

"Uh, *yeah*. She's my best friend."

"Can you tell us?

Dionne hesitated. "Only if she says it's okay."

"Can you ask her?" While Dionne tapped a text message into her phone, Lorena said, "Stevie's parents don't know where she is. They're really worried. Has she been posting anything? Instagram, Facebook?"

"I could look." Dionne stayed focused on her phone.

Lorena asked if Dionne knew about what happened to Mr. Ouelette and whether the kids at school were talking about it. Dionne nodded small affirmations but gave only a half shrug when Lorena asked if kids were speculating about who murdered him. Waldo couldn't tell whether she was using her phone to search for Stevie or to hide from them.

Lorena said, "Stevie told us she was hooking up with Mr. Ouelette."

That got Dionne's attention. "Stevie told *you* that? *God*." She snorted and said, "Actually, I'm totally not surprised. She thought it made her, like, *so cool* to be doing it with a teacher. I mean, he's not even a *hot* teacher. And, like, I *totally* could have had sex with Ouelette. Seriously. Whenever he used to make me get up and throw away my gum, I knew he was watching my butt the whole time. The boys made jokes about it at lunch. Ouelette is, like, a total perv."

Then Dionne's face fell, her disgust at the teacher giving way to the recollection of what had happened to him.

Waldo asked, "Did Mr. Ouelette ever make a move on you?"

Dionne drew back like she'd forgotten Waldo was even in the

room. Lorena scolded him with her eyes, then said to Dionne, "Did he?"

Dionne looked like she was thinking about lying, but finally said, "No." Then she added, "But I've hooked up with way hotter *regular* guys than Stevie. And she totally knows it."

"Did you say that to her? Like, when she was bragging about getting it on with a teacher?" Waldo could see that the question landed. Lorena stayed with it. "Did you say all that other stuff, too—the stuff you just said to us?" Dionne looked away. "Did you guys have kind of a fight?" Dionne nodded. "When was that?"

"Couple days ago, at lunch."

"Has Stevie talked to you since then?"

"Not really."

"Meaning . . . ?"

Dionne said that they had driven Stevie home but barely talked in the car; then Dionne fell asleep early that night and awoke to find a late-night text from Stevie saying she was sick and couldn't go to school. Lorena had Dionne read them the text.

They asked if she really knew where Stevie was, and Dionne admitted she didn't. They asked about Koy Lem; Dionne said that Stevie wasn't into him anymore. They asked if there was anyone else from school who might know more than she did; Dionne said, "You mean, besides Mr. Ouelette?" and began to tear up. Waldo saw a box of tissues across the room and brought it to her. She blew her nose. Dionne said, "Do you know where he got shot?"

Lorena said, "His apartment building."

"I mean, where on his body?"

A Chevy Tahoe made it a hat trick: after the Sedona and the Santa Fe, three straight air-befouling SUVs named for unspoiled locales of the West. What were these car companies up to—a hoodwink, or a taunt? The thought of some future Chevy Idyllwild with an extra-long wheelbase was almost too much to bear. Not that any of these monstrosities troubled Lorena; indeed, he thought he caught a smirk when she was climbing in.

At least the address of Stevie's other friend wasn't far, just a few miles away on the other side of Ventura Boulevard, where the homes were smaller and closer together. Parents in this neighborhood who sent a kid to Stoddard weren't merely adding another tractable expense; they were making sacrifices that might squeeze them forever.

Waldo rang the doorbell. A thin-haired man in baggy chinos and a UCLA sweatshirt opened the door, drooping, drained by the day or maybe by life.

Waldo said, "Are you Mr. Whiting?"

"Yeah. What's up? It's past nine."

"My name's Charlie Waldo; this is Lorena Nascimento. We're private investigators, working for fellow parents of yours from the Stoddard School—Joel and Paula Rose?" Whiting's eyes hardened; Waldo could tell he'd dropped the wrong names, but there was no turning. "Your daughter Kristal is a friend of Stevie's?"

"So?"

"So, Stevie's missing. If Kristal's around, we'd like to talk to her."

Lorena added, "We know it's late. Just for a minute or two."

The man looked at a flower bed and Waldo could almost hear him count ten in his head before speaking. "Kristal's not here," he said, slowly, evenly. Another parent with a girl on the loose.

"Do you have any idea when she—"

The man cut him off but kept the same even cadence. "Kristal's in rehab." Waldo didn't even get to say, *Oh.* "Leave my family alone. Stevie Rose has done enough damage." Kristal Whiting's father closed the door.

Three leads and nothing to show. Lorena sighed and said to Waldo, "I guess that's a night," while she started to order their next car, their fifth of the day. They waited quietly, a few driveways down, so as not to linger in front of the Whitings'. When their ride pulled up, his heart sank again: a Dodge Grand Caravan. "What the hell *is* it with Uber?" he said. "It's all SUVs."

"Yeah, XL," said the driver. "That's what you ordered."

Aghast, Waldo turned on Lorena, who was already giggling. "Lighten up, Waldo. I just wanted you to give my poor Mercedes a little love."

Willem wasn't home, so Lorena microwaved a bag of popcorn and watched the *Malibu Malice* pilot in the living room. Waldo sat nearby, cruising the internet and diving deeper into the Roses.

Their moment in the sun, he learned, had been a masterly marketing scheme of their own devising, one that made *Malibu Malice* a succès de scandale right out of the box some four years ago. Their network, a struggling cable stepchild of one of the big conglomerates, acquired in a package with a more coveted sports network and known mostly for tired reruns of second-tier sitcoms from the nineties, had decided to "go edgy," i.e., to break the same new salacious ground that thirty other networks were already breaking.

With *Malibu Malice*, its first venture into scripted programming, the network had, at the Roses' urging, eschewed traditional advertising and targeted teens only through social media. Their provocative message of *Watch it online and clear your browser . . .*

your parents will never know! suckered watchdog groups into a predictable uproar, and the creators did everything they could to build the attention into a bonfire: Joel and Paula Rose had been everywhere, from the look of it, talking about the right-wing forces of censorship and how kids were too smart to fall for it. When the initial conflagration died down they stoked it again with a second-season opener in which super-vixen Eden Conner persuades an innocent freshman to hold on to her boyfriend and still keep her virginity by having anal sex instead. Waldo found four different YouTube interviews from that autumn in which Joel Rose defended the story line with the same rationale, offered each time in the same earnest timbre: *"Believe me,"* Joel would say, *"this is happening all over. This is a real issue."* Indeed, thought Waldo, just like deforestation, or the scarcity of clean water.

Lorena got to the end of the pilot and snapped off the TV. "And now these people have Stevie Rose," she said.

"What do you think?" said Waldo.

"What do *I* think? I think some people get everything they want, *and* everything they deserve."

TWELVE

They delayed their arrival at the school to miss the drop-off rush. A police SUV sealed off the driveway, so they drove past and parked on the street. As Waldo tried to pass between the police car and the gate, the same decrepit security guard, unstrung with sudden responsibility, fumbled to ask if he had a pass. Waldo started to argue that he'd never needed one before, but the old man's eye started twitching and Waldo dropped the pushback, gave his name and asked him to call the headmaster's office for approval.

Waldo didn't recognize the young female uniform who'd gotten out of the SUV and was talking to Lorena near the street. She was already telling Lorena about some guy she was looking at; from the snippet he could make out, the suspect's name might be Weitzman. Waldo loved it: leave it to Lorena to charm a cop out of the car and a lead out of the cop before they even made it onto campus. Waldo tried to pick up more of their conversation, but the guard, talking louder than required, kept asking Waldo to repeat his name and even made him spell it twice.

Waldo wandered over to Lorena. The officer was telling her, "I love that cone. I have trouble with stilettos, though—I tore up my knee a couple years ago and it still isn't right."

Lorena turned a leg, showing off her sharp-toed ankle boot, black leather with four decorative buckles. "These might work for you. The support's more like a block."

"Really?"

Lorena said, "I bought the Stuart Weitzmans, but then I saw these and I needed them, too." Whoever Stuart Weitzman was, Waldo was pretty sure he wasn't the guy who shot Victor Ouelette. The very notion of fashion galled him, with its perpetual cycle of gratuitous consumption and disposal. He looked at Lorena's boots and said, "Needed?"

Lorena said, "I didn't have any cone heels."

"Why did you 'need' cone heels?"

"Because it's this year." The police officer laughed. Lorena gave Waldo's own worn, pragmatic ensemble a once-over, eviscerating it with a raised eyebrow and giving the cop's laugh a fresh roll. "Waldo," she said, "this is *why we work.*"

"Amen to that," said Lorena's new friend.

Waldo looked over at the guard to check if he'd gotten permission to wave them in yet but saw Hexter coming out of the gate and walking toward them instead. The headmaster steered Waldo away from the others. "It's too chaotic in there. I don't know what your role is—"

Waldo indicated Lorena. "My partner and I are working for the Roses. Stevie's missing."

"Oh, for Pete's sake." Hexter squeezed his eyes shut and pinched the bridge of his nose. "You do know the police are calling her a suspect."

Waldo said, "I need to talk to some of your teachers."

"No. I can't have you on campus. The school's a tinderbox already." The two men watched the traffic on Chandler, avoiding each other's eyes. Their ledger was already tortuous: yes, Waldo had preserved a career-threatening secret for Hexter, but the accommodation Hexter made in return was no small thing, granting second-grade admission conspicuously late in the school year to the daughter of a drug dealer who'd saved Waldo's life. It would be hard to adjudge, at this point, just who owed whom.

Lorena was still chatting with the cop but eyeing the men. Waldo kept her at bay with a slight shake of the head. He said to Hexter, "Give me *one*. His best friend on the faculty, whoever that is. Then I'll go away." When Hexter still balked, Waldo said, "You can send the guy out here."

Hexter pawed the ground with a scuffed oxford, then said, "No promises," and walked back through the gate and toward the office.

There was nothing to do but wait, so Waldo went back to the women. The police officer was saying, "But I can't really wear fuchsia."

A few minutes later a female teacher came out to see them, midthirties, with frizzy hair, a bohemian dress and army boots. She told them her name was Cheryl Falacci and that she taught art. She was a close friend of Victor Ouelette's, she said, not just at Stoddard but since they were freshmen together, and later off-campus roommates, at UC Irvine. In fact, she said, she was the one who'd recommended him for this job. The woman was jittery, brittle; it was hard to tell how much of that was her normal affect and how much was anguish at her friend's murder.

Waldo told her they were trying to find Stevie Rose. "I'm

sorry to make this even more unpleasant, but I have to ask: have you heard any rumors about her and Victor?"

Brittle or not, that set her off. "*Hateful. Yes.* All horseshit, and hateful. And see what happened?" She'd lost Waldo already. She explained: "Why would anybody kill someone like Victor? People talk hateful crap, it becomes a *thing*, and then all of a sudden it's a problem. Like Trump and Sweden. There was no terrorism at all in Sweden until Trump started talking about it. Then? Guess what."

"So you think Victor was killed because of the rumor?"

"I'm sure it didn't help him any."

"Who would do that?"

"I have no idea. There's just a meanness out there now. I was scared to leave my house *before* this."

"But you're sure it wasn't true about Victor and Stevie Rose."

"These kids—how they live, what they do with each other online—there's no privacy, there's no modesty. Everything's nothing to them. So dragging down a man like Victor? That's nothing either. And let me tell you—the teachers aren't any better."

"Did he have enemies on the faculty?"

"Enemies? No. But they were all jealous. The kids loved Victor. He got asked to advise more clubs than any of us. He coached track. He took on more independent studies. Victor Ouelette was one of the most decent men I've ever met in my life, and they killed him. This country . . ." She was overcome. "I'm sorry . . ." She turned and scurried back onto campus.

Lorena said to Waldo, "Wouldn't be the first thing Stevie made up."

Waldo was doubtful. "Why would she lie to her best friend about something like that?"

"To impress her."

Waldo shook his head and started back toward the car. "I never understood girls."

Lorena raised another eloquent eyebrow.

They reviewed the previous day's interviews with Stevie's parents, to match their impressions against what the Roses knew. Waldo told them that the Lem boy claimed that he and Stevie weren't deeply involved.

"I couldn't tell you," said Paula. "I only met Ky the one time."

"Koy," corrected Lorena. She asked if the Roses knew that Kristal Whiting was in rehab.

Paula, distressed, said, "No, I didn't know that."

Joel said, "Who's Kristal Whiting?"

Waldo asked if they'd printed out the phone records. Paula went to the kitchen and brought back a sheaf half an inch thick. "Stevie uses her phone a lot. It's mostly texts."

Lorena said, "How'd you do identifying the numbers?"

"Not too well. We x-ed out mine and Joel's, but that's about it." She said to her husband, "We should probably get Dionne's number, at least. For emergencies." Waldo was struck by the implicit optimism. Or maybe it was denial.

It wasn't hard to figure out Dionne's number, though; it showed up thousands of times during the month, a hundred or more texts in both directions every day, many through the classroom hours. The last of those, outgoing, was sent at ten thirteen a few nights earlier, presumably Stevie telling Dionne she couldn't make it to school the next day. One other phone number appeared a couple hundred times, mostly texts too, ending abruptly about ten days before, probably marking Kristal Whiting's entry into rehab.

Different numbers popped up prominently for a few days, then disappeared. Lorena said those were probably boys.

The most glaring revelation, though, and the troubling one, was that, except for scattered, unanswered incoming texts and voicemails, the phone had been used only once since that final message to Dionne, and that only half an hour later. Hundreds of calls, thousands of texts, and then nothing for two and a half days, nothing since about five hours after Waldo and Lorena had been the last to see her. Nothing since the night Victor Ouelette was shot to death in his garage.

Lorena pointed to something on the last and third-to-last calls, made on either side of the final Dionne text. Waldo looked closer: they were different phone numbers, both outgoing, one at five fifty-eight, which lasted twenty-seven minutes, the other at ten forty-seven, which lasted two minutes. Both had 949 area codes.

Waldo said, "949? Is that O.C.?"

"Irvine's 949," Lorena said, floating a possible link: that was where Cheryl Falacci said she and Ouelette had gone to school and lived for a while.

Paula said, "What do we do with all these phone numbers we don't know?"

Lorena told them she subscribed to a service called Trans-parentator, one of several available apps that work as reverse white pages, even for cell phones. She wanted to run the numbers here, with the Roses nearby, to see if they recognized any of the names as they popped up.

"You're going to do *all* of them?" said Joel, dismayed. Waldo wondered what he had to do that was more important.

Lorena handed Waldo the printout. The calls and texts ran in reverse order, most recent at the top, so they started there. He read Lorena the number of the last call, the one at ten forty-seven. She typed it in, waited a moment for the result, then read, "M. Amador." The Roses shook their heads at the unfamiliar name. Lorena said, "You're sure."

Waldo said, "Think, now."

Paula said, "M. Amador? Orange County? Sorry."

Joel said, "No idea."

Lorena said, "Okay." Waldo, skipping over the Dionne text, read off the third number on the page, the one for the longer call Stevie made around six, a couple of hours after they'd been in this room with Stevie.

Lorena saw the name and sat up. "Fuck," she said.

Waldo resolved to find a good moment to suggest she watch her language around clients. He said, "What is it?"

Lorena slid her phone to him so he could read it on the app himself. One short name, six letters total, but enough to knock a couple of teeth loose in his jaw.

Roy Wax.

Waldo said, "Fuck."

THIRTEEN

W hat?" said Joel.

Lorena said, "A name we've seen before. Do you know a Roy Wax?"

The Roses looked at each other. "Why?" said Paula.

Joel said, "He's my brother-in-law. *Paula's* brother-in-law."

Paula said, "He's married to my sister."

Joel said, "How do *you* guys know him?"

"Unrelated case. Coincidence," said Waldo, though he didn't believe it. Lorena grimaced bewilderment like someone was telling her the laws of gravity had been revoked.

Joel turned to his wife. "Why would Stevie call Roy?"

Waldo said, "Or someone with a phone on Roy's account. Does the app tell you the actual user?" Lorena was still too gobsmacked to answer.

Joel, putting it together, spit, *"Daron."*

Paula sighed exasperation and explained to the detectives. "Our nephew. Brenda and Roy's son."

Waldo said, "Stevie's age?"

That set Joel off. "Not close. Old enough for prison. You still know any cops?" he said to Waldo.

Waldo said, "Prison for what?"

But Joel was too riled for discussion. "Spoiled little prick. From when he was, what, seven? *No* values . . ."

"None," Paula seconded.

"That whole family. No *compassion* . . ."

"None."

"No—no—no . . ." He looked for it. ". . . *empathy*. Human scum."

"*No* compassion. It's all about themselves."

"Scum. *All* of them."

"Prison for what?" Waldo asked again.

"Anywhere he'd fucking hate it," said Joel, answering a different question in his head. "Anywhere so fucking awful, he hangs himself in his fucking cell."

"*Joel*," said his wife. "Maybe you should take a Xanax."

"I don't need a Xanax. I need somebody to stick that little bastard's head in a vise and pop his eyes out with a spoon."

"You need a Xanax. One of the good ones. Want me to get it for you?"

"I'll get it." Joel stood and left the room again, muttering about whether a fork might be more effective.

Paula turned to the others. "About a week after we saw them at Thanksgiving, I smelled something in Stevie's closet. Marijuana. I found three baggies, and one of cocaine—all in a business envelope from Roy's company."

"She was fourteen!" hollered Joel from down the hall.

"And Daron was twenty," added Paula.

Lorena said, "Does he live with his parents?"

"No, he's got his own apartment. In Costa Mesa, I think."

"Do you have the address?"

Somehow that question spun Paula out like her husband. "Jesus, why would I have his address? The kid *is* a menace! They *should* lock him up, and throw away the key." Then she remembered. "Oh wait, of course I have it. I needed it for the Christmas cards."

She gave them a family history lesson as she rummaged through the files on her MacBook Air. Brenda and Paula Steinfeldt had grown up in Artesia, near the Orange County line, back when the suburbs were creeping north from Santa Ana and Anaheim and tumbling south from Los Angeles proper. The sexual adventurousness of the seventies made life a little too interesting in the Steinfeldt house; divorce hit when Brenda was seven and Paula only three. They didn't see their dad much, and Kitty, their mom, was more interested in her dating life than in making sure her older daughter didn't bully her little sister. With that plus the age difference, Brenda and Paula had never been much like friends.

Kitty eventually remarried a childless plant manager for McDonnell Douglas and suddenly decided that family was the most important thing in the world, but by that point the girls were too old for reclamation, Paula a junior in high school and her big sister already in her third year at Scripps. Still, they assembled every Thanksgiving, and a year or so ago, to honor Kitty's seventieth birthday, the Roses and Waxes hired a photographer for a posed portrait of the combined family, which Paula showed now to Waldo and Lorena. Kitty and her husband, Wally, sat before the standard mottled cyclorama, flanked by the Roses on the left and the Waxes on the right, all in matching burgundy polos and khakis, looking like a wholesome family singing act from the last century. Paula said, "This was the first time Stevie was old enough for Daron to pay her any attention."

"Yeah, because she was old enough to buy drugs from him," said Joel, returning from the bedroom. "Someone should break his ankles with a sledgehammer." Waldo didn't know how fast Xanax kicked in, but it didn't sound fast enough.

Lorena said, "What else should we know about Brenda and Roy?"

"I can tell you everything you need to know about them in two words," said Joel, plopping into a seat beside Paula and crossing his arms. "They're Republicans."

Mount St. Lorena was getting close to blowing; he could feel it. They'd been bickering since they left the Roses, and nothing was working out for her. First they couldn't agree on a place to eat: he wanted to start Googling toward something sufficiently green in the Valley; she wanted Jack in the Box. Unable to compromise, they started out for Costa Mesa hungry. Waldo was better built for unfed stretches than she was and she grew cranky first. Then she insisted they follow Waze's recommendation and take the 405 rather than the downtown route Waldo instinctively preferred, only to have traffic stop dead at the top of the Sepulveda Pass. As soon as she fought her way into the carpool lane, cars started cruising by on her right. Down by Wilshire she shifted back over, only to see the pattern reverse. Waldo wisely kept silent.

When the congestion didn't loosen, even after LAX, she erupted. "I want out of this. I'm serious: let the cops find her, or let the Roses hire somebody else. And Wax—fuck, Waldo, I want to stay clear. Connected like he is? What am I going to do if he does get my ticket pulled? Be a meter maid? Work in a flower shop? Think I'd be good at that?" She looked over at him but he knew better than to answer. "You're going to say I have to tough out shit like this. If I want to get bigger than peep shows." That was the right answer, but he was careful not to even shrug with his eyes. Still, she said, "You know what, Waldo? Shut the fuck up."

A couple of minutes later she jerked into the exit lane at Hawthorne. "You're going to watch me eat a Jumbo Jack. And curly fries." Waldo still hadn't said a word. "Asshole."

While Lorena drove, Waldo called hospitals to cover the traditional bases. Daylight was gone by the time they reached the address Paula gave them, a luxury apartment complex called Puesta del Sol. Cruising past, they spotted two ways in: a gated garage, which would handle most of the residents' entries and exits, plus a double glass door for visitors and deliveries, with a vestibule and a maroon-jacketed security man at a desk, which looked like a pass-through to offices.

They both wanted to arrive at Daron's door unannounced but found themselves in disagreement yet again, this time over how to get there. Waldo thought they should loiter in the shadows near the garage and duck in behind the next exiting car, then do the same to slip past the inevitable security door beyond. Lorena was sure she could get them inside quicker by walking in the front entrance alone and talking her way past the half-assed security man, then finding her way to the garage and letting Waldo in through the gated pedestrian door. Waldo, his empty stomach starting to growl, gave in again and let her try it her way.

Lorena parked and headed for the front entrance. Waldo found a dark spot under a fern pine and perched on a short ivied wall to wait for the vehicle gate to rise, sure he'd get inside first and show her he was right. But he wasn't: in less than a minute Lorena was opening the pedestrian door and calling his name in a stage whisper. "How'd you do that?" he said, following her through the garage.

"Shit, I keep telling you: men are easy."

In the complex's North building, they took the elevator up and found number 421. Waldo stepped to the side; Lorena stood in front of the eyehole and knocked. "Daron?" The door opened. Sandy hair hung over Daron's eyes and there were patches of unshaven fuzz on his chin and lip. He wore jeans with a tear at the knee and a Deadmau5 concert T-shirt and nothing on his feet. "Hey, I'm Lorena, I live in South. We have some friends who've been telling me about you." She walked right past him and into his apartment. Men *were* easy.

Daron followed her in, flicking the door behind him to shut it. "What friends?" he said. Waldo stopped the door with his toe and stepped inside. Daron turned and said, "Hi," confounded but unalarmed. He was too soft to be much of a dealer; if the Roses were right about him selling to his cousin, he was probably just passing on his own buy to show off.

Waldo could see doors to at least two bedrooms. There were take-out food containers all over the living room and empty Ketel One bottles and dirty clothes. The place smelled like weed and greasy leftovers. Tonight's dinner cartons sat half-eaten next to a bong on a filthy glass coffee table, across from a ninety-inch TV with some multiplayer shooting game in progress, animated Special Forces types hunting bad guys somewhere in the Middle East.

Waldo said, "We're looking for Stevie Rose."

The name put him on guard. "I don't know her, man."

Lorena said, "How do you know Stevie's a her?"

Waldo said, "Play dumb about your friends, not about your cousin. That's *too* dumb."

Daron said, "Hey, what friends told you about me?" His eyes flitted to his game. "I'm kinda playing with a team . . ."

Lorena looked at Daron's half-eaten dinner cartons. "Mastro's. What you got, a K.C. strip?"

"Rib eye."

"And is that the lobster mashed potatoes? *Love* those." She looked at Waldo. "That's a thirty-five-dollar side right there."

Daron said, "Postmates." Now he was staring at his game full on. He reached for a controller on the coffee table, which was plugged into a laptop on a chair, corded into the TV.

Lorena slid the controller out of his reach. Daron shot her a *what gives?* look.

Waldo said, "When's the last time you talked to Stevie?"

"Not since Thanksgiving. For real."

"You know she's missing?" Daron shook his head, looked uneasy. "Your number's one of the last she called before she disappeared. For real."

"Are you police?"

"Private eyes. Working for Stevie's parents. We find her, all of this goes away. We don't, the police'll be here next, and they'll want to talk about the goodie bag you sent her home with."

"I don't know what they found, but I didn't give her anything."

"The envelope was from your dad's company." Daron deflated. Waldo said, "Are you always this stupid, or just always baked?"

Daron said, "I'm straight, man. I'm in the middle of a game, is all. I'm a Distinguished Master Guardian, and if I want to make Legendary Eagle, we've got to defuse this bomb—"

Waldo yanked the cord from the TV, toppling the laptop too.

Daron, infuriated, lunged at him. Lorena placed a stiletto in his path and Daron crashed to the floor. Saying, "Temper, Daron," she kicked his kneecap for good measure.

"Ow! You know, even if you got a problem with me? There are four other guys whose ratings you just completely fucked."

Lorena said, "Three nights ago—why did Stevie call you?"

Daron stayed on the ground. "She said she had some big fight with her parents. She wanted me to come get her so she could come down here and chill. I wasn't doing anything else, so . . ."

"Do you guys hang out a lot?"

"Not really. Just, like, when the families are together."

"Did she ever call you like that before? To come get her?"

Daron shook his head and rubbed his knee. "First time."

Waldo said, testing, "For real."

Daron, still on the floor, said, "Yes!" Then: "Can I get up?"

Waldo nodded. "So what did you guys do down here?"

Daron climbed onto a love seat. "Ordered a pizza. Watched some Netflix. She never saw *American Pie*."

"Then what?"

"Then she left."

"By herself? How'd she do that?"

"I don't know. She was, like, in a mood. She got all drama-rama."

"Over what?"

Daron looked cornered. "She wanted some shit I didn't have."

"What kind of shit?" Daron clammed up. "Talk to us or talk to the cops."

Lorena said, "Or my foot."

He rolled. "*Blow.* After the pizza. I'm not even *into* blow." Off their skepticism, he said, "Look, I sell a little weed sometimes, just, like, to friends. I got my green card," he said, as if that made everything legit. "But after the pizza, Stevie wanted blow. So we went to see my guy and bought a gram. She wanted to buy more than that, but I was feeling, like, responsible, you know what I mean? Because she's my cousin."

Waldo said, "I'm sure your aunt and uncle appreciate it."

Lorena said, "So what was the fight about?"

"She got all flirty with my guy. And he was into her. She let him put his number on her phone and all, and then he gave her another gram. Just *gave* it to her. She's fifteen, man. This isn't a guy you want to fuck around with. So when we got back here I told her that, and she didn't like it, said I was being all parental, and she wouldn't let it go. After she did a couple rails she just got worse about it and made, like, this big speech about how I wasn't her dad and walked out."

Waldo said, "And you let her go? Down here, where she didn't know anybody?"

"You ever met Stevie? She does what she wants, man. She's been like that since she was a little kid. Her parents let her do anything. Thanksgiving, all she'd eat for, like, three years was rice with ketchup on it, and her parents were cool with it. It's fucked up."

"Any idea where she went?" Daron shook his head. "Think she called your dealer?"

Daron didn't answer, but Waldo could see the notion troubled him.

"What's his name?"

Daron straightened up on the love seat and shut down again. He wasn't going to tell them that.

Lorena said, "It's Amador, right?" Daron startled. "First name something with an *M*?"

Daron's eyes widened and he rolled again. "Marwin."

"She left here about a quarter to eleven?"

Now he was alarmed. "I guess. How do *you* know?"

"Amador's number's on her phone. Last call she made."

"Shit."

Waldo said, "Put on some shoes. You're taking us to Amador."

Daron looked helplessly from one to the other and finally said, "Can I take my dessert with me?" Waldo nodded. "Can I put it in the microwave first? It's butter cake—it's way better served warm."

Waldo said, "Shoes."

Daron went into the bedroom. Lorena said to Waldo, "That butter cake's sixteen bucks. *Love* Mastro's."

Out on the street Daron waited in tattered high-tops while Waldo and Lorena did math problems. Given Lorena's Mercedes, which couldn't seat three, and Daron's BMW, which could, was the ten-mile trip north to Santa Ana more environmentally damaging with all of them in the Beemer, requiring a double-back to Costa Mesa before Lorena and Waldo would triple-back north for the night, or could they, as Lorena preferred, take two cars to Amador's in the first place? The respective fuel (in)efficiencies were a variable, though, and Waldo suspected that Daron's 7 Series was actually even worse than Lorena's SLK, so he took out his phone and typed in *carbonfootprint.com* to run a comparison. Daron fired up a joint. Lorena slapped it out of his hand and implored Waldo to ride with Daron while she followed. Waldo, weary of relenting, relented again.

Getting off the 5 at Grand, Daron told Waldo that Amador wouldn't like him bringing one stranger to his house, let alone two, so Waldo phoned Lorena in her car and they agreed she'd park down the street and wait for them to finish. The blocks grew shabbier as they pushed deeper into Amador's neighborhood, which Daron told him was called Lacy. For all Waldo's years in Southern California, most of Orange County remained mysterious terrain.

As the lights grew fewer and the windows more heavily barred, he grew more self-conscious about their minicaravan, Beemer and Benz. He looked over his shoulder. As if reading his mind—nothing new—Lorena slowed and let Daron's lead stretch to three-quarters of a block. She kept that distance when they parked.

Amador's bungalow looked like the others around it, peeling paint and heavy metal rods. Waldo reached for the doorbell. Daron told him it didn't work and gave the bars on the doors a clamorous rattle instead.

Marwin Amador threw open the inner door and scowled, scrutinizing Waldo from behind the security gate. His weight-lifter's frame strained a dirty blue A-shirt and his head was shaved, but his most menacing feature—not apparent until he turned his head to glare at Daron—was a small constellation of teardrop outlines tattooed high on his right cheek. They might stand for a number of different things: people he killed, loved ones he mourned, deaths he planned to avenge. Waldo squinted against the light spilling from inside, trying to decipher the ink above it, an indefinite shape above the eyebrow that did nothing to diminish the ambiguity.

Amador saw Waldo staring at it and said, "Fuck are you?"

"Waldo. I'm a detective."

Amador glowered at Daron, murderous.

"Not a cop!" said Daron quickly. "A private eye. Like Columbo."

Waldo said, "Columbo was a cop."

"He was?"

"Yeah. Lieutenant Columbo."

"Fuck's Lieutenant Columbo?" said Marwin Amador, with an accent thicker than Waldo had realized from his first monosyllables.

Daron, nervous, added, "Old TV show. I used to watch reruns with my dad." But it didn't look like that helped with Amador, who leaned closer to the bars and peered down the block in both directions.

Waldo said, "I'm looking for a girl."

Daron said, "The one I brought here the other night."

"Don't remember no girl."

Waldo said, "You gave her your phone number. She called you."

"Didn't talk to no girl." He looked at Daron. "You remembering wrong, *ese.* Maybe you left her in the car."

Daron said, "Maybe I did."

Amador stared Waldo down. "That all you wanted?"

Waldo held a beat, then said, "Yeah."

"Good," said Amador, and started to shut the door.

"*Hey,*" said Waldo. Amador turned. Waldo stepped closer to the bars himself and peered unapologetically at the tattooed blob above the tattooed droplets. Waldo tapped the corresponding spot above his own eye. "What's that supposed to be—a sponge?"

Amador's nostrils flared. "'S a fucking *cloud, ese.* Tears like rain."

"You sure? Looks like a sponge."

"*Tears like rain.*" Amador's lip twitched and he slammed the door.

Waldo put Daron in his car and sent him home. He walked down the block to Lorena's car. "Shit," he said, getting in, "I'm lost down here."

"Don't look at me. Orange County's kicking my ass this week."

"I don't even know who this Amador is. Is he a player? A punk? We need a lead on our lead."

"*O.C. Dealers for Dummies.* Who could write that book?"

Waldo had an idea and Lorena felt it.

"What?" she said. "You know someone?"

"You know him, too."

When it dawned on her whom he meant, she started to argue, but this one he wasn't going to let her win.

FOURTEEN

Waldo dialed, waited and, on hearing the bodyguard's expected grunt, said, "He there?"

The boss's voice, when it came, was impatient and gruff: "What *you* want?" Waldo wondered whether he'd made a mistake.

Don Q was the trafficker who had pressured Waldo into forcing the headmaster to let his daughter into Stoddard. Before that, he had threatened to kill Lorena, driving her underground and prompting her to fake her own murder, for which the dealer took false credit. Along the way the guy's hired muscle had bruised Waldo's ribs and twice left him unconscious. In fact, every encounter Waldo had with the dealer had ended in violence.

Then again, the last couple of times, Waldo hadn't been the *victim* of that violence, which could be seen as progress, and now Don Q looked like his quickest path to information about Amador. "I got some questions about an entrepreneur in Orange County. Do you know a guy named Marwin—"

Don Q cut him off, said, "Fuck you calling me for?" and hung up.

Lorena said, "What now?"

Waldo thought about the options. "I wouldn't mind another conversation with Papa Wax."

"Let's get him at home this time, before he leaves for work. I'd kind of like you to meet Mama Wax, too."

This left them once again with the tiresome problem of where to spend the night. Given the emission costs of the round-trip drive to Lorena's, the likely presence of Willem and the quick turnaround they'd need to fight traffic back down to Newport Beach, trying to find an environmentally acceptable hotel nearby seemed like the least bad idea. Lorena, who made a practice of keeping an overnight bag with a change of clothes in her trunk, found their way out of Lacy while Waldo opened his browser.

He grumbled at everything that came up, one gimmick after another, like the inn in Huntington Beach with beehives on the roof to make their own honey, or the so-called green resort in Anaheim that boasted of the recycled hydration system it used to water its golf course—*its golf course!* Near the entrance to the freeway Lorena pulled over and put the car in park. Waldo braced for a scolding about how difficult he'd become, but now she just looked sad and exhausted. He was burning her out.

He Googled "greenest hotel in Orange County," accepted the first suggestion without review, and in less than a minute they were heading south on the 5 to Laguna Beach and something called the Hotel La Vela.

It was almost midnight when they checked in, holding the room for a second night on the likelihood that the search for Stevie would keep them down here at least that long. Lorena said she was going to take a shower and wash the whole sleazy day off of her. Through the open bathroom door she said, "Ooh, they've got one of those rainfall showers."

Waldo stretched out on the bed and tried as hard as he could not to think about the flow rate of that showerhead nor to question the seriousness of the La Vela's commitment. The die was cast, at least for a night or two, and scrutiny would only drive him crazy and Lorena crazier.

"Hey," Lorena called from under the simulated rain, "you going to join me, or what?" He rose from the bed but hesitated, frozen by all he knew about the worldwide water shortage and the unconscionable gallons they'd be wasting while they frolicked. "*Please* tell me," she called, "that you're not out there thinking about drought!" He chuckled surrender and peeled off his shirt.

Then his phone rang, unfamiliar digits. "Fuck you doin', Waldo?" came the voice from the other end. "Callin' me on a regular phone and talkin' business."

"Only number I had. You on a burner? I need to know about a guy—"

"I still ain't doin' this on your unlimited minutes. Where you at?"

"Orange County."

"*Orange County?* Shit, man—only part of O.C. I can stand is Laguna Beach, and even *that* ain't the same since MTV fucked it all up."

Waldo knew that Q was referring to a fairly watchable reality show from a decade before, though he had no idea how it had ruined the town. "Well, that's where I am now. Laguna." There was nothing from the other end. "You still there?"

"Lifeguard tower. Main Beach. Three thirty."

"Wait—A.M. or P.M.?"

"Shit, man, *A.M.* You see me on the muthafuckin' 405 at rush hour?"

Waldo walked the mile or so up South Coast Highway to Main Beach and waited for Don Q on the bench closest to the lifeguard tower. There was a tangle of threats and debts between them, property stolen and property returned, lives spared and lives taken. Next to all that, Waldo's help getting Don Q's daughter into a second-grade class—the most recent favor—seemed trivial, but if the dealer was driving an hour to come help him, he must be more grateful than Waldo realized.

A man slumped toward him down the boardwalk, stringy hair and ratty army jacket, a green garbage bag slung over his back. In the light of the full moon Waldo recognized him: he'd just seen the same guy sleeping in the doorway of a jewelry shop, one of several homeless people he had passed on the walk from the hotel. The man stopped abruptly in front of Waldo. "Yo."

"Yo." He wanted the guy gone before Don Q arrived.

"You got any tips? I just got here today. I been in Seal Beach, but everyone says you can't beat Laguna. That Friendship Shelter always full?"

It took him a second to get a handle on the man's misapprehension, but when he did, it made all the sense in the world: looking like Waldo did, in this town, out in the middle of the night—what else would a stranger think? "I don't know. I'm not . . ."

"Not what?" The guy, suddenly intense, demanded an answer. "*Not what?*"

Waldo, pinned, said, "Homeless. I don't live on the street."

The guy looked Waldo over and burst out laughing. "Me nei-ther! I'm staying at the Montage!" The guy staggered away, cack-ling. He turned and called, "Meet me there for brunch! Eggs Florentine!" before disappearing into the night.

Don Q startled Waldo by dropping onto the bench next to him unseen, his approach covered by the sound of the waves. "Fuckin' MTV, man."

"I liked that show," Waldo said, defensive. He had, in fact, watched all three full seasons of *Laguna Beach: The Real Orange County* just the year before, when it ran on MTV Classic. It was exactly the sort of thing he liked over dinner in his own spartan cabin, and while its soapy contrivance couldn't match the purity and shamelessness of, say, *Cribs,* he'd found himself hooked by the characters' clueless privilege and sun-drenched youth.

"Ain't you too old to watch that shit, Waldo? *Damn.*" Don Q looked up and down the boardwalk and took a deep whiff of the ocean. "Man, used to be you could walk around this muthafucker and *breathe.* Take a weekend with your lady, enjoy the salty air, fish taco maybe, check out the galleries. No one hardly knew this bitch was *here.* Shit, *now?* Weekends, might as well be at fuckin' Califor-nia Adventure. And the hotels, man, they, like, doubled. I got a kid in private school—I can't afford no eight hundred a night at the Surf and Sand."

Over Q's shoulder, Waldo spied Nini, the Inuit bodyguard who'd pummeled Waldo a couple of times in the past. Waldo wag-gled his fingers at him. Nini didn't wave back. Waldo said to Don Q, "I'm looking for a missing girl. Fifteen. Dealer out of Santa Ana might know something, guy named Marwin Amador."

"Don't know him. O.C.'s a whole other nation, man. But I can ask around."

"Thanks. And thanks for coming all the way down here."

Don Q shook his head again, his thoughts elsewhere. "That private school. I wanted her in there for the quality education. I didn't realize how *liberal* that shit was. You know what they got them studyin' right now? Public sector employees. *Second grade.* I never even heard those words growin' up, 'public sector employ- ees.' Tryin' to show how important they are—teachers, *po*-lice. If teachers in the public sector are so fuckin' great, why am I givin' *these* muthafuckers twenty-two G for second grade?"

Waldo knew he was working up to something. Please, he si- lently prayed, don't ask me to go complain to the headmaster about the curriculum. "How do I fit in?"

"Homework. Dulci gotta bring one to school."

"One what?"

"Public sector employee—fireman or parole officer or child services or some bullshit. Fuck am *I* supposed to find somebody like that? She's cryin' to my wife 'bout it—new school, teacher gonna flunk her out."

"And you want me . . . ?"

"Former cop. Friend of the family."

"You want me to be your daughter's show-and-tell?"

"Shit, Waldo, you don't think I come all the way down here 'cause a' the girl *you're* worried about."

Their early start for the Waxes meant he only got a couple of hours' sleep. At least his clothes, which he'd washed in the sink after get- ting back from his meet-up with Don Q, were somehow dry. Lo- rena said, "I used the hair dryer on them before you woke up."

"Why?" he said, scandalized.

"Because I knew you wouldn't."

While she wasn't looking, he took the PLEASE CHANGE THE SHEETS card, which she'd placed atop her pillow, and slipped it back under the telephone.

Newport Beach was only one town up the coast and they reached the entrance to the gated community a little before seven thirty. The guard, fiftyish with a pinched face, slid open the window of his booth. Waldo and Lorena could hear scratchy bits of talk radio coming from inside.

Lorena said they were there to see the Waxes. The guard asked for her name and the name of the other person in the car with her. When she told him, his eyes widened and he repeated, "Charlie Waldo?" and leaned down to get a look. "I'm listening to your radio show! Right now!"

Waldo said, "I don't have a radio show."

The guard said, "No, KFI—there's a guy, I think used to be FBI, explaining how those people forced you to say all that stuff. About Pinch. And then you come driving up! It's true, right?"

"Could you please call the Waxes?"

"Oh, yeah. Sure." The guard slid his gate window shut, had a brief phone conversation, opened it again and said to Lorena, "They're not home."

Lorena said, "Then who were you talking to?"

"Ma'am, if they say they're not home, they're not home. Know what I mean?" He peered in at Waldo again. "Hey, could we call in? Bet you KFI puts us right on the air."

Waldo, speaking loudly across Lorena, said, "Make you a deal: get the Waxes on the phone again, and repeat the things I tell you, and then we can call into your show before we go in and see them."

"Really?"

"Yeah," he said. "It'll be fun." Lorena covered her face.

The guard said, "I hope my wife's listening," and dialed the house again, this time leaving the window open. He nodded at Waldo when he got one of the Waxes on the phone.

Voice still raised, Waldo said, "Tell them, 'Lorena Nascimento and Charlie Waldo are here.'"

The guard repeated it.

Waldo said, "'Stevie Rose is missing . . .'"

"Stevie Rose is missing . . ."

"'And your son, Daron, is the last person she was seen with.'"

The guard hesitated but said, "And your son, Daron, is the last person she was seen with."

Waldo slowly fed him the next line. "'How much other shit about you do I have to tell your security guard . . .'"

The guard hesitated, listened through the phone for a moment, then said, "Will do, sir," and hung up. He said to Waldo, "He could hear you," and opened the gate. "Okay, I'm going to call the radio station. I bet they don't even put us on hold." He looked down and started punching numbers into his own cell phone.

Waldo said to Lorena, "Drive." She gunned it.

"Hey!" shouted the guard after them, leaning out of his booth.

They found the street number painted on the curb. Both Waxes were waiting outside their front door. Brenda, smaller and more birdlike than she'd appeared in the magazine photos, said to them, "Stevie's missing? For how long?"

Lorena said, "Three, four days."

"And Daron . . . ?"

Waldo said, "She was at his apartment. He says they had an argument and she left. That's the last time Stevie was on the grid."

Brenda said, "Please. Come in." Lorena darted past Roy, cutting off his opportunity to protest.

Brenda directed them all to a living room decorated in coastal style, lots of blue and white and rattan. French doors led to their dock and a sixty-foot yacht.

Roy said, "This isn't our problem."

Waldo knew to ignore him. He said to Brenda, "We were working with the Roses before Stevie disappeared."

Brenda said, "On what?"

"That's confidential, but—"

Roy clapped his hands together and said, "We're done here. And everything I said to you in my office still holds: you'd better tread carefully, even with whatever's happening with Stevie."

Waldo said, "Your niece disappeared at the same time somebody was setting you up. Eighteen million people in greater L.A.—hard to believe there isn't a connection."

Roy said, "Believe it. I already figured out what happened on this end."

Lorena said, "You did?"

"It's related to my business. Beyond that: not your concern."

Waldo pressed him. "You know we won't let that alone. Police won't either, if this turns into a missing persons."

"Fine. I have an option to buy a factory in Korea, which would put a competitor out of business. This stunt with you was my competitor's way of letting me know that he's willing to play dirty. That's all you need to know."

Waldo let that angle go for the moment and turned back to Brenda. "Is there bad blood between you and Paula's family? When's the last time you talked to her?"

Roy answered for his wife. "Is that what Joel told you? 'Bad blood'? Look: we're families who annoy the shit out of each other on Thanksgiving, and then everyone's glad it's over until next year. That's it."

Waldo said, "I'd like to hear from Brenda." He asked her again: "When's the last time you talked to your sister?"

She looked to her husband before answering, as if for permission. "Thanksgiving. Five months?"

Waldo asked Brenda to tell them a little about their background, how she and Paula grew up. She described much the same story as Paula did, of the divorce and the subsequent parade of suitors. There were a couple of differences: older than her sister, Brenda had more vivid memories of their father, an assistant manager at a dairy farm, and she had a different spin on the original strain, attributing it to Paula's brattiness, her spying and sabotaging and provoking, unrestrained by their distracted mom.

"Interesting," said Lorena, "that you two started out so modestly and both ended up marrying such successful men."

The comparison set Roy aboil. "Do not compare me to Joel Rose," he said, twisting in his club chair. "Joel Rose is a smug little prick with no self-control."

"Roy . . ." said Brenda.

"You should have seen him at Thanksgiving, waving around a carving knife like a crazy man."

Lorena said, "Sounds like bad blood to me."

"It wasn't me he was upset with. He was out of his mind about the election. Trump derangement syndrome."

Brenda added, superfluously, "They were big Hillary people."

Roy snorted, then repeated, "Smug little prick. So offended by anyone who's actually pulled himself up by his own bootstraps, anyone who believes people should have to at least *try* before the government starts giving them handouts.

"*He* looks down on *me*, can you believe that? I pulled myself up by my own bootstraps"—he liked this bootstraps thing—"and now I'm giving kids a love of history, a love of their country. Meanwhile that prick does nothing but pour sludge into the culture. Ever watch their TV show? And you know what he says? 'That's how teenagers behave.' How about you teach your *own* kid to behave instead of running wild all over Southern California? That girl's a nightmare, but you could see it coming from the beginning, the way they indulged her. Whatever's happening," he said, "they brought it on themselves," and walked out of the room.

Waldo didn't entirely disagree with that assessment. Then again, he was pretty sure Roy Wax's son hadn't paid for his Postmates from Mastro's by buckling down and studying for the CPA exam.

Brenda said to them, "I wish I could help you find Stevie, but we truly don't have any contact with them." She thought for a moment, then added, "It's not easy for us. Paula and Joel have a lot of hate in their hearts. And Roy is right about their values. We make choices in this life, and sometimes they lead us straight to hell."

Lorena said, "Well, they're definitely going through hell right now."

Brenda Wax let out a condescending sigh. Waldo knew she had something warmer in mind.

FIFTEEN

The address texted from Nini's phone turned out to be a two-story gallery on Forest. Don Q wore a straw fedora and was so still as he studied a nude on the upper floor that Waldo almost didn't notice him even though the room was nearly empty. "Look at that," the drug dealer said. "Rosemary."

"That's her name?" said Waldo.

"No, man. The shit you put on chicken. *Rosemary.*" He pointed to the figure's pubic hair. "Look—pushed it right into the canvas. This here bitch musta really wiggled his churro. This artist, Hampton? He did those, too." He pointed to two large wooden boards, one with a painted gorilla and one with a tiger. "I got the giraffe."

"What, at home?"

"No, I drive around with it strapped to my roof. Fuck you think?"

"What happened to 'kid in private school, I can't afford the Surf and Sand'?"

"It's a *investment*, Waldo. This muthafucker gonna pop. His shit make you feel good, you know? Make you happy.

"So," Don Q said, dropping his voice. The only other people in the expansive space were a middle-aged white couple in the far corner bickering unselfconsciously about whether to buy a piece downstairs that the husband thought overpriced. "This dude you asked me about. He's a *raitero*. You know what that is?" Waldo didn't. "*Raitero:* it's like Spanglish—dude gives you a ride. But what it *really* means is *scumbag*. You know temps?"

Waldo shook his head again.

Don Q got impatient with him. "*Temps*—shit, Waldo, what *do* you know? Company gotta unload a truck, need to hire some oompa loompas for a day. Or their secretary calls in sick—"

"You mean a temp, like from an agency? Like, legit? I know what *that* is."

"Okay, so a *raitero* nominally—you understand 'nominally'?" Waldo nodded. "Muthafucker *nominally* works with the temp agencies, on the books. IRS be askin', just a workin' stiff, drivin' a van, freelance-like. But really bitch does *everything*—goes in the hood, tells 'em where to line up, picks who gets to work, *all* that shit. Then he scrapes off mucha every fuckin' paycheck as he can."

"How?"

"However. Exploitin' our own. *Cabrón*."

Cursing in Spanish wasn't something Waldo had seen before from the dealer, nor was this suggestion of an ethical code. Waldo said, "And the drugs?"

Don Q rebuked him without a word and scoped the room again. The squabble had broken down: the man was gone, the woman still with them, now studying an African folk sculpture.

Don Q turned back to the rosemary painting and lowered his voice even further. "Perfect with his other business—got the van for cover, and he meets a lot of people, know what I'm sayin'? But it ain't just dealin'. This girl of yours—she ugly?"

"No. Why?"

"Better if she was, man. One more source a' income for this piece a' shit—he gets some girl in that lineup looks lost—runaway or whatnot, maybe over the border, cut off from her family—he hooks her up with this pimp called Tesoro. Next thing you know, like it or not . . ." He shrugged, *what can you do?*, and said, "Why you lookin' at Amador?"

"Missing girl had a fight with her cousin. I think she called Amador right after."

The dealer looked at him: it was a bad answer.

Waldo said, "What can you tell me about the pimp?"

"Sure you wanna know?" Waldo nodded. "My man say he's one of them five-one dudes, tries to make up for it by roidin' up like a tank. Ponytail, bad skin. Hang in front of a Burger King in Santa Ana, 'cross from a club called Headlights. All the girls wor- kin' that block, they're his."

"I'll check it out."

"Hope you don't have no luck there, man. He's an adult dose, this *cabrón*. Marks his girls, cuts 'em right here." He indicated a spot on his own hand, the webbing between his index and middle fingers.

"Why?"

"Hurts like a muthafucker—ever get a paper cut there? Keep 'em scared and shit. Somebody oughta one-eight-seven this *hijo de puta*, he give you half a reason. But that ain't gonna be you, Waldo. You ain't that tough." Waldo registered the gratuitous shot. "I'm just sayin'." Waldo nodded thanks and started out. "Wait," said Don Q. "One more thing."

"Yeah?"

"My kid's school bullshit—week from Monday. I've driven down here twice now—don't even *think* 'bout fuckin' me on that."

They placed the gentlemen's club called Headlights on North Harbor Boulevard in Santa Ana and found the nearby Burger King. It anchored a strip mall; Waldo scoped the parking lot as they cruised past, couldn't see anyone who matched Don Q's description of Tesoro. Lorena drove another three blocks and pulled over to let him out. "Should I park, or circle?"

"Around here? Circle. I'll text you."

He walked back to the strip mall. A couple of banger types in dark T-shirts, too tall to be Tesoro, leaned on a Chevy, telegraphing enough trouble that civilians between their cars and the BK didn't dawdle. Waldo crossed the lot and went inside.

No Tesoro in here, either. It was well past dinnertime but the place was doing business. There were two couples in their twenties, an obstreperous gaggle of teenage girls, a trio of boys peacocking for them and an old woman in a corner with the glazed look of a transient, though after last night in Laguna, Waldo wasn't making presumptions about anybody else.

The girl at the cash register eyed Waldo warily and said with careful politeness, "Welcome to Burger King, can I take your order?"

Waldo knew that to stay inconspicuous he needed to buy something; even the probably homeless woman was nursing a small coffee. He looked up at the busy menu panels and took a deep breath. Nothing here would be acceptable, not even the risibly named "garden salad." The challenge evoked one of the more contentious issues of the past month. Lorena had singled out his vow to avoid food that had ever been packaged as his most unreasonable and had been chipping away at it without letup. Strictly speaking, his self-formulated prohibition was against *eating* anything packaged, not against *buying* anything packaged; if it would help camouflage his surveillance tonight, couldn't he sit with the untouched food in front of him and watch the action outside?

Or maybe that was a distinction without a difference. Only days earlier he'd read about a report from the Silent Spring Institute that found that an alarming percentage of fast-food wrappers contained man-made polyfluoroalkyls, advantageous for things like stain and stick resistance, but not so advantageous for things like cancer resistance. And once these PFASs started leaking out of a landfill, they wouldn't give a damn whether Waldo had actually eaten the sandwich or not.

A thirtyish guy, probably some sort of manager, was watching him now too. Waldo thought about Stevie Rose and the trouble she might be in down here, threw conscience and immunity suppression to the wind and asked for a MorningStar Veggie Burger. He took another look at the old woman in the corner and, resolving to offer the food to her when he was finished not eating it, added a small onion rings. He used to like them better than fries, back when that was relevant.

While he waited for the counter girl to put together his order he went to the window and scoped the parking lot again. The bangers had been joined by a pint-size bruiser with a ponytail: Tesoro, no doubt.

The girl said, "Veggie burger?" and Waldo collected his tray. He carried it over to the corner and put it down in front of the old

woman. Homeless for sure, now that he got a closer look: the coffee cup was empty, her hair was matted, and the feculence of her
clothing cut right through the smell of the greasy meal.

"What's that?" She was missing a bunch of teeth, too.

"Veggie burger. And onion rings. For you." She stared at it like
she was waiting for it to explain itself.

Waldo left her and went out to the parking lot. A skinny
young woman was talking to Tesoro in Spanish now, in platforms
and a spangly halter and half a skirt. She handed him some bills.
Tesoro said something and his two goons laughed, but the woman
didn't. He tipped his head and she obediently tromped back out to
the boulevard.

Waldo followed her, glancing back at the homeless woman in
the window. She was staring at him. When they made eye contact
she gave him the finger.

Tesoro's girl had thirty yards on Waldo and he sped up to
close the gap. Half a block before the strip club, she turned to let
him approach. "Hey," she said.

"Hey. How much?"

"For what?"

Closer, he could see past the makeup: she wasn't skinny, she
was a kid. He'd never worked Vice, hadn't been around this enough
not to be struck dumb by how young she looked.

She said, "You a cop?"

"No."

"What you want? *You* gotta say." She'd learned enough English to set up an entrapment defense, at least.

"Sex."

"Hundred."

"Okay."

"Wonderland Motel, past the club." She half gestured with her thumb. "But walk five minutes that way, then come back and meet me in room six." Her English was better than he was expecting. "Make sure nobody's following you." She turned and walked off.

Waldo started back toward the Burger King as directed, then turned around. Nobody followed him, except Tesoro and his bangers with their eyes.

The Wonderland was a trio of two-story stuccos around a quarter-full parking lot. Room 6 was up the stairs to one of the buildings, at the end of a catwalk. He knocked and the girl let him in. The room was illuminated, sort of, by an under-watted standing lamp with a torn and dingy shade. Thin fabric curtains didn't really cover the window. He closed the door while she sat on the badly made bed, the only furniture in the room, and fished a condom from her tiny purse. "What's your name?"

"Alice." Right, he thought, like every tech support guy you got on the phone from Bangalore was named Steve. Alice. Alice at the Wonderland. He wondered if it was somebody's sick joke.

He said, "How old are you?"

"Eighteen." He wouldn't have believed her if she said fifteen. "The money first, okay?"

He took the bills from his pocket. He sat next to her and she started to lift her halter. "Wait," he said, grabbing her hand to stop her. He saw the mark and turned her hand over in his. The scar, a deeper color than he'd have expected, ran across the webbing and into a second scar across the ball, forming, from Waldo's angle, a clear letter *T*.

She took her hand back. "You want to do it or what?"

He pulled the photo of Stevie out of his shirt pocket. "Have you seen this girl?"

She pulled back. "You a cop? You said you're not a cop."

"Private eye."

"Shit!" She stood up.

"I'm not going to get you in trouble. I promise. Could you sit down, please? I just want to ask you a couple of questions."

She didn't sit but didn't leave either. "You're supposed to give me a hundred dollars."

He counted out a hundred for her, and then gave her an extra twenty. "Those scars on your hand—is that supposed to be a *T* for Tesoro?"

He was making her nervous. "Can't we just do it?"

Waldo shook his head. "I only want to talk. When did he cut you?"

"He didn't."

"Who did?"

"My stepfather." She held his eye, daring him not to believe her.

"Could you look at this picture again? This girl is missing, and she might know Tesoro." He held it toward her for a closer look. "Please. Help me. This girl's parents are very worried."

The simple play backfired; she got colder and said, "Lucky her."

"You know Marwin Amador?" Alice didn't answer. He gave her another twenty. "Is that how you met Tesoro?" She offered a tiny, diffident nod. "Can you tell me about that? Did Amador drive you to work? To some job?"

Painstakingly, he pulled the basics of the story out of her. She'd arrived in Orange County knowing no one; a woman at a KFC told her she could line up behind the Dollar Tree and maybe get picked for work at a factory. At the end of the first day, Amador asked her if she wanted a cheeseburger and introduced her to Tesoro at the Burger King.

"What was that like?"

"He was real nice. My shoe was broke, like the buckle, so he bought me some new ones?" She did the Stevie Rose question-mark thing. "And this necklace?" She showed Waldo the thin silver chain with a heart of fake diamonds hanging from it. Alice said, "Why you askin' all this? It don't matter."

"I'm trying to find out what happened to this girl." He gave her another twenty and waited for her to say more.

"I started staying at his apartment, being kinda his girlfriend. I was, like, the special one at the beginning, you know? He's still nice to me sometimes."

"How long till he made you start working?"

"I dunno, like, a week maybe till he was bringing people over? Then, like, another week till I was on the track."

"How long ago was that?"

"Last summer."

He showed her the picture again and offered her another twenty.

She said, "There's a couple white girls but I never saw one looked like that."

"Do you know all Tesoro's girls?"

She shook her head. "He got, like, two other tracks, I think."

"Do you know where they are?" She shook her head. "But this girl—she could be working one of them, and you wouldn't know her." She nodded. "When did he do that to your hand?"

She hesitated but this time told the truth. "The night before I went out on the track. He said it meant I was part of the family."

She looked toward the door. "I can't be talking about it no more, okay?"

He couldn't just leave her to go back to work. "Listen—do you want to get out of here?"

"Let's wait like another couple minutes, so they think we really did it."

"I mean, out of here totally."

She took a step backward. "I'm safe here. Don't mess with me."

"Safe? How is this safe?"

"Nobody fucks with me, 'cause a' Tesoro. I don't have to get in cars or nothin'. I met girls it's way worse. Let's go now. I'll leave first, okay?"

She reached for the door but Waldo sprung from the bed and stopped it with his hand. Now she looked full-on scared. He said, "Where's your real family?"

"I don't wanna talk about that shit." When he didn't move his hand she said, "San Mateo. Can I go?"

"One more question." It wasn't important but it had been nagging at him. "Most girls go to Hollywood—why'd you come here, if you didn't know anybody? Orange County." She shifted her weight and stared at his hand on the door. But he wouldn't move it.

She finally said, "Disneyland. When I was a girl, I always wanted to go. Tesoro say he gonna take me someday." She almost smiled, thinking about it. Waldo dropped his hand from the door and she bolted out of the room.

He sat on the bed and looked at Stevie Rose in her school photo: fresh-faced, healthy, optimistic. There were probably pictures like that of Alice too, somewhere. *When I was a girl.*

Could Stevie be in anything like this kind of trouble, this

quickly? In most ways she didn't fit the usual profile of the vulnerable girls who ended up getting trafficked. But he knew things sometimes went to violence and force a lot more quickly than they had for Alice; he'd heard stories from the Vice guys. Could pissed-off Stevie have walked out on her cousin to go see what else Amador had in his bungalow, and before she knew it found herself in way over her head?

Could Tesoro have her in some apartment somewhere?

Or was Waldo just wasting his time chasing one wispy branch off one thin lead, compelled by the horror of the possibility?

Then again, that one thin lead, Stevie's final call to Amador, was all they had.

He texted Lorena to meet him across the street from Headlights, left the room, traversed the catwalk and trotted down the stairs. Turning at the first landing, he saw Tesoro waiting for him at the bottom, leaning against a Pepsi machine and blocking Waldo's egress to the parking lot. He stopped halfway down the lower flight, regretting, for the first time on this visit to L.A., that he'd left his Beretta back in his cabin.

Tesoro said something to him in Spanish. Waldo's incapacity to master the language at any practical level was a shortcoming that had frustrated and shamed him throughout his years in the department. He'd tried a night class, he'd tried Rosetta Stone, and he could handle, say, a written vocabulary quiz about animals or occupations or months of the year. But on the street his attempts to speak would trigger looks of frustration or, worse, pity, and his interlocutor's words—like Tesoro's now—sounded to him like gibberish on speed.

Tesoro finished talking, read Waldo's incomprehension, and said, *"Sastre—comprende?"*

Waldo had no idea what had preceded, but these last two words were at least familiar, if confusing: with *"comprende,"* Tesoro was asking him if he understood the preceding word—and Waldo did! Unfortunately that word, *sastre*, meant *tailor*, and had no apparent relation to this context. So Waldo mimed a needle and thread and repeated, *"Sastre?"* as a question, to show that he was at least partially keeping up.

He must have gotten even that wrong, though, because Tesoro let loose a quietly menacing tirade, it, too, faster than Waldo could handle.

Waldo reached into his pocket. Tesoro, reacting, went for something in his own. Waldo froze, held up his other hand to show that he would move slowly and unthreateningly, and did.

He withdrew his iPhone, featured it for Tesoro, then called up Google Translate.

He typed in *tailor*. When *sastre* came up, he moved toward the pimp so he could read it. Tesoro gave him a quizzical scowl and reached for the device. Waldo pulled it out of reach; he wasn't about to let his phone out of his hands. He typed in *Do you have a phone?* and showed the Spanish translation to Tesoro, who scowled again.

Waldo took a second look and realized that he had typed in *Do you have a phony?*

He made the correction and showed that to Tesoro, who nodded and took his own phone from his pocket. He tipped his chin to say, *show me*. Waldo stood next to him and demonstrated how to get to Translate.

The pimp typed in some Spanish and displayed the English to Waldo: *this is not the neighborhood for you.*

Tesoro typed in a second sentence in Spanish, which came out:

find your next neat in another barrip. Then Tesoro nodded at him with a curled lip, to make sure Waldo knew that he meant it.

Waldo, puzzled, looked at Tesoro, who typed in a third bit to complete the warning: *or you will have a disaster.* Waldo picked up the cognate and looked at the last Spanish word on the input line: *disastre.* Okay, so not *sastre.*

Waldo typed *I am looking for this girl* into his phone and showed the pimp the result. He handed him the picture of Stevie.

Tesoro typed into his phone and presented the English to Waldo: *I've seen her.*

Waldo looked to him hopefully.

Tesoro shook his head *no.*

Waldo was confused. He shook his own head *no,* but with a questioning look.

Tesoro shook a definitive *no.*

Waldo typed in *Look at the photo again.*

Tesoro did, leered, then typed and showed the English to Waldo: *Pretty mouth.*

Then: *She will become a rich man.*

Then: *I have not seen her.* Tesoro shook his head. Waldo was pretty sure there were no typos in that last one.

He reached to take the photo back. Tesoro sneered and put it in his pocket. He typed again into Translate: *I will keep this.*

And: *Put it under my lunch.*

Having gotten the last word, Tesoro pimp-rolled into the night.

Waldo made off in the other direction, through the parking lot, keeping his ears pricked for an ambush there by Tesoro or his men.

It didn't come. He walked undisturbed to Harbor and started down the deserted boulevard. He'd cross at the corner by the strip club and the break in the tree-lined center median, to the side where Lorena was supposed to be waiting.

He heard two pairs of footsteps and glanced over his shoulder: the pimp's bangers from the Burger King had fallen in behind him, a quarter block away.

Waldo picked up his pace. They did too.

He looked back at them again. Beyond, down the boulevard, two pairs of headlights were approaching, probably pushing fifty on the empty boulevard. Waldo darted into the street and, using the speeding cars for interference, made a run for the median, praying that Lorena would be where she was supposed to.

He sprinted down the grass strip, staying left of the line of trees. There were a number of parked cars ahead, but the glare of the headlights in this direction made it impossible to know whether Lorena's Mercedes was one of them. He dashed into the street and toward the far sidewalk, well ahead of the oncoming car. He looked back to see how much distance he'd put between himself and the bangers with his first maneuver.

They were running straight across the median, out onto Waldo's side. They veered and ran down the left traffic lane, waiting to let the car whiz by in the center before cutting over to the far sidewalk to chase Waldo down.

Waldo recognized Lorena's Mercedes just as she threw open her door and slammed it into the lead banger, who went down hard. His partner stumbled over him. As the latter regained his balance, the Mercedes screeched to a stop beyond and went into reverse, Lorena gunning it right toward them again. The banger on his feet dove for the median. The one she'd already hit had gotten up on all fours; Lorena swerved to bounce him off her taillight and stayed in reverse until she reached Waldo.

"Nice timing," he said, sliding into the passenger seat.

"I was waiting down the block. You were late." She threw the car back into drive and floored it, aiming straight at the man still on the ground.

Waldo said, "If you're going to hit him again, let me get my seat belt."

The banger rolled out of the Mercedes's path just in time.

"He looks okay," said Waldo as they passed.

"Seriously?" said Lorena, *"He's* what you're worrying about? Fucking car is two months old."

SIXTEEN

W hat the . . . ?" Lorena turned the pillow over. "There's a lipstick stain! They didn't change the sheets! I put the—" She
looked at Waldo. "Did you take the card off the pillow?" He didn't
deny it. "Goddammit, Waldo, could you please just chill a *little*?
You want to wear your clothes wet, fine, I won't blow-dry them for
you. But for two-fifty a night I don't want to sleep on yesterday's
lipstick, okay?"

On the way back to the hotel he'd told her all about Alice
and then she'd been quiet for a long time. The explosion didn't
come until now, when she was getting into bed. "You waste all
your energy on this OCD-psycho-environmentalism—meanwhile
here's a girl who's a fucking *slave*. Why don't you pull your head
out of your fucking ass and spend your energy on *that*?"

He'd gotten to know this Lorena too well in the old days, the
one who'd misdirect legitimate rage at Waldo, the nearest target.
He knew she'd be sorry for talking to him like that as soon as the
words left her mouth. But he could take it; somehow he was built
to ride out her flash storms. It was one of the ways they fit.

He even knew how long to wait before saying, "What now? Back to Amador?"

"Yup."

"He's not a talker."

"He hasn't met me yet."

In the morning, while Lorena went to the front desk to check out, Waldo walked out to the street and thought about the night, which had never fully gotten back on track. Echoes of the unpleasantness were still hanging around the hotel room when Lorena had turned out the light—expecting him to reach for her and fix things that way, Waldo guessed. But he couldn't: he'd found himself pinned to his side of the bed by flashbacks to the lonely, crushing nights long ago, nights when they'd turned to their reliable physical consonance to save them, only to find afterward that it hadn't been enough. Lorena stayed on her side, too, possibly frozen by the same memories.

They'd set the alarm for quarter after five so that Lorena could make it to the Dollar Tree parking lot where Alice had told him women lined up hoping for Marwin Amador's favor. Lorena would first have to overcome a wardrobe challenge: she'd never pass for a factory day worker in her usual couture, so she'd have to engineer a change of clothes, too, no simple task at an hour before anything was open. The plan was for Waldo, meanwhile, to spend the day on the phone taking an exhaustive round of blind shots, widening the net to include the hospitals in both counties, plus the jails and coroners too. He decided he might as well place the scores of calls from the enchanting Laguna boardwalk rather than from some parking lot in Santa Ana.

The valet brought Lorena's car. Waldo tipped him and waited for her to come out of the hotel. When she did she offered Waldo a ride to the beach, but he said he'd prefer to walk. Her good-bye peck felt obligatory.

The phone work proved as fruitless as expected. Waldo broke up the tedious day by rewarding himself with three long walks, one through the heart of the quaint beachside town, the second barefoot along the mile or so of unbroken beach to the south, and the last, after he'd struck out with his last cold call, a random climb through the steep, winding inland streets to the multimillion-dollar homes overlooking the Pacific.

Lorena sat heavily on his mind. Her marital surveillance was mostly stuff for rich white people, nothing like the diverse world of victims and perps Waldo naturally encountered as an L.A. homicide cop. He wondered if Amador and Tesoro being Latino embarrassed her, if it had anything to do with her misplaced anger.

She'd never introduced him to any relative, not even the aunt who raised her, and had offered Waldo only a sketch of her up-bringing. He did know that Lorena's mother, in the country from Zacatecas without documentation, had tried to tough out a second pregnancy without health insurance or prenatal treatment and died of toxemia diagnosed too late. Her dad, also here illegally, had been working two full-time jobs; not long after losing his childhood sweetheart and their unborn second child, he collapsed of a heart attack and died. He was thirty-eight. Lorena was seven. Lorena once told Waldo that she couldn't hear the term "anchor baby" without wanting to tase someone.

After that, Lorena was raised by her father's divorced younger sister. About those years she said particularly little. Waldo knew she'd considered the academy but enrolled instead at East Los

Angeles College with an eye toward a career in accounting. The turn came when a neighbor's pickup got stolen and Lorena managed to track it down, found it sitting with fresh paint and new plates in the driveway of the owner's niece's boyfriend. That led to her first paying gig: another neighbor's husband had run off with the jackpot from the woman's winning Fantasy 5 ticket; the jilted wife, a hotel maid who couldn't afford a traditional investigator, offered Lorena a quarter of whatever she could recover. Lorena found the prick at a blackjack table in Reno—ahead, miraculously. With a sudden thirty-four thousand dollars in her first-ever savings account, Lorena dropped out of school and found a third-rate PI in Los Feliz willing to take a flyer on a kid coming off a big win. The real flyer the guy was hoping for, of course, was that this hot twenty-one-year-old wannabe would be up for a spin with the boss. Lorena managed to keep him out of her pants for the six thousand working hours she needed before the state of California would let her hang her own shingle.

Waldo's phone buzzed in his pocket: Lorena was on her way back from Santa Ana and wanted to know where to meet him. He suggested the easiest landmark in town, the same lifeguard tower where he'd met Don Q.

He got there before she did, found an empty bench, stretched his arms across the back and enjoyed the clouds as they started to turn pink over Catalina. He closed his eyes, breathed the ocean air, slow and deep, and dipped into a happy drowse.

Something landed on his lap, startling him awake. "Rough day?" Lorena settled in next to him, holding a take-out soda. Waldo reached into the white bag and found a wrapped sandwich, a Jumbo Jack. Lorena plucked it out of his hand and tore into it.

Waldo looked in the bag and saw another burger and a cardboard box full of fries. "I'm not eating this."

"It's not for you. I haven't eaten in twelve hours. Wait till you hear *this* shit." She was still in a ferocious mood. For the moment, though, he didn't seem to be its target and he was thankful for that small mercy.

He said, "Start with the outfit." Her attire couldn't be more non-Lorena: fraying jeans, a nondescript gray sweatshirt with a torn seam at the wrist, blue Keds. Her hair was pulled back with a rubber band.

She told him that she'd looked for a woman her size behind the Dollar Tree and offered a trade: her entire couture ensemble plus a hundred dollars for the woman's work clothes. The woman took the deal and also spelled out the drill. The *raitero*, Amador, would show up around seven and look over the women hoping for work. If he picked you, you had to give him eight dollars for the ride, cash. When he was almost full he'd start asking for an extra five for the last spots and would always find desperate takers. At the end of the shift the temp agency would give your pay to Amador, not to you; he'd drive you to a check-cashing store, which, like it or not, would take out another four dollars and give you what was left.

Amador had arrived in an old school bus repainted blue. From the hundred or so hard-up women, he picked sixty-four, by Lorena's count. She was one of the first and, best as she could tell, the only one who wasn't an immigrant. Amador was pocketing money every which way on each of them: eight-plus for the ride, some kick from the check-cash store, probably a couple of bucks per working hour from the temp agency—say twenty-five dollars a woman in all, times sixty-four, that would be sixteen hundred bucks a day, most of it in cash. Each woman, meanwhile, was taking home, for her eight hours (eleven, really, counting three of unpaid travel and waiting at the factory before the time clock started), seventy-two dollars, minus withholding. That is, the lucky women who got picked at all.

"And here comes the good part. Where do you think he took us to work?"

Waldo didn't have a guess.

"Independence Infants."

"Wax's . . . ?"

"I spent all day sewing Born in America Babies. Baby Barack. At least it was a president I *liked*." Waldo wanted to sort through what the coincidence meant, but Lorena kept railing, exercised by the politics. "Wax wants his pro-business Republicans in there, so he bankrolls two anti-immigrant hard-asses, while the very people they want to build a wall to keep out—*they're the ones making his fucking toys!* And then he gets all offended by his *in-laws'* hypocrisy in Hollywood—"

"Wait," said Waldo, cutting her off. "What are the chances Amador would take you to Roy Wax's factory?"

"Not an accident." The tumblers clicked for Waldo even before she laid it out. "That's how Daron *knows* Amador. And why Daron didn't seem all that afraid about taking us to his house that night: end of the day, Amador works for his daddy."

Waldo said he had no idea Lorena knew how to work a sewing machine. He certainly couldn't imagine her sitting behind one all day.

"Fucking miserable," she said. "Eight hours, no lunch break. My neck's killing me. Look at my nails."

"So how'd it work? End of the shift, Amador picks you up, takes you to the check-cashing place . . ."

"Yep."

"Did he offer to buy you dinner and meet a pimp?"

"I was expecting it." Waldo was being facetious: no way in hell could this woman make herself look vulnerable enough to be mistaken for that kind of prey. But he could hear in Lorena's voice a little disappointment, even offense; she was so oversensitive right now that she took even this as a snub, one more sign of her vanishing youth.

From the check-cashing store, she'd followed Amador into a nearby dive bar, where she cornered him coming out of the men's room and leaned on him, using what she'd picked up during the day and the Wax connection.

Waldo said, "Really? That got him to talk?" Amador's racket was surely amoral, but if it was actually illegal, it wasn't by much.

"I didn't threaten him with the cops. I told him I'd go to the *Orange County Register.* You know Roy Wax doesn't want his Newport Beach buddies reading about him and Marwin Amador." It was the smart squeeze: Amador's fear of losing this sweet job— eight grand a week in bus fare—would lubricate a conversation for sure.

Still, though, Amador hadn't been able to give her much. He admitted knowing Daron through his father and also that Stevie had indeed come inside the house the night Daron bought the coke.

"And Stevie's phone call?"

"He said she sounded kind of wasted, hung up, that was it."

"He say anything else?"

"Yeah, he said, 'That girl don't need *me* to find trouble.'"

"You believe him?"

"Who knows. The phone call was only two minutes, right? Maybe it was nothing. Or maybe that was long enough to set up a place for him to pick her up . . . and then, whatever."

They were nowhere. All the Orange County leads were dead ends or stone walls. "What now?" said Waldo.

"Now I eat my other Jumbo Jack. Gimme."

They reviewed their options while she ate. They could fight traffic back up to the Valley and talk to the Roses and Dionne again, try to pull some more names of Stevie's friends they could interview. Or they could stay in Orange County and lean into the worst possible scenario, try to find Tesoro's other tracks in Santa Ana and talk to more of his girls. On top of the Stevie problem, they faced the usual nuisances of deciding where to sleep and an acceptable dinner for Waldo.

Lorena's phone rang and she checked the caller. "Wax."

Waldo was sure it wouldn't be good news. "You think Amador told him you went undercover in his factory?"

She said, "Why would he?" But it gave her pause. She watched the phone ring, and Waldo could see her picturing her career in flames. They didn't come any tougher than Lorena Nascimento, but this guy had her petrified.

Waldo said, "Put it on speaker."

She did, connecting the call. "Hello?"

Roy Wax said, "I know where she is."

SEVENTEEN

Wax was brief and to the point. Stevie had texted his son, Daron, and then they had spoken on the phone. Daron was able to get an address from his cousin and Wax had insisted Daron give it to him. The girl had been in L.A. since she'd left his son. That was all Wax knew. He was passing on the address to Lorena and Waldo, on some street called Cheltenham Drive, and trusting that they would find Stevie safe and sound. Assuming they did, he'd consider their business concluded and then he expected them to leave him and his family alone.

Waldo and Lorena walked from Main Beach to her car, which was parked at a meter near the gallery where Waldo had met with Don Q. The two of them were on the same page at last. They shared a take on the timing of Wax's call: Amador had indeed reached out to Wax after Lorena shook him up; Wax in turn leaned on his son, who either found out or knew all along where Stevie had been hiding. The ticktock didn't matter, though. As long as Stevie really was where the Waxes said she was, they'd take it. They'd deliver her to her parents and smooth the meet with Cuppy, and once the family Rose was hooked up with a lawyer they'd extricate themselves as quickly and cleanly as they could.

Lorena started the engine and plugged the address into her GPS. "That little cooz."

"What now?"

Lorena showed him on the dashboard map. "Look. She's half a mile from her parents' house."

A white-haired woman opened the door, a senior flummoxed by unexpected visitors after sundown. Lorena said, "We're looking for Stevie Rose. We were told she was staying here."

"Yes, while her parents are out of town. Who are you?"

"My name's Lorena Nascimento. This is Charlie Waldo." The woman, who hadn't recognized Waldo without the prompt, now couldn't keep from gawking. Lorena told her that the Roses were, in fact, at home and had hired them to find Stevie. The woman said her name was Marilyn Lambert and that she was Clara's grandmother, assuming they'd have an idea who Clara was. She said she'd go get Stevie and disappeared into the house without inviting them inside.

Stevie glowered at Waldo and Lorena as she strode past them and out to the street, leaving without a good-bye or thank-you to her friend Clara, who lingered in the doorway, or to Clara's grandma. Waldo did thank Marilyn Lambert and they followed Stevie.

Waldo and Lorena hadn't made a plan for getting the girl home in the two-seat Mercedes. Waldo said, "We could walk."

Lorena said, "*You* could walk. We'll meet you there."

Stevie said, "Yeah, fuck that, I'm not walking. It's like two miles."

That torqued Lorena enough to take the hills in her heels. "We're *all* walking." Stevie heaved a supremely annoyed teenage grunt. They started their hike. Lorena said, "So who's Clara?"

"That girl."

"Who *is* she?"

"My best friend. Not that it's any of your business."

"I thought Dionne was your best friend."

"Who told you *that?*"

"Your parents didn't even mention a Clara."

"You talked to my *parents?* *God.*"

"They hired us to find you."

"Figures. Leave it to Paula to turn everything into a great big drama."

"You've been missing for five days."

"I wasn't missing. I was right here."

"You were in Orange County."

"*When?*"

"After we saw you at your house. You called your cousin and he came and got you."

"No. I called Clara, because Clara has a car and I figured you two would snitch on me for being home when my parents were away."

"Snitch to who?"

"Whoever. The school."

"You haven't been *going* to school. You think they weren't going to notice?"

"I've been going to school," she said, as if annoyed at their incompetence.

"When's the last time you were there?"

"Today. I skipped a couple of classes, but I *went*."

Waldo knew it was the usual Stevie obscuration but Lorena was treating it like a deposition and letting the girl's inconsistencies spin her out even more. He could tell Stevie read all that and was relishing the game.

Lorena said, "Oh, really. If we went to your school right now and asked them—"

"It would be closed. Because it's *night*?" Stevie said it with such overbearing smugness that Waldo thought Lorena might slug her.

Before she could, he said, *"Hey,"* and stopped walking. "Do you know that Mr. Ouelette is dead?"

Stevie stopped walking too. "Yes."

"Do you know that the police want to talk to you?"

Stevie shook her head.

"Your parents are paying us to be on your side, and we're pretty much the only ones who are. So you need to stop bullshitting us, understand? You need to tell us everything that happened from when we left your house that day."

Stevie glowered some more, then looked away. Finally she said, "I was just hanging out. I felt like getting high and I was bored. So I called Daron."

"Why Daron?"

"Because I knew it would piss off Paula and Joel. Especially if I was down there with him when they got home."

He said, "Why did you want to piss them off?" She hiked a shoulder. "So what did you and Daron do that night?"

"We smoked some weed and stuff and then he started being a dick."

"Being a dick how?"

"There was some guy he didn't want me talking to." It was a pretty soft telling of the drugs and of Marwin Amador and his teardrop tattoos, but at least it was more or less consistent with Daron's account. "I didn't need my cousin all, like, telling me what to do. So I left."

"Where'd you go?"

"Well, then I was shit out of luck, because my phone was dead. I got some guy outside a CVS to lend me his and I called Clara and told her where I was. She's a senior."

"And she drove down to Orange County and got you?"

"Yeah. I slept over at her house. The next day we ditched school and went to Venice Beach. And then this other girl Shannon texted Clara about Mr. Ouelette and I was totally freaked out, so I just stayed at Clara's. I didn't want anybody to know where I was."

"Why not?"

"Because of what I did with you guys, hiring you to mess with him. I didn't want to get in trouble." She told them that starting the second day, Clara would drop Stevie off somewhere on her way to school and Stevie would hang out alone at Fashion Square or the Galleria. "It was probably stupid," she said, "but I was, like, too freaked out to deal. Do they know who killed him?"

Waldo said, "How did Daron find out where you were? Did you call him, or did he call you?"

"I didn't *call* him. I *texted* him, like, on the first day, from Clara's phone."

"Why from Clara's?"

"Because I was keeping mine off so I wouldn't have to deal with *this*," meaning anyone coming to get her.

"Why did you text Daron, then? What did you say to him?"

"Just something normal. You know: *'It's Stevie, friend's phone,*

OMG my teacher got killed,' or whatever. But he was still all weird about that guy down there and I stopped answering."

"How did he get Clara's address?"

"I don't know. Maybe he texted her and she snitched me out. Apparently I can't trust anyone for shit."

"What about Amador?"

"What's Amador?"

"The guy you called. Marwin." Stevie shook her head like she didn't know what he was talking about. "The guy you bought the coke from."

She stepped back, thrown. "Oh. Yeah. I thought his name was, like, *Marvin.*"

"You called him after you left Daron's."

"No—I called him while I was *at* Daron's. While we were fighting. To piss him off." It was a versatile motivation.

"Daron didn't tell us that."

"Maybe he doesn't remember. He was pretty fucked up."

Waldo ran it all through again in his head, then said, "Let's walk." They started again toward the Roses'.

He believed Stevie was telling something in the vicinity of the truth. Too much matched what they'd heard elsewhere, with no obvious inconsistencies. Still, one thing didn't feel right. "You knew your parents were back from Hawaii?"

"I guessed they were. They were supposed to be."

"Ouelette was murdered, you were scared . . . why didn't you call them?"

"You don't get it. You don't know Paula and Joel." Her voice had a different tinge, something that sounded darker under the teenage sneering. Waldo looked over at Lorena to see if she heard it too.

Lorena rolled her eyes.

When they got to the Roses', Stevie unlocked the door but paused before opening it. "This is going to suck." She turned to Waldo. "Could you go in and talk to them first? Like, soften them up or something?"

Lorena said to her, "I'm waiting out here with you."

Stevie said, "Don't worry, Lorena," again the put-upon, superior teen. "I'm not going to run away."

"Fucking A, you're not."

Waldo shook his head and opened the door, glad for the brief respite from their hostility. He started to call for Stevie's parents, but before he could make a sound the beast was upon him—a brown bear, right in the house, lunging out of a darkened hallway, fangs first.

Waldo raised his right hand at the last second to protect his face and throat; powerful jaws clamped his forearm and the creature's flying weight slammed him into a wall. The back of Waldo's head shattered a mirror.

On the ground now amid the shards, the bear champed his arm without letup. Waldo screamed and clubbed at its snout with his other hand, to no effect.

Then the world went red and his brain exploded. Every muscle seized at once, a full-body paroxysm, agony like nothing he'd ever conceived of, so excruciating that he completely forgot there was a beast trying to slaughter him.

And then it was over.

The pain. The attack. Everything.

Waldo leaned against a wall and started breathing again. He tried to get his compass back, to make sense of what had just happened. The bear was sedate too, lying on the ground a few feet away. Lorena knelt beside it. Stevie was running into the darkened hallway. He heard a door slam.

Waldo closed his eyes, concentrated on drawing a breath as slowly and deeply as he could. He let it out and did it again.

Then Lorena was pulling him to his feet and out the front door. The pain flooded back into his arm. Lorena pulled the front door shut behind them.

Waldo leaned against the doorjamb and said, "Where the fuck did these people get a bear?"

Lorena broke into a laugh so convulsive that she actually fell down. Seated on the ground, she said, "Fuck, *that* broke the tension. Oh, that's good."

"*What?*"

"It's not a bear. It's a Presa Canario, I think."

"What is that?"

"It's a dog. It's banned in a couple countries."

"What did you do?"

"Tased it. Couple times. I might have caught you on one of them. It was a little tight. Sorry."

"*Oh.*"

Lorena said, "Was it good for you?"

He almost chuckled. "My arm's pretty messed up."

"We should get you to a hospital."

"Yeah." He started down the driveway.

"Where are you going?"

"To your car."

"Uh, no. Ambulance." She was already dialing.

"We'll get to your car faster." She wasn't hearing of it and waved him off. He said, "You just don't want me bleeding all over your Mercedes."

"That's why I love you, Waldo: you understand me." She gave the address to the 911 operator and came over to take a better look at his bleeding arm in the light of the Roses' motion detector security lighting. "Yeah, that's pretty bad. Let's get you sitting down." She guided him to a cedar porch glider.

Waldo worked his good arm out of its sleeve and wrapped the shirt around the wound, applying what pressure he could. Lorena said, "You want me to do that?"

"Nah, I got it."

Lorena put her arm over the back of the seat and stroked his hair, a rare moment of chaste affection. They waited quietly for a few minutes, rocking gently. At one point she said, softly, "Where'd these people get a bear?" and they both smiled.

The door opened and Paula Rose took three furious steps in their direction. "*What*—" she said, "*did you do—to my dog?*"

Lorena said, "I tased it."

"What is *wrong* with you? What kind of person *does* that to an animal?"

Lorena said, "Shut the fuck up. Now. Or I'll *shoot* the fucking dog, and tase *you*." Paula gasped. "And by the way," said Lorena, "your daughter's home."

EIGHTEEN

H e didn't feel like a lucky man, certainly not the lucky man the doctor in the St. Joe's ER kept telling him he was. She was tall, this Dr. Baggett, over six feet, given to hunching to downplay it, and also given to repeating herself. "You are a lucky, lucky man," she said, her eighth and ninth "luckys." He knew they were the eighth and ninth because Lorena was trying to distract him from his pain by counting them off discreetly on her fingers. The searing puncture wounds were an infection risk, but the dog had chomped the meaty end of his forearm and Waldo had gotten away without either the lacerated flexor tendon or fractured ulna Dr. Baggett feared. The dog had had all its shots, too; the first thing the doctor did was tell Lorena to step outside and call the Roses to ask. Paula, incredibly enough, had been snippy about it.

The X-rays, the MRI and the rest of the attention kept them there past midnight. Arm in a sling, Waldo was finally released with detailed instructions for keeping the wound clean and prescriptions for both oral and topical antibiotics and Percocet for the pain. He could live with counting all the medication as one Thing, but the sling had to be a second, and he had few Things in L.A. to shed. He silently resolved to discard his two pairs of underwear and go commando until his arm healed, if he didn't come up with a better idea before bedtime.

They had waited until they were through at the hospital to call Cuppy and let him know that they had Stevie in hand and could bring her in to the station for a conversation tomorrow. "No way," the detective said to Waldo. "I'm talking to her tonight."

"Give her a break. She's been through a lot."

"Tonight, or it won't be a chat, it'll be an arrest."

All Waldo wanted was one of those Percocets and some sleep. He wasn't getting either soon. "Meet you at the Roses' house in an hour. Stevie'll be there."

Cuppy said, "Forty-five," and hung up.

Waldo didn't want Lorena on the phone with Paula again, so he dialed Joel's number himself and told him.

Lorena said Stevie deserved whatever trouble Cuppy was about to bring down but Waldo still felt protective and talked her out of finding a twenty-four-hour pharmacy and getting the scrips filled first. As recompense he let Lorena, who was beyond fed up with the Things at this point, win both halves of the argument about exempting the new ones: he agreed to treat the medicine as he'd treat food (that is, intrinsically not a Thing), and the sling as he'd treat a cast (that is, a temporary bodily extension and thus not a Thing either), even though the latter was a blatant cheat.

Lorena pressed the button on the Roses' call box and the gates opened right away. At the top an unfamiliar blue Lexus was

parked where the EMTs had tended to Waldo hours before. Joel
Rose stood in the doorway. Lorena said, "What'd you do with the
puppy?"

"In the laundry room. He's useless now."

Lorena said, "Good," and walked past him and toward the living room.

Joel muttered, "That was a three-thousand-dollar dog." To
Waldo he added, offhandedly, "Sorry, by the way."

It was past midnight and everyone else looked rumpled and
exhausted, but the woman in the living room with Paula was fresh
as a sun shower and dressed like she'd stepped out of a window on
Rodeo Drive. Waldo's heart sank. This was Fontella Davis, the
celebrity lawyer, whose collaboration on the Pinch case he'd enjoyed only slightly more than tonight's with the Presa Canario.

Joel told Waldo, "Fontella and I are on a couple of boards together: City of Hope and Esperanza." Waldo recognized these as
a chain of cancer hospitals and an immigrant rights group, respec-
tively. "We thought it would be smart to have an attorney here."

"Hey," Waldo said, "you're looking for someone to handle a
dog-bite case, you couldn't do better."

Paula said, "That's not—"

"I know what she's here for."

Davis said, "Delighted to see you again, too."

Joel was thrown by the tension. "Is there a problem?"

Waldo and Davis measured each other. Waldo shook his head
and Davis said, "No." Then she said, "We should talk to Stevie
before the police get here."

Lorena spoke up. "Wait—first this dog thing."

Joel said, "We bought him yesterday. He was just supposed to
be a barky dog. "

"It's fucked up."

Paula said, "I know—we should have gotten a rescue dog instead of buying. But they didn't have anything this big at the shelter we went to. We're offsetting it with a contribution to Dogs Without Borders."

"I don't give a shit about that. I'm talking about Waldo could have been killed. What are you doing with a big fucking monster like that?"

Joel said, "Paula's been a wreck since the thing with Stevie's teacher. She's been terrified to stay in the house alone."

Waldo said, "You might be safer with a gun."

Paula and Joel exchanged an eye roll. Paula said, "I'd think a former law enforcement officer would be aware of the statistics." She spelled it out for him. "People purchasing guns ostensibly to defend their homes, only to end up with the wrong person getting shot?" She left the room to get Stevie.

Lorena said to Joel, "Are you on any boards about domestic violence?"

"No. Why?"

"Because I'm thinking, if you hit your wife, I won't have to."

Waldo said, "O-*kay*." When the time was right he'd also suggest Lorena try not to threaten the clients, either.

By way of apology, Joel said of his wife, "She's distraught. All this with Stevie . . ."

They let the thought hang and stood there awkwardly with Joel and Fontella Davis until Paula returned with her daughter. The latter was wearing loose gray shorts and a little pink tank top, probably what she'd changed into for bed. She was saying to her mother, "Nobody gives a shit what I'm wearing."

Paula said, "This is the *police*."

Stevie gestured at Paula's own wardrobe. "Oh, is that who *you* dressed up for? With that stupid dashiki thing, and those beads?

What are you going for—like, 'I wish it was still the seventies so I could blow up a post office'?"

Paula said, "Fine. Maybe he'll arrest you for looking like a hooker."

"Maybe he'll arrest *you* for wearing *batik.*"

Joel stepped in. "Stevie, this is Fontella Davis. She's going to be your lawyer."

"Hi, Stevie."

Stevie didn't answer. She looked at Waldo's injured arm and rolled her eyes to tell him the whole exercise was yet another way her parents seemed intent on embarrassing her.

Davis said, "We only have a few minutes. Why don't we sit down, and you tell me about the day you ran away."

"I didn't 'run away.' *God.*" She said to her father, "This is my *lawyer*? I am so fucked." She flopped onto one of the sofas. Davis sat on the opposite one.

Joel said, "Let me get a couple of chairs," and left the room.

Davis stared at Stevie until the girl offered a better answer, albeit with an attitude that made clear how much this was inconveniencing her. "All I did was call my cousin and go hang out with him, and then my girlfriend picked me up and I slept over at her house. It's no biggie."

"Mr. Waldo and Ms. Nascimento came over here to talk to you earlier that day. Is that correct?" Davis was actually asking Waldo and Lorena, who nodded confirmation. She turned back to Stevie. "And is it true that you hired them?"

"Yes."

"To do what?"

"I told them I needed them to find my brother. But what I really wanted was for them to go talk to Mr. Ouelette."

"Why did you want that?"

"Because he's a total creep and something, like, really, really shitty had to happen to him, and I knew nobody else was going to do it if I didn't."

Fontella looked to Joel, who was returning with two low-backed leather chairs, probably from the Roses' dining room. "We need to do some work before we let Stevie talk to the police." Waldo and Lorena sat on the chairs. The Roses sat on the sofas, Joel beside his daughter and Paula next to the lawyer, who said to Stevie, "When the detective's here, you're not to answer any questions unless I specifically tell you to. After he leaves, I'll teach you how to answer in a way that won't get you into trouble. Okay?"

Stevie said, "Whatever."

Joel said, "Maybe Paula and I should have a conversation with the officer first, without Stevie."

Davis shook her head and said, "He's going to want to talk to her."

Stevie said, "Yeah, Joel. It's not all about *you* for once."

Her father said, "Don't call me Joel."

"Okay, Joel."

Joel strained to keep his anger in check. "Young lady, we're paying a top lawyer thousands of dollars to come out here in the middle of the night to keep you out of prison. Now, straighten up. Be respectful. And go change your clothes before the police get here, like your mother said."

Stevie said, "Have another Xanax, Joel."

Waldo got off the chair and came over to Stevie on the sofa. He crouched to talk to her eye to eye; Stevie sighed annoyance and looked at her fingernails. He said, in a softer tone than the others had been using, "I know the cop who's coming over here today. I know him really well. You think *we're* all assholes? *This* asshole is *really* an asshole. And he wants bad things to happen to you. So listen to Ms. Davis. Don't talk unless she tells you to. And after he leaves, let her coach you. Trust me, okay?"

She finally met his eye.

Everyone else held a careful silence.

A bell rang. Joel went to the intercom, buzzed open the gates and left the room to answer the door. The others stayed quiet and listened to Cuppy introduce himself to Joel, who led him into the living room. He said, "This is Detective Cuppy."

"I'm Fontella Davis, attorney for the Rose family." Cuppy took a deep breath at that news and blew it out. She told him, "Stevie's not going to be answering any questions tonight. She's a minor, it's late, and I've just met her myself. I suggest we meet you at North Hollywood Division tomorrow morning at eleven and pick this up then."

Cuppy said, "Sure, we could do it that way."

"Thank you."

"Second option, she could answer a few questions here now, informally. Third option, we do this with handcuffs and a sleepover. Come to think of it, we're not going with the first option."

Davis, stuck, looked at Stevie and weighed how to play it. She said to Cuppy, "Only questions about Stevie's activities on the day of the murder. You ask; I tell Stevie whether or not she should answer. If I say stop, the interview's over and you can do what you will." Cuppy nodded agreement. Davis added, "And I want everyone out of the room. Just the three of us."

Joel and Paula conferred wordlessly; then Joel said to Waldo and Lorena, "We can all wait in my office."

The Roses started to lead them out, but Stevie said, "Hang on. I want him here." She tipped her chin toward Waldo.

Cuppy said, "Not a chance."

Davis said quickly, "Agreed."

Stevie said, "Fine. Arrest me." She held out her wrists for handcuffs.

Davis and Cuppy met eyes, gave in together. The others left the room.

The questioning played out the way Fontella directed: Cuppy posed a series of simple queries about Stevie's day, and, with step-by-step permission from her lawyer, the girl walked through the timeline, from school hours through Waldo and Lorena's visit, then through her phone call to her cousin Daron and his bringing her down to Costa Mesa. When Cuppy asked what they did down there, she said they watched some movie; she couldn't remember the name but some guy had sex with a cake.

She told them how Clara Lambert had picked her up and about how she'd stayed at Clara's house without telling anyone until today. Waldo chimed in at that point, corroborating that that was where he and Lorena had collected her earlier in the evening. Cuppy asked him how they knew Stevie would be there; Waldo said that he received a phone call from Stevie's uncle, Daron's father, who'd known that he and Lorena had been looking for her in Orange County.

Cuppy said he was going to need all of Daron's information and Clara Lambert's too. Stevie said she'd have to get it from her phone and Cuppy let her go to her room for it.

Waldo could see Fontella Davis starting to breathe easier. It could have gone a lot worse.

Stevie returned with her phone and the contact information. Then Cuppy asked her the same question Waldo had earlier. "When you were at Clara's for so long, why didn't you contact your parents?"

"Because we're, like, always fighting."

"What do you fight about?"

Stevie said, "They're just, like, *horrible*. They're, like, constantly . . . *abusing* me."

Davis jumped to her feet. "Okay, we're done."

Cuppy said, "Wait a minute, abusing you *how?*"

"No. We're done." Davis said to Waldo, "Go get Joel and Paula."

Waldo left the room to find the Roses. Behind him he could hear Davis telling Stevie to go to her room and Stevie snapping back, "I don't have to listen to you."

Waldo followed adult voices to Joel's office and told the Roses that they could come back now. Lorena asked with her eyes how it went, and Waldo, the same way, answered that it had been a disaster.

Back in the living room, Cuppy was saying to Davis, "You'll explain to them how child services works?"

Paula said, *"Child services?"*

Cuppy said to the Roses, "Yeah, they'll be dropping in for coffee and cake. In the meantime, make sure your daughter doesn't go running off again."

Stevie said, "Yeah, because they were so good at that the last time," and stomped off to her room.

Cuppy gave business cards to Fontella and Joel, said he'd be in touch and left.

The moment the door closed, Lorena turned to Paula. "So, mission accomplished: Stevie's home, safe and sound. I'll send you a bill. Good luck."

Joel said, "Wait—you're not leaving us now. We still need you. Until she's cleared."

Waldo cut Lorena off before she could demur. He said to Joel, "We'll call you tomorrow."

Lorena shot him a look but he touched her elbow. She took the cue and went with him to the door.

As they left, Joel said to Waldo, "I still want to talk to you about that other thing." Waldo thought he must mean the dog. But Joel said, "You know: the rights to your story. I'm *telling* you . . ." he said, with a meaningful look, the meaning being, presumably, money.

Out on Ventura, Lorena said, "First I thought that girl was a train wreck. She's not—she's a carrier. Bad shit's going to keep happening if we stay with this one. Plus she shot the guy. I know it in my bones."

He thought of Stevie sitting on that sofa, in her nightclothes, her bare legs folded under her, vulnerable, surrounded by Cuppy's animus, Fontella Davis's thirst for publicity, her own parents' uselessness. "We can't walk away," he said. "She's fifteen. Who in that room do you think's going to look out for her?"

"Nobody, Waldo. Nobody but you. Her hero."

"Don't start this . . ."

"Looking up at you with those big eyes. 'I want *him* here.'" She gave the quote a breathy Marilyn Monroe reading. Waldo didn't respond.

She pulled onto the 101 to head back to her house. Waldo silently nursed his own doubts about whether he was doing the right thing. What he really wanted, but knew he couldn't say, was to spend the night in his tiny loft, where there wasn't room for two.

NINETEEN

Waldo woke from a restless Percocet sleep with his forearm throbbing, and once more alone. He heard laughter, struggled one-armed into his dry set of clothes and went out to the kitchen. Willem was juicing again, in workout gear this time. Lorena was drinking coffee and leaning on the counter in an aquamarine cowl-neck blouse and a black pencil skirt. She stopped giggling when Waldo entered. He got the feeling he was interrupting something.

Waldo said, "I didn't hear you."

"I didn't want to wake you. I've got a meeting, prospective client."

"Oh." She hadn't mentioned it.

"It came in last night, while you were in the MRI. Marital—which is starting to look better. You going to be all right on your own?"

He didn't know if she was telling the truth about the new case or if it was just a way to slide out of Stevie Rose's without another argument. He felt Willem's eyes on him and wondered how much he knew. Probably none of it, based on the sketch Lorena had given Waldo of their marriage, but still her ex-husband had to sense the strain. Waldo said, "Sure."

Lorena rinsed her cup, said, "Good. Check in later?" and made a quick exit. Waldo had an apple and some dry granola, then went back to Lorena's room, where he showered carefully and treated and re-dressed his wounds lefty.

Feeling strong enough to try the day without the sling, he biked to the Red Line and rode it back up into the Valley, a solo act again.

Their romantic morass would take time to figure out, but the professional side was becoming clear. This case would be another one-shot à la carte like Pinch was. The Roses had agreed to three thousand a day, which meant Waldo's chosen charity would be entitled to at least fifteen hundred. Actually, he'd have an argument to make for two thousand, the amount he'd negotiated for Pinch and which he'd deserve again if he was going to start working Stevie's case himself. It reminded Waldo that he'd received no confirmation that the network had actually made the contribution of the Pinch money—sixteen thousand dollars by his reckoning— to the Sierra Club. He ought to ask Fontella Davis about it next time he saw her.

Maybe he'd steer the Rose fee to Greenpeace, or Ecotrust. Or maybe, Lorena's censure from the other night reverberating, he should stretch beyond environmentalist groups and give it to people trying to help girls like Alice.

Meanwhile, Stevie. Following Hexter's disquisition on teenage brain development, he had done some reading on his own. One doctor's article, seconding the thesis about teen brains resembling those of insane adults, advised any parent with a problem teen to hang on and wait for these hellish years to pass, and in the meantime just keep the kid alive. Maybe he should forward that article to the Roses.

Of course, it'd be nice if they could keep everyone *around* Stevie alive, too.

"He was one of our most beloved teachers, you know. You can't imagine the effect it's having on the campus—the fragility, the utter grief." Hexter closed his office door behind them. "I tried to explain that to the detective, but he's been a bull in a china shop."

"Jim Cuppy?"

"You know him?"

"What has he asked *you* about?"

"Victor's background, how he fit in at the school. His classes, the clubs he supervised. How he got along with the faculty, with the students."

"Did you get into the relationship between Ouelette and Stevie?"

"Her accusations?" It was a subtle but pointed correction.

"Yes."

"I did."

"What was Cuppy's reaction?"

"Detestable."

"What did he say?"

It was like a turd in Hexter's mouth. "He said, 'Bet you wish you did something about that, huh.'"

"You still don't believe anything happened."

"I didn't believe it before Victor was killed, no. And now you want me to believe it was the motive for the murder you want me to believe she didn't commit."

"I'm not saying who committed the murder."

"She's your client, isn't she? You're trying to prove she didn't do it."

It was a truth he'd yet to fully acknowledge to himself. During the Pinch case he had wrestled with precisely this issue, the inherently corrupt nature of the PI's role, so different from the objectivity of police work. Somehow with Pinch he'd walked that line to his own satisfaction: he kept thinking of himself as a legitimate investigator who happened to be hired by someone with an interest in Pinch's exoneration, but he never thought himself a champion *for* that exoneration. He followed leads as cleanly and thoroughly and honestly as he could, and his solution had borne out the legitimacy of his process.

But this was different. Somewhere along the line and without realizing it, he'd indeed become invested in protecting Stevie Rose. He said to Hexter, "Did Cuppy ask you about anything else? Any subject you weren't expecting?"

The headmaster pumped a knee a few times. Waldo could tell they were veering toward another tough subject. "Drugs. Drugs on campus. He dug in on that."

Waldo asked whether that was a particular problem at Stoddard. Hexter said it was an issue at every private school and talked about Stoddard's zero-tolerance policy, which had led to seven expulsions during the current school year.

"What drugs were they expelled for?"

"Six for marijuana, one for cocaine."

"How about Adderall?"

"Prescription drugs are a different issue, with their own challenges. Some parents are complicit, and some doctors."

"Ever hear anything about Victor Ouelette selling Adderall to students?"

"What? No. Is Stevie Rose claiming that, too?"

"Cuppy didn't ask about that?"

"Not about Adderall."

It was too careful an answer. "But he asked if Ouelette was selling drugs?"

Hexter stood, discomfited. "I wish people would remember that Victor was the victim here."

"Look, a case like this, there's usually something going on in the victim's life that people around him didn't know about. I understand it's a delicate time, but could you arrange for me to talk to more of the faculty? And I'd like Ouelette's emergency contacts from your records, or any other family members you might know about." Hexter nodded sadly, resigned to the continuing intrusion. Waldo said, "Anything else about Cuppy? Anything that surprised you?"

"He asked me about a number."

"A number?"

"Seventy-nine. He asked if seventy-nine meant anything to me."

"Did it?"

Hexter shook his head. They heard a hubbub coming from the outer office. Hexter said, "May I?" and they both went outside.

The staff was clustered around one assistant's desk, staring at her computer, which Waldo saw was open to the neighborhood website Nextdoor. "Look," one of them was saying, "there's a link to KABC. Maybe they're showing it."

"What's going on?" said Hexter.

"There's a fire. I live near there. I got an alert."

The link took them to aerial footage of what looked like a very large hillside house, one end of which was in flames. LIVE and SHERMAN OAKS filled the bottom of the screen next to the Channel

7 bug. There were at least three trucks in the shot and a couple dozen firemen trying to knock down the blaze.

Waldo said, "Is that close to here?"

"Not *that* close. But it's a Stoddard family."

Hexter said, "Dear God. *Who?*"

Waldo didn't need to hear the answer.

He could smell it all the way up from Ventura Boulevard, acrid and metallic. He started coughing, dismounted his Brompton halfway up and walked the rest. The trucks were still there but the firemen on the street seemed unhurried. He said to one of them, "How's it looking?"

"We think we got it all, but we're still going through the house."

"Anybody hurt?"

"Looks like we're good. Family got out quick."

Waldo left his bike at the bottom of the driveway. One truck was parked at the top. The near side of the house looked intact, but the roof damage started only ten yards past the front door. Paula, in tears, came around from the back, Joel a step behind, both looking up, surveying the damage. Waldo said to them, "What happened?" Paula couldn't speak. Joel answered with a lethal glance toward the glider where Waldo and Lorena had sat waiting for the ambulance the night before. Stevie rocked on it now, wrapped in a blanket, staring at the grass.

Joel put his arm around his wife and guided her away. Waldo went over to Stevie.

She was defiant, provocative. "It was an accident."

"You didn't go to school?"

"Paula and Joel said I could stay home today. After everything."

"And . . . ?"

She recited it in a bratty singsong, oh so put upon at having to tell it again. "And I was smoking in bed, and I fell asleep for a minute. I thought I put it out, but I guess I didn't."

"What were you smoking?"

She answered by not answering.

His phone rang in his pocket and he took a look. *Burner.* It took a second to realize that had nothing to do with the blaze, that it was only the blind appellation Waldo had attached to the number that Q had called him from the other day. He pressed a button to forward it to voicemail.

Waldo stepped back to take in the damage. The house was so huge that they might even be able to live there during the reconstruction. An older fireman, probably the chief, was talking to Joel and Paula now, pointing to various sections of the roof. Paula was crying too much to pay attention, no doubt mourning irreplaceable mementos lost. She'd get past that more easily than she could imagine, Waldo knew from experience; people always think they need more Things than they really do. Joel seemed fixed on what the fire chief was saying, though he threw one or two glances Stevie's way. Waldo wondered at the insurance implications of your fifteen-year-old burning down the family mansion with a careless doobie.

"I am so fucked," Stevie said. "Paula was *already* talking about sending me away. After you left last night? That's like all she did, look online at boarding schools for 'problem girls.' They probably think I did this on purpose, because I hate them or something."

"Do you?"

Stevie studied her toenails. "Sometimes."

Waldo wanted to get away from this quagmire, to get back to handling something easy, like a homicide with no clues.

"It's perfect that I destroyed my own room, right?"

"What do you mean?"

"I fucked everything else up. I wouldn't know how to find my way back anymore if I wanted to."

"*Do* you want to?"

"Of course. But to what? My parents are so done with me." It was the first time she hadn't referred to them by their first names. "Look at them." The fire chief was walking away from the Roses. Paula was running her hands down her face, Joel putting a hand on her shoulder, the pair a picture of utter defeat.

Stevie looked up at Waldo. "Can you talk to them for me?"

"What do you want me to say?"

"Tell them I didn't kill Mr. Ouelette. If it comes from you, maybe they'll believe it. Could you do that for me, Waldo? Please?" There was no attitude, no posturing. She was just a girl, earnest and urgent and frightened. "Tell them I fucked him," she said, "but I didn't kill him."

TWENTY

He glided down to the boulevard. Maybe the best move was to try Ouelette's apartment building, talk to that nosy neighbor and anybody else who was home. He should also go back to Stoddard and see what Hexter was able to line up for him. If Ouelette had a darker side—bearing in mind that, at this point, they were going only on Stevie Rose's word for that—had he really managed to hide it fully from his coworkers? Were they all like that clueless hippie art teacher? He should concentrate on the males on the faculty. And he should find out if there were any other teachers who'd been accused of improper relationships with students; Hexter would hate like poison to share those names, but it might be Waldo's best shot at finding somebody Ouelette opened up to.

He stopped at Coldwater and decided to work his way left after the light and turn north on Whitsett. Hit the school while everyone was still there and save the apartment for later, at the time of day people were more likely to have seen the teacher around anyway.

All at once the world went dark, some kind of hood pulled over his face. Something knocked him off balance; his legs tangled in the bike and he toppled to the curb on his right, his shoulder taking the brunt. Breathing came hard through the hood. Then someone was pulling his arms behind him; that shoulder was screaming and his bitten forearm was crying. Plastic handcuffs cut into his wrists.

An iron grip yanked Waldo to his knees, then to his feet. He let himself be pushed sideways into what felt like the height of an SUV or minivan and onto its floor. Doors slammed. How many were there? It wasn't his biggest problem right now, but bye-bye to that expensive new bike.

At least inhaling was starting to come easier. It was musty under the dark hood, but they'd left it loose and it felt like some kind of porous cloth. The car made a series of turns. If this had something to do with Roy Wax or Amador or Tesoro, then he was probably on his way back to Orange County. He waited to feel the afternoon sun hit him on the back of the head as they drove south, but that heat never came.

They drove for what felt like half an hour, mostly freeway. There were slow stretches but no full-on start and stop; that probably meant they were heading away from town, deeper into the Valley, the 101 or maybe the 170. Then there were surface streets, and then the driver killed the motor. That same rugged grip pulled Waldo out of the car. He only heard a single set of footsteps plus his own. Could all that muscle come from one man?

They stepped onto deep carpeting. His captor wrenched him to a stop. The plastic cuffs were sliced off. Waldo was shoved backward onto a cushy sofa. The hood was jerked from his head.

Waldo's eyes teared as they adjusted to the light. He was in a wealthy man's study, mahogany and leather. But it seemed like a free-standing structure, not attached to a house: windows on two sides looked out on well-tended gardens in the reds and purples of a late-spring bloom, the third side onto a cedar woods, and sound and sunlight poured in from the door behind him. The desk looked to be an elaborate antique, the chairs plush, with good lamps beside them. Bookcases on every wall overflowed with worn paperbacks, not matched sets of classics or antique books bought by the yard by a decorator trying to make some arriviste look learned. This was the library of a real reader who happened to be rich.

"I warned your ass, Waldo, do not trifle with my daughter's education." Don Q entered the room through that door behind him and crossed in front of Waldo, then sat opposite him in a leather wingback.

"I didn't trifle with—what the fuck is this?"

Don Q looked beyond Waldo's shoulder and said, "Go get Dulci." Waldo half turned and saw Nini leaving the room. Q said to Waldo, "What you *think's* gonna happen, you let my shit go to voicemail?"

"I couldn't talk to you right then. My client's house was on fire—"

"Bitch, I don't care if your *client* was on fire. I fulfilled *my* obligations; I got you the four-one-one. And I know all about you goin' down to O.C. and followin' up on it. Now *you* owe *me*. My little girl needs you to prepare for her presentation—that's *my* fire."

"Okay, chill. I'm here." Waldo looked around. "This your house?"

"Yeah, it's my house. And don't be askin' what part of town it is, because I don't need you knowin' that shit. That's why I shrouded your trip in mystery. Get it, Waldo—shroud? That's what you call a 'bon mot.'"

"Hidden Hills?"

Don Q darkened. "Mutha*fucker*! How you figure that out?"

"Direction we were driving. And it smells a little like horse."

"It do, don't it? My wife say she don't smell it, but I swear I got that shit in my nostrils since the day we moved in." There were a lot of horse properties at the west end of the Valley. This study was probably a converted barn.

A girl in pigtails raced into the room and jumped right into the trafficker's lap. "Daddy, can we watch *Nicky, Ricky, Dicky & Dawn?*"

Don Q looked like he was hit with an instant sinus headache. "You don't got kids, do you, Waldo." Waldo shook his head. Don Q sighed. "Yeah, we can watch tonight, baby, after your homework is all done. This my friend, Mr. Waldo."

Don Q told his daughter that Waldo was going to be her very own public sector employee, which seemed a big relief to her. The three of them went to work. Dulci read flawlessly a list of ten carefully curated questions, including why Waldo wanted to be a policeman, what his favorite part of the job was, why he decided to stop, and whether he missed getting to play with the siren. Waldo answered everything honestly except the question about stopping; to that he only said that he wanted to live in a different town, where they didn't need so many policemen. He gave his answers slowly, at her winsome admonishment, so that she could meticulously transcribe them into a hardback notebook, her father looking over her shoulder and gently correcting her spelling. Dulci was bright-eyed and clever and adored her daddy. Waldo was transfixed.

Don Q explained that Dulci would turn this into a written report and then would ask Waldo all the same questions in front of her class on Monday. He asked if he could count on Waldo to be at her Stoddard School classroom at eight thirty, or whether he needed to have another limo arranged like this time. Waldo said he'd get there on his own. Don Q made sure Dulci said thank you and then asked Waldo if he had any questions before Nini gave him a ride home.

Waldo said, "Yeah, one. You know anything about seventy-nine?"

Don Q said, "Dulci, go in the house. Tell your mom I'll be in in a bit."

The little girl took her notebook and started out. "Bye-bye, Mr. Waldo!"

"And close the door behind you." When she was gone, Q exploded. "Fuck is wrong with you? Talkin' 'bout shit like that, in front of my little girl? She don't know what I do!"

"I'm sorry. I don't even know what seventy-nine is—is it a drug? It came up in this case I'm working."

The trafficker started to cool down. "Just watch it in front of my girl, understand?"

Waldo apologized again.

"I don't know that much myself," said Don Q. "I just started hearin' 'bout it. It's a synthetic—I think from, like, Iceland or shit."

"Is it the same as fentanyl?"

"Nah, it's its own thing. Letters and a number, like A-H-seventy-nine-somethin'. Ain't no business for me, man."

"Why not?"

"First, you got a marketin' problem right out the box. Shit don't even have a good name. A-H-seventy-nine-whatever? Sound like you tryin' to get your high from the fuckin' IRS.

"Second, price point. I like a porterhouse at Cut much as the next muthafucker, but Cut ain't in the Dow Jones like Mickey D, know what I'm sayin'?"

"So where's it moving? BH? Westside?"

Don Q shook his head. "All I heard is it landed in *your* neighborhood."

"*Idyllwild?*" That made no sense and would be one coincidence too many.

"Your *new* neighborhood, Waldo. Gold Coast. O. muthafuckin' C."

Don Q instructed Nini to drive Waldo back to the east Valley, anywhere he wanted to go, and told them both that the hood could come off once they hit the 101.

In the dark again, Waldo considered what he knew, or more accurately, what he didn't. Why was Cuppy asking Hexter about seventy-nine? Did they find some in Ouelette's system? In his apartment? What was a San Fernando Valley private school teacher's connection to a new designer drug that was only moving in Orange County?

That last one was less mysterious than he'd like it to be.

Stevie was the common denominator. One way or another it was looking like the girl was hooked into a drug killing. Maybe she was getting this seventy-nine from her cousin and moving it to her old teacher? Or maybe she was working directly with Amador. Either way . . . *shit.*

Nini pulled the hood off, mute as always, and Waldo found himself sitting in the back seat of an Escalade. He took out his phone and started tapping the letters and numbers into Google. Don Q's breakdown was right, as far as it went: AH-7921 was a synthetic opioid, gaining traction in England and Northern Europe. It was developed as an analgesic for medical purposes but never got as far as testing in humans. Hard to come by, usually a powder, usually sniffed, particularly dangerous because of the difficulty of regulating dosages, and the known cause of a couple dozen deaths scattered about the world. Little mention of use in the United States.

Waldo texted Lorena to let her know about the fire, then dialed Cuppy's number and told him they needed to talk. Cuppy said he was at the Harvard Room. Waldo knew it as a dive bar on Oxnard whose sense of humor extended only as far as its name. He'd been there a couple of nights in the old days, back when Cuppy used to hold court with his partner Dub Gerhardt, two cocks of the walk with the world by the balls.

Nini let Waldo off in front of the bar and popped the hatch. Waldo was only half-surprised to find his Brompton intact. He chained it to a street rack and went inside.

The place was running on inertia: there were more wall signs for defunct beers than there were patrons. Cuppy hunched over a draft—probably not his first, or even second or third, from the look of him. "You know how fucked I am, Waldo? I'm so fucked, *you're* lookin' like good news."

Waldo waved to the bartender and asked for a Bud. He still wasn't much of a drinker, but with an Anheuser-Busch plant right in the Valley, a Budweiser on tap might be, oddly enough, one of the least environmentally pernicious items he'd consume today. He said, "Tanaka?"

"Ouelette didn't land on my desk, bitch'd have my gun already. I gotta close this one." Waldo's old colleague Pam Tanaka had become division commander at North Hollywood. Ambitious and starting to catch fire, she no doubt saw Cuppy as a career stain waiting to happen; she had to be as astounded as Waldo that Cuppy hadn't tumbled with Gerhardt in the investigations that followed Waldo's noisy exit from the force. But it wouldn't be hard for her to find a new charge or suspicion she could use to take Cuppy off the board, bury him somewhere monitoring surveillance cameras or checking vehicles in and out while the department slow-walked an investigation and the union pounded sand.

It would kill him. It was killing him already. "I gotta close this one."

Of course, Waldo didn't give a shit. "So close it."

"I know it's the girl," said Cuppy. "Teacher was doing her, right?"

"Can't say."

"Yeah, can't or won't. Jesus, Waldo, give me *something*."

"For old times' sake?" Cuppy blew a grunt through his nose and shifted his weight onto an elbow, which just missed the edge of the bar.

Waldo said, "I got his next one," to the bartender, who was delivering Waldo's Bud.

Cuppy drained the glass in front of him and grumbled about Tanaka. "Bitch is *made* for downtown. And just what they're looking for now: not white, not male, check all the fucking boxes."

Waldo said, "How much seventy-nine did they find?"

"Half a gram! You know what that costs?" Cuppy blurted before he had a chance to process the question. Then his wits started creeping back in his direction and he studied Waldo through narrowed eyes. "How'd you hear about that?"

"How much *does* it cost?"

"I'm not telling you."

Waldo chuckled. *"That's* where you're going to draw the line? I can Google *that."* He pulled out his iPhone and asked the bartender, "You got Wi-Fi?"

Cuppy gave in, waving off the phone. "Fuck it, I found that online, too. Sixty-five G a gram." A porterhouse at Cut, indeed. "That's ordering through the Caymans. But even then you need a note from your doctor. Who better be the surgeon general."

"So, what—private school teacher had thirty grand of this shit in his apartment? And the tox report?"

Cuppy shook his head. *"My* turn to ask a question. Where'd Little Miss Muffin go for five days?"

"Best I can tell, her friend's house."

"The friend with the grandma."

"Uh-huh."

"She leave the gun there?"

Waldo conjured the most enigmatic smile he could, baiting the hook. "Tox report," he said, letting Cuppy know he'd only get the info he wanted in trade.

Cuppy said, "Clean."

"Anything else in the house? Coke? Crank?"

"Nope and nope."

"Adderall?"

Cuppy scoffed. *"Adderall?* No, Waldo. No fucking Adderall. Jesus. No Midol, either. No Anbesol, no Tylenol." He shook his head. "Fucking *Adderall."*

So no drugs in Ouelette's apartment except the better part of a year's salary in an obscure designer synthetic.

The bartender brought Cuppy his draft. The cop said, "So, the gun—what, she left it at the old lady's house?"

"No idea."

Cuppy, pissed at being suckered, leaned in to Waldo. The same elbow slid off the bar again. "What about the parents? They keep a gun? They don't have a permit."

Waldo shook his head. "They're allergic."

"So where'd the girl get it, you think?"

Waldo said, "Give me some more about seventy-nine; then I'll tell you what I think. There a lot on the street?"

"Yeah, if the street is Piccadilly Circus. Champs-Élysées. Whatever fucking street runs through fucking Stockholm. Even DEA hasn't heard shit about seventy-nine on the West Coast."

Which put Don Q a couple of steps ahead of the feds. Surely not for the first time.

Cuppy said, "Now: where you think she got the gun?"

"What *I* think?" said Waldo. "*I* think . . . the girl didn't kill him."

"Really. You think that."

"Really I think that."

"What the fuck, Waldo, you her publicist now?" Waldo shrugged. Cuppy said, "But you know whether she was doing him, don't you."

"I do."

"Well?"

Waldo said, "I need one more answer before I give you *that*."

Cuppy finished his beer and said, "Go ahead: ask."

Waldo shrugged helplessness. "Unfortunately, Cuppy, I'm all out of questions." He slid off his stool.

Cuppy, chafed, said, "Know what *I* think, since we're getting all BFF-y? *I* think . . . *you're* doing her. How is the lovely Lorena liking that?"

"Go fuck yourself, Cuppy." Waldo put a twenty on the bar and headed for the door.

"I *could* fuck myself," Cuppy grumbled into his empty glass, "but I'd have to get in line."

Waldo left a message on Lorena's voicemail, telling her that he was going back over to the Roses'. He also said he might have a link between Ouelette and O.C. but that he hadn't sorted it out yet and they should talk later. He didn't want to leave too much on the recording. Especially since he didn't even know if she still gave a damn.

Paula Rose wasn't as lit as Cuppy when she let Waldo in, but she was on her way. The house reeked. She said they were indeed going to try to make a portion of it livable while they sorted out the rebuild. Waldo told her he was looking for Stevie, that he had some new questions for her. Paula said, in a tone dripping with irony but with words that didn't actually contain any, "Stevie's room is uninhabitable, so she's moved into the pool house. You can find her there." She swept her arm in that direction and faltered a little on the stairs.

Waldo crossed the pool area to the guest cottage beyond. He knocked on the wooden casing to the screen door, his eyes averted for Stevie's privacy. He could feel the cold air blasting from inside, halogenated chlorofluorocarbons pumping into the troposphere as the Roses generously air-conditioned Sherman Oaks.

"Waldo! My first visitor! I was hoping it would be you!" Stevie slid open the screen for him. "Want some schnapps?" she said, continuing the theme of the evening.

"No. Maybe you shouldn't be drinking that either."

"I *definitely* shouldn't be drinking this. It tastes like Robitussin. Unfortunately it's the only thing I found out here. I have no idea who left it."

The pool house was about twice as big as his own cabin in Idyllwild. There was a full-size daybed with a wrought iron headboard, a small sitting area with a couple of club chairs and a kitchenette, plus bathroom. "Can I sit down?"

"Do it."

Waldo sat on one of the chairs. Stevie stepped up onto the bed and stood on the mattress with her glass in hand, bouncing lightly. "How do you like my new apartment?" She was wearing an oversize Dodgers T-shirt and below-the-knee shorts, easily the most modest outfit he'd seen her in.

"Tell me about Victor Ouelette and drugs."

"Drugs? He didn't even drink."

"What about him selling Adderall? And other stuff?"

"Come on, Waldo—keep up, will you?" She bent to put the glass down on a nightstand, then flopped onto the bed and threw her legs over the side. "Mr. Ouelette wasn't into anything except sex."

"How about seventy-nine?"

"Off by ten." She giggled, took another slurp of schnapps and peered at Waldo over her glass. He saw a flicker and didn't want her going there, but didn't know how to stop her. "When you were a cop, did you ever do it with somebody you were investigating for murder?"

"When you told us about him dealing—that was all made up? Completely?"

She wasn't listening. "I bet you did. Was it hot? Thinking maybe she'd stab you right in the middle of it—like a movie?"

"We're definitely not going to talk about my sex life."

"You want to go swimming?" She started to peel off her T-shirt.

"*Hey.*"

"Chill, Waldo. I have a swimsuit under this."

"Leave your clothes on."

"I want to go swimming."

"And I want to talk about Mr. Ouelette."

"Fine, I'll change in the bathroom."

She went behind the bathroom door but didn't close it. She was completely visible in the mirror over the sink. Waldo looked at the floor. "Did you ever bring him anything, for anybody else?"

"Like what?"

"Designer drugs, maybe?"

Stevie said, "Should I try to find a suit for you, or are you cool swimming in your underwear?"

"If you even need *that*." Waldo startled at the voice. It was Lorena, outside the screen door.

Waldo jumped up and slid it open for her.

Stevie emerged from the bathroom in a fire-engine-red two-piece. Waldo was completely rattled and sure he looked it.

Lorena pursed her lips. "How's the interview going?"

Stevie beat him to an answer. "Not very well. Waldo asks all the wrong questions. Actually, I think I might be more likely to open up to another girl."

Waldo didn't know what her angle was but said, "Okay," and stepped outside.

Turning back to slide the door closed, he saw Stevie grin at Lorena and finish the thought. "Especially one who remembers what it was like to get hit on all the time." It was a sly and wicked shot. Even from outside he could feel Lorena's shoulders tense.

He found Paula in the kitchen opening another bottle of wine with an electronic gadget. She said, "I have no idea what I did to deserve it, but I raised a total cunt." Her intensity made him recoil even more than the word. "I mean, I was shitty to *my* mom sometimes, but nothing like this. You should hear how she talks to me. The *contempt*." She refilled her glass, didn't offer one to Waldo. "I'm her mother—I know I'm supposed to believe she didn't murder anybody. But you know what? The way she looks at me? I honestly think she'd kill *me* if she could get away with it. Tell you something, Waldo: it makes believing in that girl kind of hard."

TWENTY-ONE

On the way to Lorena's house, Waldo downloaded her on the seventy-nine and what he learned from Don Q and Cuppy. "Maybe when you're messing around with a student you want to keep it secret, but there's no point being a dealer without anyone *knowing* you're a dealer. So I'm thinking tomorrow we—"

Lorena groaned exasperation.

"What?"

"Listen to yourself—you're like a pretzel, trying to twist this into something that lets her off the hook. You're in denial."

"No," he said, defensive, "I get that she's probably involved. She could be part of Ouelette's connect to Orange County—"

"*She murdered him.* And she planted the designer shit in his apartment, before or after, to throw off the investigation. Took his keys to get in, then went back and left them next to him."

"A fifteen-year-old came up with that."

"It's not that brilliant."

"And Marwin Amador just gave her thirty grand worth of junk, to plant."

"We don't know he *gave* it to her. She could have bought it."

"With whose money?"

"Maybe her cousin, with the lobster Postmates."

"And he gave it to her, why . . . ?"

"I don't know. Maybe she put on her little red swimsuit. Turns men stupid, apparently."

The fuzzy logic wasn't remotely like her. There was some burning anger driving it, an anger Waldo didn't understand—at *him*, it sure felt like, and definitely more than was warranted by whatever Lorena thought she saw in the pool house.

She didn't turn right on Vine like he expected her to. "Where are we going?"

"Santa Ana. Talk to Amador."

"Now? For what?"

"Find out if he's dealing seventy-nine, and if he gave it to Stevie."

It was all upside down: maybe his own objectivity *was* compromised, but she seemed hell-bent on proving that their own client was guilty.

He sighed and settled in for the ride. He had no choice. Nothing made a man feel less in control than riding shotgun when Lorena Nascimento had the wheel.

Amador's house was dark. Lorena reached for the doorbell. Waldo told her it was broken and gave the bars a violent rattle like Daron had. No answer. They got back in the car.

Waldo said, "Costa Mesa? See what Daron can tell us?"

All she said was "Nah," and started driving again. Daron was the obvious next move; she was only rejecting it because Waldo suggested it. Her pique itself was now steering the investigation. He closed his eyes and settled in for the return drive to L.A.

A few minutes later he realized they were back on Harbor Boulevard. "What's here?"

"Maybe Amador's with Tesoro."

"Why would you think that?"

"Why *wouldn't* you?" Her opposition was automatic by this point, not to mention wearisome.

They cruised the Burger King from the far side of the street. He didn't see the pimp, but one of his thugs was in the parking lot again. "That's Tesoro's guy. Probably the one you didn't run over."

"Uh-huh," she said, not interested, peering down the sidewalk. "Tell me if you see that girl."

"Who, Alice?" Suddenly he got it. "You're not looking for Amador."

"I'd talk to him if we saw him."

"What do you want with Alice?"

Lorena hiked a shoulder. "Help her."

"Jesus."

She snapped. "What's wrong with that? How about we start doing something for a girl who *needs* help?"

"Like what?"

Lorena took a U at the light and headed back toward the Burger King. Waldo saw the girl and shifted in his seat. Lorena read it. "Is that her?"

Alice was walking alone thirty yards ahead. Lorena decelerated. The girl turned, like she might have a customer. Lorena pulled up to the curb. Waldo got a better look at Alice as she leaned toward the car: there were new bruises around her left eye. Lorena powered down his window. But when Alice saw Waldo she frightened and backed away, then started again down the block.

Waldo wasn't sure what he was supposed to do. "Hey," he called to her, feeling foolish.

"Leave me alone," said Alice, eyes averted, walking faster.

Lorena put the car in park and jumped out. "Whoa," said Waldo, "what are you—?" Alice broke into a trot.

Waldo sat in the car, flustered and impotent, and watched Lorena race after Alice. The girl's platforms weren't made for running; even in heels Lorena caught her easily, seized her by the arm and talked at her. Alice retorted, the exchange escalated and soon they were shouting over each other in Spanish. Lorena let go of Alice's arm. The girl didn't run away this time, but whatever Lorena was trying to sell her, she wasn't buying.

Meanwhile, sitting alone in the passenger seat of a high-end Mercedes with the engine running was feeling less and less wise, especially given the block party the locals threw the last time they were in the neighborhood. Waldo got out and crossed behind the car to the driver's side. As he opened the door he glanced to the right and recognized Tesoro's squat frame almost a block away and heading in their direction. When the pimp spotted Waldo he pulled out a phone and made a quick call, then picked up his pace.

Waldo slid in behind the wheel. Beyond Lorena and Alice he could see Tesoro's goon come out of the Burger King lot and head their way from the other end of the street. Waldo pulled the car even with Lorena, reached across to the passenger door and threw it open. "Get in! Goddammit, let's go!" Lorena grabbed Alice by the arm again. "Leave her alone!" he shouted.

Instead, Lorena tugged hard, pulling Alice right off her platforms, then shouldered the stumbling girl toward the open door and bulldozed her into the passenger seat. Alice screamed.

Lorena jammed her way into the car too, squeezing in on top of her. "Drive!"

Waldo tore away from the curb with the passenger door still wide open. Lorena was reaching for the handle when it clipped a parked Jeep, slamming it closed.

"Shit!" Lorena said.

"You okay?" Waldo shouted over the girl, who was caterwauling a torrent of Spanish.

Before Lorena could answer him they heard two gunshots. Waldo swung left in front of an oncoming pickup at the next break in the median.

"Go back!" Lorena shouted. "Run that fucker over!"

"We'll come back and do that another time."

He ran surface streets until he saw a sign to the 22 and hopped on, hoping he remembered correctly that it would run them into the 405. Alice was shrieking in the passenger seat and Lorena, atop her, was bracing herself with an arm on the dash. Waldo tried to hold a steady forty-five in the right lane.

Eventually, Alice's protests receded to a whimper. Waldo glanced over: the girl was terrified. Lorena kept talking to her in Spanish, her voice dropping lower and lower. In time the girl calmed and even answered a couple of Lorena's questions. Coming into Long Beach, Lorena told Waldo to look for a place to eat.

He found a Denny's past the airport. When they got out of the car, Alice looked around and Waldo thought she might run, but she didn't. Inside, she asked for a French Toast Slam. Waldo ordered a grilled cheese sandwich and when it came pushed it in front of Alice; she tore through that too. They ate in silence: Waldo had eyes only for Lorena, Lorena only for Alice, Alice only for her food. Waldo had no idea what Lorena had in mind as a next step, let alone an endgame. But she was so focused and fearsome right now that he didn't dare ask.

In the parking lot she and Alice had another brief discussion in Spanish, this one hushed and tranquil. The two of them looked over at Waldo like there was a question on the table; then the girl answered it. Lorena said to him, "You drive again."

Apparently by agreement, this time Lorena got in the car first and told Waldo, "Drive to Hollywood. I'll tell you where to go."

The girl wedged in and folded onto Lorena's lap. Waldo checked her before backing out of the space. He said, "You going to be all right there, Alice?"

Lorena said, "Her name is Mariana."

TWENTY-TWO

Everything about the night left him mortified at his own ignorance. He didn't know enough Spanish, didn't know enough about this realm of human exploitation, didn't know that this organization, the Los Angeles Trafficking Rescue Emergency Action Network, even existed. As a homicide cop, in fact, he'd barely been aware of the shift toward thinking of these girls *as* "trafficked"—that is, as victims, as *slaves*—rather than arrestable young hookers. But this outfit had probably been sitting here, on the upper floor of a two-story above a falafel joint on Hollywood near the Egyptian, since back before the area Disneyfied.

Lorena had known all about it, though, and had called on the ride up from O.C. to arrange for someone to come into the office to meet them. She and Mariana had gotten out of the car and gone inside without a pleasantry, leaving him to wait on the street, and now she was coming back out alone. Waldo pointed east and they started toward the car. "Anybody asks," she said, "we picked her up on Figueroa—downtown, not O.C."

"How come?"

"Just do it, Waldo, okay?"

"I didn't say I wouldn't; I'm just asking why."

"If they knew she was on the street out of county, they wouldn't be able to place her without a shitload of red tape. Biggest shelters wouldn't even touch her. She could end up back out there, even worse than before."

"You know a lot about this."

"You should, too. You were a cop."

"Well, I don't. I didn't even know that *you* knew this much." Her silence felt like yet another reprimand. "So, what, they do placement?"

At the car, she reclaimed the driver's side and held out her hand for the keys. "Placement, all kinds of victim services. Assistance through the court system. Education."

"For the girls?"

"Not just for the girls," she said, getting behind the wheel. "They try to make law enforcement less ignorant, too."

He didn't see her face as she said it, but it was the kind of shot she'd usually take with a smile. He figured he could help get things back on track by joking back. "They could use a better acronym, though."

"What do you mean?"

"L.A. Trafficking Rescue Emergency Action Network? LATREAN?" He saw her face now, as she turned to him under the car's interior lamp. No smile.

How had it gotten this bad, this fast? Could it really have been only weeks ago that they couldn't get through a day without their clothes coming off more than once, Lorena relentlessly pitching him a vision of the life they could build together, an investigative power couple on an endless romantic adventure? It had been intimacy—full intimacy, not the facsimile he'd recently shared with Jayne White that helped him back into the world, not even the halfway, safety-on version he'd known with Lorena when they were younger—and the whole thing, the real thing, was so intoxicating that despite the grooves three years of solitude had worn on his soul, he'd let her maneuver him into using this case as a trial run.

Some power couple. They couldn't agree on where to stop for lunch, let alone whether their client was some kind of teenage black widow. More ominously, the working relationship seemed to be snuffing out the physical. It had been three nights now. The first two of those she'd curled up against him, but last night she'd given his hand a squeeze and rolled away.

Then again, sex had gotten them into this and maybe it could get them out. Get back on track tonight, that's all, and back to where they were before they'd ever heard of Stevie Rose.

Sometimes she showered with the bathroom door open, an explicit invitation; more often she left it closed but unlocked, available for a happy surprise. As he undressed, he had a flicker of insecurity: might she have bolted it tonight?

Or had she not, hoping he'd cross the divide?

There could be no better test.

Naked, tremulous, he queried the knob, this brass oracle from Restoration Hardware that knew his future.

It surrendered to his turn.

Behind the pebbled glass, Lorena stopped lathering. He pulled open the shower door. "Hi."

"What are you *doing*?" The doorknob had lied. "No. *Jesus.*"

Mortified, he closed the bathroom door behind him and pulled on his jeans. He'd gotten it all wrong again.

He lay down on the bed and waited, staring at the ceiling and reviling himself. Think where *her* mind had been. Mariana. LATREAN. What was he thinking? Trying to repair their relationship through sex, on a night like this? Jackass.

When she emerged, again encased in the grannyesque flannel, he said, "I'm sorry."

"You're a *fucking asshole*. To go from all that tonight to *sex*?"

"I said, I'm sorry."

"What, did that turn you on?"

"For God's sake. I didn't know, okay? The door was unlocked . . ."

"Fine, I'll start locking the fucking door!" She stormed back into the bathroom and slammed it so hard he could hear the frame crack. He hadn't seen her in the red zone like this, not since they'd been back together. He'd been lulled into thinking it was something she'd left in her twenties.

"I don't think you're being fair," he said through the door, hoping to settle her down with reasonable words and a gentle tone. "You shouldn't be angry at me over what's happened to that girl. I didn't do anything to hurt her."

The door flew open. "That's not why I'm angry at you."

"Why, then?"

"She told me."

"Who told you what?"

"That you came on to her."

"Mariana—you mean on the street, when I was trying to—?"

"*Stevie.*"

"*What?* When?"

"In the pool house."

"That did not happen. Not even close."

"Well, *something* happened. When I walked in there, you could cut the vibe with a knife."

"It's in your head."

"Uh-huh. She's got you hypnotized, Waldo. Don't even try to deny it."

His jaw moved, but that was pretty much all he had.

"She makes me sick, that girl. Look at her next to Mariana—did you see her hand? That scar?" Waldo nodded. "Did she tell you what that shitstick did to her? He cut her and poured *ink* into it, to *mark* her. The rest of her life she's going to have to look at that. Every single day." The revulsion made his throat tighten. "Maybe—*maybe*—she can stay off the street, but that girl is never, ever going to be 'normal.' The world has totally fucked her over. And then you've got your precious little Stevie Rose, who's been given *everything*, and what does *she* do with it? *She* fucks the *world* over. And *you*"—her disenchantment with him, her disgust, was bringing her almost to tears—"you don't even see it."

She disappeared again into the bathroom. He realized there was nothing he could do to get past her fury tonight. He took off his jeans again and slipped under the comforter in his boxers. He'd leave the nightly laundry for the morning. The safest thing now was to be as still as he could. He didn't have any energy left anyway.

A few minutes later, Lorena came out and got into bed herself. After the long night of crossed signals, suddenly she could read his mind: "I don't know where this is going either, Waldo. Let's just get through this goddamn toxic case and then see what everything looks like."

She turned her back to him and switched off her light, to wait for sleep, alone together, inches and a million miles apart.

TWENTY-THREE

Lorena sat on the bed and Waldo stirred. His head was jumbled; the pain had woken him up around three and he'd taken another pill. "How's your arm?" Her tone was gentle and she took the fingers of his damaged arm in her own. She was dressed already, more casually than yesterday, in a navy blouse and loose slacks. "I got that gig I met on." The one he doubted was real. "I'm going to work it today. Think you can keep anything else from burning down while you're on Rose?"

Rose. It was a carefully neutral label. He said, "What's the new case?"

"Peep-show classic." If she was lying about it, she was doing it easily, but that didn't surprise him. "Investment banker, thinks his trophy wife's jumped the pedestal. Stakeout in Brentwood—going to use it to break in my young guy." Waldo felt a glimmer of jealousy, then wondered, through his thick Percocet haze, if that had been her intention.

Hours later, when he woke up for good, he didn't even remember Lorena leaving the room.

He tended to his wound and reconsidered his day, or what was left after sleeping half of it away. He'd been planning to focus on Ouelette, but Lorena's critique of his Stevie blind spot nagged at him and he decided instead to reconstruct a ticktock of the girl's five days off the radar. Daron's role in hiding her was suspicious, his father's in finding her even more so. Waldo wanted another shot at Roy and Brenda together, which meant another trip to Newport Beach. With the late start, he'd get there, conveniently, around dinnertime.

Traveling to O.C. without a partner in stilettos let him cut a couple of bus rides off the front of the trip. In fact, if it weren't for his arm he'd be tempted to take most of the forty-five miles by bike. In the event, though, by the time he reached downtown it was throbbing so badly that he was grateful to be able to rest it on the MetroLink.

He extended his stop in Long Beach, searching on his phone for a farmers market and finding one set up for the day in a parking lot near the Denny's where they'd taken Mariana. He feasted on a late lunch of unpackaged foods: homemade garlic jack cheese, strawberries and a scrumptious bagel—pumpernickel—baked, the vendor swore, by reformed members of the Latin Kings.

After that, he returned to Wardlow Station to catch the bus that would take him back over the county line. Before all this he'd thought of O.C., when he bothered to think about it at all, the way most Angelenos do, as a bland, bloated suburb, a negligible stepbrother, so irrelevant to the real city that even their Major League team couldn't inspire a decent rivalry. Now, though, he was starting to see Orange County more like a junior version of L.A. itself: glamour, grime and divertissement in separate and incongruous but proximate stretches, the golden coastline of Roy and Brenda hard by the grubby boulevards of Amador and Mariana, hard by the fresh-scrubbed Main Street of Mickey and Minnie.

Waldo transferred to the OCTA bus down PCH, traversing the Beach cities—Seal, then Huntington, then Newport—where, shadows growing long, he got off an easy pedal from the Waxes' house. The conspiracy theorist security guard he'd left hanging was on duty again.

Waldo said to him, "Hey, sorry about last time, but I had to get in there."

"Uh-huh."

"Besides, I can't go on the radio and talk about the Pinch murder. You understand that, right?"

"Depends what you're hiding."

"There's nothing to hide. The story is the story."

"Good story," said the guard. "Before this? I was Seal Beach PD," he said, significantly. *"Three years."*

Waldo looked the guard in the eye and spoke as earnestly as he could. "What the cops say happened, happened. *I shot the guy.*" In fact, Waldo hadn't shot the man, but it was so much closer to the truth than the fables they were peddling on the radio, he was almost convincing himself. "Okay?"

"Okay."

"So," said Waldo, hopeful that he'd put the crazy talk to rest, "could you tell the Waxes that I'm here?"

"They're not home."

"You sure? Could you call and check?"

"I've seen them both drive out today."

"Separately or together?"

The guard, pleased with himself, said, "The story is the story."

"I'll wait."

"Not in the driveway." He closed his window.

The other side of the street was a line of low-slung luxury apartments. Waldo breathed in the salt air and contemplated another minor O.C. mystery: who would be filling these, at probably seven figures a pop for a two-bedroom? Hollywood weekenders? Rich locals like Daron Wax, parents parking them until the inheritance kicked in? Could there be that many of those kids?

He found a shady spot close enough to the guard gate to get a read on a driver, and a brick planter where he could sit until someone chased him away. There were few cars on this out-of-the-way street and no pedestrians. Waldo bored quickly and found his Kindle. He broke off from World War I at the occasional sound of tires and looked up to see if they were turning into the Waxes' community. Two luxury cars did get waved through in the first hour without being stopped, but neither was driven by a Wax.

A little past seven, Roy wheeled into the drive in an electric blue Porsche Targa convertible. The gate rose immediately but Wax paused anyway to trade a few words with the guard before continuing in. Waldo gave Wax five minutes to get to his house and settle in, then biked back to the kiosk. He said, "Call him for me now?"

"Call who?"

"Roy Wax."

"Told you, he's not here."

"I just saw him. In the Targa."

"That wasn't Mr. Wax. That was another resident with the same car." Waldo didn't know if the guard was running interference at Wax's direction or just screwing with him freelance. Probably the former.

Eight-foot stone walls extended from the guard gate in each

direction. Waldo went south and cruised to the next corner. The wall turned there and ran downhill with the side street to the water. There wasn't a good spot for scaling, but the least bad was a crumbling stretch where he might be able to wedge a toe. A couple of nearby oaks would obscure him from the main road, another benefit.

He'd done this before, and all too recently, successfully circumventing more fearsome guards up in Beverly Park in pretty much the same way. The déjà vu renewed his misgivings about this new career. He could hear Lorena telling him to throw a better shine on it: he was turning into a pro, getting his reps in.

He looked around to make sure no one was watching, then braced the Brompton against the stones and stepped up onto the seat. He tested a crack with his boot. No luck: the wall just crumbled a little more. The Brompton shifted beneath him and he had to grab the top to steady himself. A shaky toe toppled the bike and he barely managed to catch the wall with his other hand too and hang on, nose pressed to the wall. He chinned himself to where he could grip the far side with both hands. He could almost see over the top now, but not quite. The strain tore at his wounded forearm. He hung there for a moment in limbo: should he try to pull himself the rest of the way over, or let himself fall and start the whole process again?

Two quick *woots* from a police siren made the decision for him. He dropped to the ground. A pair of uniforms were getting out of a Newport Beach Police SUV.

"Turn and face the wall, please, sir?" Very polite.

"Afternoon, Officers," he said without obeying. "Good thing you came along when you did."

"How's that, sir?"

"You were able to stop me right before I accidentally tres-passed. Could have gotten myself in trouble."

"Hands on the wall, please?"

"I haven't done anything wrong."

"Hands on the wall."

Waldo did as he was told. One frisked him while the other whipped open his expandable baton. Waldo said, "I'm former LAPD," not knowing whether that was even currency down here. The frisking cop took his wallet and his phone. He told Waldo to put his hands down, then slipped Waldo's backpack off his shoulders and took that too. He slapped a cuff on Waldo's bad arm. "You're kidding, right? Hey, in front, at least? Professional courtesy?" The cop pulled Waldo's other arm backward and cuffed him behind. The baton cop guided Waldo into the caged back seat. They tossed the backpack in after him and slammed the door.

The windows were all up and the air-conditioning had already worn off. He could see both uniforms walking past the rear of the vehicle, in no rush. He wished they'd talk to the gate guard and put together who he was. Not that the truth would win him any fans, but it would all work out more quickly and smoothly than if the NBPD treated him as what he knew he looked like, one more homeless guy hanging around a beach town until he got into trouble.

One of the cops made a brief phone call, but mostly the pair chatted idly and left him roasting in the car. The vehicle had a funk that rose with the temperature, dried vomit apparently un-liberated from the upholstery.

The smell of sick had always been suggestive to him. It had been that way since the first grade with Mrs. Rothbell, when he was left in the hallway with five other kids whose parents, along with Waldo's mom, went inside for a group parent-teacher conference. The children were instructed to sit quietly against the wall and stay there until the parents emerged. Waldo's classmate Wanda Martinez, sitting beside him, suddenly vomited on the floor without warning or explanation, the way small kids do. A hushed, inside-voice debate ensued among the children as to whether Wanda should go in and tell the grown-ups now or should wait as instructed until her mom emerged. The little girl chose stoic patience. The fetid spew on the marble floor beside him filled little Waldo's nostrils; he couldn't take his eyes off of it. Suddenly he threw up, too.

Shawana Council was next, then Joey Parlapiano, followed by, pretty much in unison, the last two kids, whose names Waldo couldn't remember. But he vividly remembered the parents and Mrs. Rothbell emerging to find the six classmates sitting there with vomit all over the floor and their school clothes, and Mr. Parlapiano saying, "What the fuck have you shitbirds been doing out here?," making it an unforgettable day on the vocabulary front, too.

The stench of the SUV brought that afternoon rushing back and threatened to bring the Latin Kings' half-digested pumpernickel rushing back too.

The cops opened the back of the vehicle and tossed in Waldo's bike, then climbed back into their seats in front. "Goddamn," said one. "Smell's just getting worse."

Waldo said, "What is that?"

"We picked up a drunk last night. Didn't make it."

They started the car and rolled down their windows. Waldo said, "Mine too, huh?" But they left the rear ones up. The motion of the car further roiled his stomach. "Hey," he said, trying to be heard over the rushing air up front, "what do you have on me?

Seriously—it's not trespassing if I never made it to the other side of the wall!" Shouting heightened the nausea, so he stopped.

They drove him through the unfamiliar beach town. He wanted to resolve this before they got to the station and started putting him through the system, chewing up what was left of the day. "I really was a cop!" he yelled, queasiness be damned. "I'm a PI—I'm working a homicide!" Neither of them even turned around. "There's an LAPD detective, you can check me out with him! Jim Cuppy!" Either they didn't believe him or they just didn't care.

They crossed a bridge, giving Waldo a good view of the pleasure boats bobbing on the shimmering bay. "I guess I see why the money comes here," he said, this time softer and to no one in particular.

To that one of the cops responded, the one in the passenger seat. "Yeah, it's beautiful. Idyllwild's nice, too. I were you, I'd go back."

They knew exactly who he was. Which, Waldo realized, wasn't better at all.

He sat in the back seat, parked behind the police station, aching in the cuffs. The front windows had been mercifully left down, at least, and with stillness his nausea receded. But they left him there for hours, not returning until long past nightfall. By then the point had been made: Waldo wasn't getting in to see Roy Wax again, not at home, not in his office, not without an invitation.

The baton cop opened the door and unfastened the cuffs. The blood flowed back into Waldo's arms, which relieved the discomfort everywhere except the spot the Presa Canario had crunched, which felt worse. He started to climb out of the SUV but the cop said, "Stay there. We're taking you to Long Beach. Train station."

"That's awfully decent of you."

His partner said, "Buses aren't reliable this time of night. We want to make sure you get on that Blue Line to L.A., nice and safe." The day was wasted, but things could be a lot worse. "Next time we're not going to be that friendly about it, understand?" Finally able to sit normally, Waldo settled back and even buckled his seat belt. He put the backpack on his lap, closed his eyes and rolled his shoulders to work the kinks out of his neck. What to do tomorrow? He could come back down here and try to work the Daron angle: the son would be easier to get to than the father. Or maybe give O.C. a rest for a day and work Ouelette and the school.

They reached the Long Beach train station quicker than Waldo expected them to, and when they opened the door and let him out, he saw why: they weren't in Long Beach at all, nor at a train station.

They were in Santa Ana.

North Harbor Boulevard, to be specific, across from the Wonderland Motel.

The cop said, "You have a nice night," handed Waldo his wallet and phone, and got back in the car. Orange County wasn't made of separate, incongruous pieces at all. It was more like the moon, with a bright side and a dark side, but all one. The cops knew the Waxes, who knew Amador, who knew Tesoro. And now they all knew Waldo.

"Hey!" he shouted as the cops pulled from the curb. "My bike!" He lunged at the SUV and managed to slap the back hatch twice. But that didn't stop them from driving off with it.

Waldo was in trouble.

He jogged across Harbor toward the Wonderland and the relative safety of its lights. A twentyish kid with a pompadour and hoops in his ears manned the desk, young for the night job, a stickup waiting to happen. A terrified look in his eye, he said, "Help you?" Waldo shook his head, trying his best to look reassuring. He took out his phone and, tossing aside every belief that once had saved him, tried to save himself now by finding a cab. He'd concoct some counterpoise later; maybe he'd squeeze to Ninety-Nine Things for a year.

The scared kid disappeared through a door to the office; a second later, when Tesoro came out the same door, it became clear that it hadn't been Waldo who was frightening him. Waldo spun for the exit and straight into a left cross from the Burger King thug who'd survived Lorena's demolition derby. There were two more bangers behind him.

They tackled Waldo and laid into him with boots and fists. One against four: he couldn't get off a single lick of his own. One of them noticed the bandaging on his arm and stomped on it. Waldo screamed.

Another banger stood on his good wrist, pinning him. Tesoro knelt over him and drew back a muscle-bound arm. The last thought Waldo had was almost comforting: if he was still alive, it probably meant that they wanted him that way.

Someone was slapping his face awake.

Waldo was in a bathtub, his sleeves rolled and his hands bound with bungees to the rusty metal knobs overhead. A grungy plastic shower curtain was gathered by his feet, whitish tiles all around him stained by a half century's worth of hotel guests of slowly descending quality.

Tesoro perched beside him on the edge of the tub. A girl a few years older than Mariana stood in the doorway. Tesoro spoke in Spanish; then the girl said, "He says, he told you this ain't the neighborhood for you."

Waldo said, "Tell him I took a wrong turn."

The girl put it into Spanish. Tesoro nodded at Waldo: *you sure did.*

Waldo added, "Tell him I'm looking for Disneyland. 'It's a Small World' fell out of my head and I have to get it back in."

The girl hesitated. "That's stupid. You really want me to say that shit?"

"I don't think it matters a lot."

Tesoro, displeased at the side conversation, turned on the girl. They had a brief dialogue. Then the girl said in English, "He says, 'This time we send you home with a souvenir.'"

Waldo said, "Cool. I'll take one of those Goofy caps, with the long ears."

The girl sighed annoyance and shook her head.

Tesoro snapped open a small knife and placed it on the edge of the tub. He reached into his pocket and took out a wide-mouth bottle of Parker black ink. He opened it and laid out the bottle, the cap and an eyedropper at the curtain end of the tub.

He ripped a tatty white towel from a bar and spoke a couple of sentences in Spanish. The girl translated for him: "Some pimps, they mark their bitches with tattoos. This is better—gives you an experience to . . . what's the word?" She looked for it, found it. *"Remember."*

Tesoro leaned down and held Waldo's nose closed and, when Waldo opened his mouth to catch a breath, stuffed the towel into it.

The girl said, "It'll be less bad if you don't fight it." Her own contribution.

But Waldo balled his fists and squeezed them tight as he could. He could feel the effort straining the stitches on his arm, the one farther from Tesoro. Tesoro called out and one of his bangers pushed his way past the girl and into the bathroom. He stepped into the tub, bracing his foot between Waldo's sternum and the wall. With both hands the banger pried open Waldo's left fist, knuckle by knuckle. Tesoro carefully positioned the knife against the webbing between Waldo's ring finger and pinky, then flicked his wrist. Waldo felt the wicked sting and, looking up, saw the red on his forearm, first drops and then a steady trickle.

It would do him no good to watch the bleeding. He looked away—and through the banger's legs saw the ink bottle on the side of the tub. Waldo torqued his body, then whipped his far leg, kicking the glass jar clean across the bathroom; it shattered on the ceramic tank behind the toilet. At least he'd be spared Tesoro's crude tattoo.

"*Cabrón.*" The pimp answered with his knife, adding a second laceration between Waldo's ring and middle fingers, slicing a little deeper this time. He did the third web, too, and then the coup de grace across the ball. The blood streamed onto Waldo's face. Waldo grunted into the towel.

Tesoro stood and rinsed his knife in the sink. He said something to the girl and left the room, his banger behind him.

The girl came over and unbound Waldo's hands. Everything was staining red. She took the towel from his mouth. Waldo wrapped it around the bloody hand as tightly as he could, tasting the salt of his blood as it traversed his mustache.

Tesoro came back and said something from the doorway.

"He says, come back here again, he cuts a *T* in your throat." The girl looked at Waldo with concern and apology. Tesoro kept talking and she translated, in pieces. "And that bitch with the Mercedes? . . . He's gonna cut all kinds of *T*s into her . . . He has her license plate, so tell her he'll see her soon . . . She don't even have to come to him." The pimp turned and left again.

The girl leaned in and whispered, "Are you the one who took Mariana?" Waldo nodded. "Is she okay?" Waldo had no idea.

Tesoro called for her. She tossed another towel to Waldo and scurried out of the bathroom. Waldo heard them all leave and the outer door slam.

His phone was in his back left pocket. He reached around for it with his right arm—pathetically enough, his better one now. Behind the instant smears of blood, he managed to find 9 and 1 and 1.

For the second time in three nights Waldo reclined on an emergency room bed, taking stitches. These were more agonizing for the same reason Tesoro picked that spot to cut, the concentration of nerve endings in the fingers. This doc, a young guy named Pfeffer with a mane of orange frizz, wasn't telling him how lucky he was. He wasn't buying Waldo's claim of a can-opener accident, either.

Waldo distracted himself by chewing over what the night meant to the case. Why did Wax want him out of O.C. so badly? Their knowledge of the *raitero* business couldn't be enough to trigger all this, could it? What would that be to Wax, really, beyond bad PR? Then again, would Wax necessarily be told what Tesoro would do to Waldo? Was dropping him on Harbor just Amador's suggestion, with Tesoro taking it this far on his own, retribution for stealing one of his girls? Did Wax even know Tesoro at all?

The drug connection to Ouelette was still murky, but the immediacy of the violence made their involvement in his killing feel more plausible. But again—what did "they" even mean? Was Wax connected to Ouelette, in more than a secondhand way through Stevie? Could *he* be the seventy-nine link? He'd have the kind of friends who could afford big-ticket designer pharmaceuticals. Even if it was hard to see Roy Wax personally waiting for Victor Ouelette in his parking garage with a gun, he could have sent Amador. *Tears like rain.* But the links were thin, the motives opaque.

Shit upon shit, and Waldo was still nowhere.

His cell rang and he managed to work it loose from his pocket midstitch, to the doctor's consternation. He looked: *Joel Rose.* Good God, what now? What could Stevie possibly have left for an encore?

"Joel," he said, trying to keep the weariness out of his voice. "What's up?"

Joel Rose answered through racking sobs. "It's Paula. She's dead."

TWENTY-FOUR

While a nurse finished the bandaging, his phone dinged with a text from Lorena. *At Roses—meet me here.*

A minute later it dinged again: *If you take a fucking bus I'll kill you.*

Steadying the phone on his leg, he downloaded the Uber app one-handed. He declined the nurse's offer of a sling: the compromise he'd made toward peace with Lorena still nettled him; his first sling was sitting on the floor beside her bed, and there was no way he was going to pretend *two* slings weren't Things. Then he had a lengthy debate with the ER desk nurse in charge of billing, more contentious than the analogous one two nights before, about why he needed to keep all his insurance information in his head instead of carrying a card. After that they let him go, so he ordered a car and waited in front of the hospital.

The driver talked at him all the way to Sherman Oaks, half the time about the "Netflix-type pilot" he was writing about a vampire hit man who drove for Uber, half the time about how this Infiniti station wagon burned so much gas that the gig was barely worth it. Everything about the ride gave Waldo's stomach a fresh turn.

He texted Lorena when they got off the 101 and she was waiting for him when the Uber let him off at the foot of the Roses' driveway. She made eyes at his mummified left hand but he waved the question off with his right. "You first."

"Gang's all here," she told him as they scaled the drive past the parked black-and-whites. "Joel, Stevie, Cuppy, your favorite lawyer. FIU's still in there with the body."

"What do we know?"

"Joel says he was working late on the show, came home, found Paula on the kitchen floor. Two shots at close range, no struggle, looks like they're pulling a third slug out of the wall."

"Where was Stevie?"

"In the kitchen, shooting her mother." He lowered his chin, raised his brows and waited for a better answer. "*She says*, out in the pool house. Earbuds, Florence and the Machine. Didn't hear a peep."

"Where is she now?"

"Back in the pool house. Cop stationed outside, making sure she doesn't run."

"Where's Joel?"

"In his study with Davis. Cuppy wanted to do residue tests on both him and Stevie but Davis jammed him—she said not without an arrest, and Cuppy can't decide yet which Rose he likes better."

"What about Fido?"

"Double homicide."

"Shot?"

"Poisoned. Antifreeze in the doggy dish out back."

He started inside but she stepped in front of him.

"What's with the hand?"

He recounted his whole O.C. trip, from Wax's brush-off through the Wonderland bathtub. As soon as he said the name Tesoro he could feel the heat rise; for her this was picking up where the Mariana story left off.

"I'm going to cut his fucking hands *off*."

"Yeah, okay."

"You think I'm kidding." She was edging back in the red zone again.

"Well, you may not even have to fight traffic." He told her about Tesoro's translated threat to come looking for her. She rolled her eyes. He told her to take it seriously. Whether or not the pimp was bluffing about having her plate, the cops knew who Waldo was, so Tesoro could probably find out, too, through Amador through Wax, and the step from Waldo to Lorena wasn't a big one. In any event, Don Q had been right: Tesoro was an adult dose, and she needed to be careful.

Lorena said, "Bring it. I'll cut his balls off, too," and headed inside.

A cocktail party's worth of uniforms and plainclothes filled the big house. Waldo recognized half of them. The guest of honor herself was slumped against one of the twin Sub-Zero refrigerators, her blood seeping into grout between the mosaic of gray and white tiles. The Field Investigation guys were still at work, photographing, measuring, taking samples. Most everyone ignored Waldo and Lorena, but a couple made a point of stopping their work to eye-fuck him. Around LAPD, he'd get that forever.

"Hey, hey, hey!" barked Cuppy when he saw them. "Out! You can sit in the office with the lawyer, but out of the kitchen!"

He pointed in one direction but Fontella Davis appeared from the other. "I'm right here." Off Cuppy's confusion, she said, "I was in the pool house with Stevie. She'll only talk to you," she said to Waldo. "Alone."

He went out through the glass doors, feeling Lorena's eyes drill holes in his neck.

Stevie was on the daybed, wrapped in an afghan, makeup running, a box of Kleenex at hand and a dozen crumpled tissues at her feet. She looked up at Waldo and said through sniffles, "I didn't know if you'd even talk to me."

He turned one of the club chairs to face her and sat, keeping the length of the room between them. "Because you told Lorena I put a move on you?" Stevie nodded. "Why'd you do that?"

"Is she here?"

"Uh-huh. In the house."

"She thinks I killed my mother, doesn't she. She hates me. Plus you can tell she thinks she's really hot. I bet she's already dying her hair."

"What can you tell me about tonight?"

"I didn't do it. I have an alibi."

"You might not want to phrase it that way. You told them you were out here all night?"

"I *was* out here all night. But I wasn't alone. I have this friend, Dionne?"

"Dionne was here with you?"

Stevie shook her head. "Her boyfriend, Conor." Naturally. Stevie stopped crying, anyway, distracted by her own story. "He came in and out through the side gate, by the garbage cans, so no one would see him? He left, like, two minutes before the police got here. Promise you won't tell anyone. It would be, like, nuclear for the whole school. I'm only telling you because it's important you believe me."

"Other people need to believe you, too."

"If *you* believe me, I know you can fix it with them." He got her to tell him that the boy's last name was Jacoby and that he was a junior at their school. "But," she said, "we kind of had a fight?"

"What about?"

"He said he should get at least a blow job—you know, if he was, like, cheating on Dionne and everything? I didn't like his attitude—I mean, she's *my* best *friend*. So I said if that's how he felt, he could leave, and he did." Somewhere in there was an ethical stance in which Stevie seemed to take pride, but Waldo decided not to try to tease it out. "You have to promise not to tell anyone. Especially Lorena."

"Why not Lorena?"

"She'll burn me with Dionne. You know she will."

He promised to keep her secret, knowing it wouldn't last the drive home.

A remark of Alastair Pinch's on the last case flitted across his mind: that it tells everything about how people really feel about marriage that the first suspect is always the husband. It made him wonder what Paula and Joel's carefully rehearsed story might have been built to hide. He said to Stevie, "Tell me about your dad. Does he have a temper?"

"Joel?"

"Yeah. Ever see him get angry at your mom?"

Stevie snorted. "Not hardly. Joel's a wuss. Like, totally pussy whipped. I swear, it's painful to watch."

"I heard he got pretty crazy at Thanksgiving. Something about the election and a knife?"

"Uh, *no*? That was Uncle Roy."

"*Roy* was waving the knife around?"

"Yup. Uncle Roy was *so* obnoxious, because he was, like, Mr. Total Trump Fan? And Paula and Joel were already flipped out about Hillary—so they started getting on Uncle Roy's ass about how his factories are all full of illegals and how they were going to go to what's her name, that annoying lady they're always watching on MSNBC? And Uncle Roy was holding the knife for the turkey, you know? And he started yelling at them to go ahead and see how that works out for them."

"You're sure that's how it went. Because I heard it a different way."

"Uh, I was, like, *there*? Uncle Roy is always way aggressive. One Thanksgiving? Aunt Brenda had on these big sunglasses and she kept them on, like, the whole day. She told us she had pinkeye but my mom said . . ." Stevie stopped and let out a moan of suddenly recalled grief, then broke down completely and wept. Whatever was underneath, it didn't seem like an act.

Stevie lay on her side and pulled the blanket over her head, disconsolate and probably embarrassed. She seemed her age for a change, or even younger. Eventually her sobs tapered to sniffles. Waldo said, "You going to be okay?" He wasn't going to leave her alone out here until he was sure she could handle it.

"I could use a hug." She was still buried under the covers.

"Maybe you could get a good one from your dad."

It was a while before she said, softly, "He thinks I did it." The weight of that hung over them both for another while before she sat up, looked at him and said, "Please, Waldo?"

He went over to the bed and sat beside her. She shed the blanket and threw her arms around his neck. He was struck by how little there was of her under her T-shirt, all bones and angles. He recalled that first dinner, her barely touched salad. This girl's problems had no beginning and no end, and now she was down to one clueless, hapless parent to help her find her way through.

In his arms, her breathing settled and quieted. Waldo wondered if she was falling asleep. He knew he needed to hold on to objectivity, but *man* did he hope this wouldn't all end with him figuring out that this girl had murdered her teacher, let alone her mother.

Stevie said to him, softly, "I don't . . ." and trailed off.

"Don't what?"

"I don't like boys my age."

Waldo let go of her and stood. He stepped back from the bed. "You know, until things settle down, you might want to take a break from *any* boys." Or better, he thought, give them a break from you.

She looked up at him with the glittering eyes that once upon a time must have sirened Victor Ouelette to her door in his swim trunks. "Be honest, Waldo: if you could be sure nobody would ever find out . . . isn't there *anything* you'd like to do with me?"

Waldo thought about it, seriously thought about it, and had to nod. "Yeah." Before she could say, *I knew it,* he said, "Buy you a cheeseburger."

"What a bucket of crap." Lorena was taking the canyon way too fast again.

"Which part? That this Conor kid came over?"

"No. That she was messing with her BFF's boyfriend? *That*, I believe. That she didn't *blow* him? Bullshit."

He was reminded again that this game—kicking the case around with Lorena, detective to detective—wasn't going to get him anywhere closer to solving it. She had always been a more than competent PI, but her Stevie derangement syndrome wouldn't let her see anything clearly. He told her about the rest of the pool house conversation, up to but not including the hug. He also told her that he believed Stevie's grief was genuine, but even that was another trigger.

"Who do *you* think killed Paula?" she snapped. "Joel? Because I don't see that."

"I'd like to know what Roy Wax was doing tonight." He knew he was swinging wildly but felt he had to throw out a name.

"Roy Wax? *Why?* Because he got really, really mad when Paula accused him of hiring illegals—*last Thanksgiving*? You're doing it again, trying to protect Stevie." Was he? His ability to resist the girl sexually didn't mean she wasn't putting some kind of voodoo on him. Lorena said, "At least check out her fucking alibi before you swallow it."

She was right. He said, "Okay. Tomorrow."

But it wasn't enough. "Every step of this, you've been protecting this girl. Why don't you protect Mariana?"

"Mariana? What does—? We *protected* Mariana. How could we have done any more to—? Why even bring her up?"

But Lorena shut down. Like she had already taken something too far.

"What?" said Waldo. "What aren't you saying?"

She didn't answer, all the way down the canyon, all the rest of the way to her house.

When she put the car in park, though, and killed the engine, she didn't dash into the house the way he expected her to. She sat behind the wheel for a long while. He waited her out.

Finally: "I told you about after my father, right?"

"Not a lot."

"But my aunt . . ."

"Who raised you? His sister?"

"Yeah." She studied a cuticle in the weak glow of the garage opener. "There were two of us."

Waldo kept very still, hanging on the rest.

"I had a sister. Sofia. She was born; she didn't die with my mother." It flew in the face of everything she'd ever told him and for a minute he had trouble accepting it as true. "Around when I finished high school my aunt got married again. I was eighteen, and with the husband—the house felt small, you know? So I moved out. A year or two later . . ." She had trouble saying it. "I was into myself . . . I had school, and a room in a house with some people, and there were boys . . . and Sofia was twelve, thirteen . . . I wasn't paying her a lot of attention . . . and all of a sudden . . . she was gone."

Waldo watched her carefully, waiting to see if that meant what it sounded like.

"Looking back, I don't know, maybe this new 'uncle' was doing stuff to her. Whatever it was . . . she disappeared, and nobody ever heard from her again.

"So the thing is, whenever I see a girl like Mariana . . ." She stopped a tear with a fingertip before it had a chance to happen. "Every time."

"Jesus."

She looked at him. "You understand what I'm telling you?"

He took a deep breath and said, "Yeah. That there's a difference between Stevie Rose and girls with real problems."

He reached for her hand but she pulled it away and looked him in the eye without warmth or communion.

"No, Waldo. I'm telling you, a lot of people have real bad things to get past." The garage opener light clicked off, leaving them in the dark. Slow and hard, she said, "But not everyone lets it turn them batshit."

TWENTY-FIVE

He hit the Percocet and she pretended to fall asleep right away. When he awoke in the morning, she was already off to wherever, this time without so much as a note.

The bus downtown was rush-hour crowded and he stood most of the way, declining offered seats and clinging to the bar with his right hand, keeping his left close to his chin to keep the fresher wounds from being jostled. The ride was half an hour of start and stop, plenty of unstructured time for Lorena's words to echo. *Batshit*. She had instigated their reunion and been its motor, so he'd taken the depth of her investment for granted, luxuriating in his own doubts without a thought that all this time she'd been harboring her own. Now she was forcing him to look at himself through her eyes and it was sobering: he *wasn't* the man she'd been expecting when she first came up the mountain. Yes, she'd given it a game try, holding on to the dream she'd nursed during his missing years, and, yes, the connection had come roaring back, in its fashion, but still: he was not that man.

Damaged, Jayne had called him. Kinder than *batshit*. Anyway, he was work now, a lot of work. And when the physical connection began to fray, why *wouldn't* Lorena start to wonder whether he was worth it?

And face it: maybe he wasn't.

It wasn't stormy, like all their other endings, and that discomfited him even more. Maybe that meant this was the one that would stick.

Waldo got off at Broadway and walked to the store where he'd bought his original Brompton before the move to the mountain. He was lucky to find a P6L in stock, though only in racing green, not his preferred black. With tax, it was going to run him close to two thousand dollars, a fifth of the amount he kept steadily in his Idyllwild checking account. It was a legitimate expense by any measure, but now one half of the client couple was dead, and could he really imagine presenting the survivor with a bill for a new bike?

Of course not. But Lorena could. Which was why she was the one fit to build a business in the first place.

All of which reminded him that now they'd have money issues to settle too. The prospect of their weeks—their years—ending in a cold coda of financial reckoning was almost too depressing to bear.

"I'm here. Meet me out front." He'd agreed to meet Cuppy at North Hollywood Division but wanted to avoid going inside and facing the bile and the ghosts if he could. He hung up and, working essentially one-handed, managed to chain his bike to the rack near the entrance, recalling the high drama even that simple act had led to last time he was here.

He waited for Cuppy and leaned on the rack, looking out toward the parking lot and the traffic on Burbank beyond. Sure enough, one of those ghosts pulled up in a blue Prius.

Captain Pam Tanaka got out of her car and headed toward him. She was a force of nature, blessed with beauty, intellect and killer political instincts, all of which fueled a dizzying rise to division command. Back in the days of conflagration around the time Waldo left the force, Pam was the rare friend who hadn't turned on him completely. On his return this spring, though, he'd repaid that loyalty by embarrassing her in front of her charges when he felt she was stonewalling him on the Pinch case, a moment he still felt bad about.

"Waldo," she said with an ambiguous smile.

"Pam."

"These noisy ones have a way of finding you."

"I was right," he said now.

He was trying to strike a tone of apology, but it must not have landed like he intended. Tanaka twitched and said, sharply, "But you've been wrong." The reminder was unnecessary: Lydell Lipps was never further away from his thoughts than the Hundred Things were. He was stunned by its quiet cruelty.

Waldo heard a grunt of surprise and turned to the entrance, where Cuppy paused midstride, flat-footed and awkward.

Tanaka said, "Are you two meeting?"

Cuppy said to his boss, "Waldo had some info to share."

"I hope you're not sharing back with a PI working for our suspect. Especially when you told me it was a done deal."

"Understood."

Cuppy was a foot taller but the eyebrow she raised before continuing into the station lopped off a good eight inches.

When the door closed behind her, Waldo said, "What's a done deal?"

"We're going after Stevie for the deuce. Ouelette *and* the mommy."

Waldo said, "You got a match?" Ballistics linking the murders would be bad news for the girl. He needed to know.

"You heard her," said Cuppy, tipping his head after Tanaka. "I give you anything, she takes my *other* nut." He straightened to full height, trying to reestablish the illusion of at least a little potency. "Anyway, I got this."

"Yeah? What if you don't?" Waldo didn't need to spell it out: if there *was* a ballistics match and Stevie's alibi was good, then Cuppy was oh-for-two and thus—with Tanaka, at least—double-fucked. Cuppy's eyes flickered, giving Waldo an opening. "Okay, I'll give first. Seventy-nine's stateside now. Moving right where Stevie went when she was off the radar. O.C. Gold Coast."

"What, you think you know shit DEA doesn't?"

"Now you do, too. Share it with them. Score a couple points. Hey, maybe they're hiring." Cuppy's face fell. Waldo had been unable to resist the shot; Cuppy just pushed his buttons.

But it had been expensive: the detective closed down, started for the entrance. There was no getting him to talk about the ballistics now. Waldo would have to offer something else.

He said, "Stevie's the tie to the seventy-nine. I can even give you the dealer she knows down there."

Cuppy turned back, intrigued. "I'm not stopping you."

"Name's Marwin Amador. Santa Ana."

"Fuck is Princess Peach doing with a mook in *Santa Ana* named *Marwin Amador*?"

"Amador works for her uncle. She knows him through the son,

her cousin. Give you a bonus: Amador's tied in with a scumbag named Tesoro. Gut says he's the trigger." That was pure smoke, but maybe peripherally useful: if LAPD buzzed the pimp, it could slow down whatever he might be planning for Lorena. Waldo said to Cuppy, "Now you."

Cuppy waved off Waldo's info. "Duck tales. Usual Charlie Waldo bullshit."

"Makes you so sure?"

"Your O.C. beaners—you going to tell me they had a problem with Paula Rose, too?"

There was his answer. "You got a match."

"Same forty. Best link between the vics are the two Roses left standing. And I don't see Papa Bear poisoning the pooch."

Shit, thought Waldo. And Cuppy was making sense about the Presa Canario, too: Joel looked comfortable with the beast, but Stevie had been away when they bought it and he could imagine it freaking her out, especially since she'd been living off in the pool house since. If she *was* going to shoot her mother, why not get the mom's guard dog out of the way first?

So it was going to come down to this Conor Jacoby and the timeline, how late the kid had been there with Stevie and what he was willing to tell. The rest of Stevie Rose's life could be hanging on how pissed off some sixteen-year-old was about being sent home for the night without his blow job. Once again, Waldo was ready to quit the PI business. He said, "When you planning to arrest her?"

Cuppy crossed his arms.

"Do one thing for me," said Waldo. "Give me twenty-four."

Cuppy snorted. "For old times' sake?"

"For a fifteen-year-old girl whose mother just got shot." Cuppy held up his palms. *Who just shot her mother.* "Girl says she's covered on the mom."

"I'm sure she does."

"I've got a name. Boy who wasn't supposed to be there."

"Her specialty. You check it out?"

"Not yet."

"Give it to me, I'll do it."

"Right. I'm going to give you another teenager to bigfoot." Cuppy shrugged indifference.

"Hey," Waldo said, *"you'll* want to know if it checks—blows out your theory, but at least you can get ahead of it with Tanaka." He was flailing; he'd already played that card one more time than was probably useful.

Cuppy split the difference. "*Six* hours. And I want to hear from you every two."

Waldo took the deal.

This time he had no trouble getting onto the campus and into Hexter's office, where the headmaster braced himself against his desk like he was afraid to come out from behind it. He had already heard the rumor that Stevie Rose was now a suspect in her mother's murder as well. Waldo asked to speak to the student Conor Jacoby, but Hexter said that giving access to students was a line he couldn't cross. Waldo told him that he'd already interviewed Dionne Shapiro and Koy Lem and that he didn't have the time to wait until after school to chase down Conor. He explained everything, again betraying Stevie's confidence about betraying her bestie.

Hexter didn't want to hear any of it. He squeezed his eyes shut and slowly rocked his head back and forth.

Waldo said, "If I can't confirm Stevie's alibi, LAPD's going to walk in here and cuff her right in geometry class."

Hexter emitted a tiny, defeated moan. He rose and asked his assistant to find and fetch Conor Jacoby, and then to try to get one of Conor's parents on the phone.

The poor bastard was such a wreck that he didn't even bump at Waldo's obvious bluff. Stevie Rose, of course, wasn't at school today and wouldn't be coming anywhere near it for weeks.

Hexter told Conor Jacoby, a beanpole with a wild thatch of red hair, to sit down. He told him, "You don't have to answer any questions you're uncomfortable with, and you're allowed to leave anytime you want. Do you understand?"

Conor nodded. The kid was literally shaking. He'd probably never been written up for breaking the dress code.

Hexter cued Waldo to start. Waldo returned his gaze until the headmaster realized that he was expected to leave Waldo alone with the boy. "For Pete's sake," he muttered on the way out.

Waldo asked Conor where he had been the night before.

"At home, studying physics. Finals are coming up."

"Alone?"

Conor said, "No, I had a tutor."

"Uh-huh." The kid was so jumpy that Waldo checked to see if there was a puddle at his feet. "Did you see Stevie Rose last night? After the tutor left?"

"No! She was there until eleven. Her name's Jamie. She goes to Valley College. You can ask my parents. Nobody else came over afterwards—we have an alarm and everything."

"So you weren't at Stevie's house? Alone with her?"

The jumpiness surged to full-blown panic. "*No! God!* Did she say that?" He read Waldo's hesitation. "Shit! She's trying to use me to mess with Dionne!" The boy was distraught. "Don't tell Dionne Stevie said that, *please*? She gets crazy jealous, like of anything! Stevie *knows* that." He put his face in his hands. "Why does that girl have to lie? *All the time!*"

TWENTY-SIX

There were no police cruisers at the Roses' house now, no fire engines, no pricey attack dogs, no pricey attack lawyers, just a man looking more like the senior citizen he was. Waldo said, "Anyone else here?"

"Only me," said Joel. "Stevie's in the guesthouse."

"Nobody watching her anymore?" Joel shook his head. "I need to talk to her again."

"The kitchen is still . . ." Joel choked on the rest of the thought. "There are special cleaning people coming." He led Waldo out to the pool and asked him to swing by his study when he was finished with Stevie.

Waldo saw her through the locked glass door, huddled under a blanket on the daybed with her computer and earbuds. He rapped on the door, had to bang harder to get her attention. Under the blanket, she was wearing jeans, a hooded sweatshirt and a woolen beanie, explained by the Siberian Freon blast when she slid open the glass.

Waldo said, "I talked to Conor Jacoby."

"I told you that was a secret!"

"He said he wasn't here last night."

She went back to her bed and her computer. "Not my problem."

He pushed her laptop closed.

"What the—?"

"Every time I stand up for you, you make me look like a sucker."

"Yeah, Waldo. Make this all about *you*." The stream of venom he'd seen her turn on others was starting to gurgle in his direction. "Was it *your* mother who got killed? I don't think so, *Wal-do*." She said his name with an ugly, mocking English.

"Tell me what really happened last night."

"What—*you think I killed my own mother*?"

"The police do. They were ready to arrest you until I stopped them by telling them about Conor."

"You told the *police* about *Conor*? Oh. My. *God!*"

"If I didn't, you'd be in lockup right now."

"And of course you believe Conor, not me."

"I *completely* believe Conor, not you."

She huffed through her nose and stared lightning at him. Then she said, "I *had* to lie," with a choler that gave Waldo a Paula Rose tingle.

"Why did you have to lie?"

"Because I was out here by myself. I had no proof of anything. And everybody already thinks I killed Mr. Ouelette."

"Look, if you *didn't* do anything, you . . . *cannot* . . . *tell* . . . *lies*."

"You're such a piece of shit, you know that? You act like you're my friend—"

"I'm not your friend. I'm a hired detective—"

"What you *are* is a total *fucker*. A fucker and a *freak*. Why don't you go take a shower for a change? Jesus Christ. How does your girlfriend even *stand* it, *touching* you? And when's the last time you got a haircut? *God!* You're like this nasty-ass cross between a werewolf and a . . . I don't know, like a *warthog*—"

"Okay," he said, trying to steer it back to the productive. "The point is, you can't lie anymore—"

She went volcanic. *"Everybody* lies! *You* lie! All you *do* is lie!"

"When did I lie?"

"When you said you'd keep my secret!"

"About Conor? That secret wasn't even true!"

"It was a test! And you failed! And it's exactly why I can't tell the truth! Everybody lies to me, they *say* they're not going to repeat things, but they *do*! And then they end up getting *killed*! You know what, Waldo? I hope somebody shoots *you* in the head, too. I hope you get killed, on your *own* kitchen floor, and then *you* can feel *all good* about repeating everything I said to you in confidence!"

With another poison stare, she put in her earbuds, reopened her computer, and left the room without going anywhere.

Waldo retreated to the main house and found Joel in his study. There was some kind of teen bacchanal playing on an oversize screen, Joel watching but not really watching. His sofa had a pillow and mussed bedding on it. Waldo said, "Are you sleeping in here now?"

The question dragged Joel slowly out of his catatonia. At length he shut off the television and said, "There's hardly any house left we can use."

Waldo said, "The police are probably going to charge Stevie."

"With both?"

Waldo nodded.

Joel said, "Will you stay with us? On the case?"

"If that's what you want." Waldo was speaking for himself. He and Lorena could relitigate her involvement later.

"I do. I want you to find out the truth, even if it *is* Stevie. And I want to hear it from you personally, because I don't trust the police in this country to handle it honestly. Jesus, watch the news." Waldo didn't need to, of course; he'd been on it enough himself.

He put Joel through all the obvious new queries about his daughter: where she might have gotten the gun, whether she had any bad-element acquaintances. Each question he couldn't answer made the producer seem smaller in his chair, adrift, inadequate. Finally he held up a hand to stop Waldo from asking anything else. He blew his nose again. "This is what happens when you have a midlife-crisis baby. I'm twenty years too old for this."

"No one's the right age for this."

"It's what I get, right? For leaving my first family. Sixty-five years old, living in a half-gutted house with a teenage daughter I'm afraid to be alone with."

Waldo biked over to the Shapiros' to ask Dionne whether she knew anyone who had access to a gun. She didn't.

Dionne had a question for Waldo too: "Did Stevie kill her mom and Mr. Ouelette?"

"I don't know yet. What do you think?"

Stevie's best friend forever said she didn't care; she was done with her. From where Dionne Shapiro sat, the lies Stevie told about Dionne's boyfriend were also a capital offense.

Waldo rolled down to the boulevard and found an empty bus stop kiosk with a bench where he could at least get some late-afternoon shade while he made two unpleasant phone calls. First he gave Fontella Davis the heads-up on Stevie's imminent arrest so that she could try to orchestrate it in the least damaging and humiliating way. She thanked him before hanging up, an uncharacteristically gracious fillip.

Next Waldo had to swallow his teaspoon of shit and call Cuppy. It was well over six hours, plus he hadn't been checking in the way Cuppy had instructed. Now he'd have to tell him he'd whiffed on the alibi, too.

"About time," said Cuppy.

"Yeah, see—"

"Man of the hour. Your lead checked out."

Waldo was nonplussed.

"Amador. Guess what we found at his house."

Waldo said, "Seventy-nine?"

"Winner winner chicken dinner. Ever meet this beanie baby? With the ink? We're pulling that shit out of his house, *and* guns, *and* coke—Teardrop keeps going, I'm only a bus driver. *Conductor de autobús.* Says he drives 'guest workers.' Love that. And who do you think owns the factory where he chauffeurs all those undocumented citizenitas?"

"Stevie Rose's uncle?"

"That a guess, or did you know?" Before Waldo could answer, Cuppy said, "So I ran this Uncle Roy Wax through the California gun registry, and guess who owns a cute little Walther forty-caliber? Keeps it in his walk-in, behind the cummerbunds." He sounded wired, on an adrenaline rush at least.

"So what—you like Wax for both of them now?"

"More than *like* him. I just put Richie Rich in the car."

"Where are you?"

"Newport Beach. Ten minutes I'll have him on the freeway."

"You couldn't have run the gun yet."

"Bringing it up with me. Lab's working late tonight."

Waldo was astonished that Cuppy would make an arrest, especially on a heavyweight like Wax, before getting an affirmative match tying his Walther to the two killings. "You got balls."

"Didn't have a choice. You should've seen Tanaka this morning, after she saw me with you. I'm fucked, Waldo—my only play *left* was shoot the moon. But if the gun matches? I clear the deuce and I'm golden. Bitch can't touch me; I'll be there longer than her." It was insane, but not: Wax, through Amador, was the only tie between Ouelette and Paula Rose other than Stevie, and Wax's forty—a slightly unusual caliber, too—could close the deal.

Waldo said, "Still. You're going to catch hell, holding this guy."

"Like I'm not catching it every day already? Anyway, if I *didn't* take him now, the fucker'd be halfway to Fiji. You should see the bucket he's got tied to his dock." Waldo had, of course. "And you know Tanaka would nail *that* to my ass, too."

"How about motive?"

"TBD on Ouelette. But Santa Ana PD brought in Amador; we'll flip him and figure it out. The sister-in-law I think I know. There was a phone call—that's the other thing I got."

"What phone call?"

"Rose house to Wax house, landline to landline, afternoon she got shot. Here's how I like it: your baby girl heard there was seventy-nine at Ouelette's and told Mama Bear how deep Uncle Wax was; Mama Bear picked up the phone, called him on it; Uncle Wax came up and killed Mama Bear to cover up the first murder." It was all a little loose, but of course that was Cuppy the cop; that plus shakedowns. Well, he'd live or die on the ballistics match.

Waldo never would have played it that way. Cuppy probably

wouldn't have, either, if Pam Tanaka hadn't driven him desperate. Now it would land on her, too, either way: she and Cuppy would both look brilliant, or they'd both pay for it.

Waldo didn't want the girl dragged in any deeper, so he held back from Cuppy one more thing he knew. *Everybody lies to me,* Stevie had said to Waldo. *They* say *they're not going to repeat things, but they* do*! And then they end up getting* killed*!*

Jim Cuppy wasn't the only one who thought Paula Rose had gotten killed for challenging Roy Wax. Stevie Rose thought so, too.

He rode toward the setting sun without a plan, under the 405 and out to Encino. The pain was mounting again but he didn't want to stop moving. When he got to Hayvenhurst he thought of the park to the north: Lake Balboa, concrete rim, reclaimed water reeking of chemicals. The place used to repel him but now it was calling to him; in its unnaturalness, its innate, ineffable *wrongness*, it felt somehow like this resolution, like this whole stinking case.

He wheeled into the park and took easy counterclockwise turns around the lake while he took inventory of his discontent.

If Cuppy was right about Roy Wax, Waldo should be glad, sort of, for Joel Rose. Paula's murder was horrible, but the alternative explanation and aftermath would be so much worse.

Ditto for Stevie, in spades.

And Waldo himself should be more pleased than he was feeling. Case closed, troubled teen exonerated, venal businessman implicated.

On the other hand . . . he hadn't solved it himself. Cuppy, of all people, had beaten him to it. Big Jim Cuppy—talk about venal, for God's sake.

Far worse, if Waldo *had* been able to crack it, and just a couple of days faster, Paula Rose would still be alive. Joel Rose wouldn't be a widower. And Stevie Rose wouldn't have lost her mother, just at the point in her life—much as Stevie would loathe hearing it—that she needed her most.

And then there was Lorena. The case had broken them.

There was nothing left for Waldo but to go home. He'd find a hotel for the night, set out in the morning for his cabin on the mountain. All the Things he'd brought down from Idyllwild were already in his backpack; he'd packed them before he left Lorena's house this morning. On some level he'd already known.

The sun was starting to drop and Waldo was getting tired. The pain in his hand was growing unbearable. He saw a copse that reminded him, in a very small way, of his woods, and decided it would be a good place to pop a Percocet and recharge before they closed the park. He lowered his bike to the grass and shrugged off his backpack. He texted Lorena, saying that he wouldn't be home tonight.

He rested his head on the backpack, closed his eyes and tried to let the evening breeze console him. Lorena wasn't answering his text. It occurred to him that she should know Cuppy had arrested Wax on both murders, so he sent her another message.

She didn't answer that one, either.

TWENTY-SEVEN

The buzzing in his pocket jerked him awake and into pitch-blackness. He squinted against the piercing brightness of the phone and began to piece things together through the Percocet fog.

Lorena was calling.

It was two nineteen. He must have slept through the park closing.

She'd been doing something somewhere that kept her from responding to him for half the night.

He swirled that all together and it came out as "Hey."

"Hey," she said. "So, Wax."

He staggered through a muddled recap of his conversation with Cuppy.

She said, "You think he's right?"

"He'll need the lab to come through, but that would seal it, I guess."

"You said Wax the other day."

"I was talking out of my ass. I didn't have it."

They were quiet together. It was a freighted moment for them—likely, they both realized, a conclusive one. He knew he should be processing all the valedictory emotions and finding something worthy to say, but mostly he was afraid of insulting her by falling asleep midconversation. He rapped his lacerated hand a few times with his good one, hoping the fresh throbbing would keep him from drifting off.

She said, "You're going back."

"In the morning, yeah."

"I guess Santa Ana's a good place to leave it. We're square now."

Waldo said, "Yeah," and wished he were lucid enough to know what that meant.

"Well." A deep sigh. "Bye, Waldo."

He sighed himself. "Bye."

She clicked off first.

What *was* that about Santa Ana? He typed it into Google with one woozy, fumbling thumb, then scrolled down the results to the news. A link to a piece from the *Orange County Register* website teased—

SANTA ANA POLICE SAY MAN FOUND BEHIND BUR . . .

—and Waldo tapped that.

SANTA ANA POLICE SAY MAN FOUND BEHIND BURGER KING HAD CONVICTIONS FOR PIMPING, PANDERING

SANTA ANA—The man whose body was found behind a Burger King on North Harbor Boulevard previously served two and a half years at the Richard J. Donovan Correctional Facility for pimping and pandering, according to Santa Ana Police Department Cmdr. Reuben Singleton.

Police were called Tuesday night at 10:20 when Aron Naranjo, whom police said went by the name of "Tesoro," was found by a group of juveniles behind a dumpster on the 800 block of North Harbor Boulevard with apparent slash wounds to the neck . . .

Good God, that's where she'd been tonight. *We're square now.* Suddenly he wasn't groggy anymore.

Was it even possible? Could she have done this? Sure, she'd once mutilated a corpse, she'd once tased a man into a heart attack, and he had no doubt she could kill in self-defense if she needed to.

But this was something different—this was, Waldo had saved her life when she was deep in it with Don Q, and now, to punctuate their long affair, she was reciprocating, cutting the throat of the man who'd mutilated him. A man who was also, by the way, threatening her and destroying the lives of scores of girls.

Of course she could have done it. That's why she called: not about Wax, but to make sure Waldo knew. *We're square now.*

Fucking Lorena.

It was almost three. At this point he might as well spend the rest of the night in the park. He remolded the backpack under his head until it was comfortable.

Still, there was a wrong note somewhere. Something about Cuppy and Wax, something he couldn't put his finger on, something just . . . *off.* Maybe it felt that way because someone else had cracked the case instead of him, maybe because the someone else was Cuppy, maybe because the case wasn't really quite *solved,* not really, with no clear motives, just a bad cop getting lucky on a ballistics match.

Or maybe there wasn't even a wrong note.

Maybe it *was* just the Percocet, and Lorena.

Fucking Lorena.

Five hours later he awoke in the sunshine, clearheaded. There was no activity yet in the park, which probably didn't open until eight or nine.

His phone showed three texts from Cuppy that somehow hadn't roused him. The first read: Got a match. The second read: Golden. The third read: Up Tanaka's ass.

The Tesoro murder came rushing back; for a moment he wondered if it had been just a druggie dream. No, it was real. He and Lorena had been dragged over the line into Orange County, it had wreaked havoc on them, and in the end they'd returned the favor.

Wait: dragged down to Orange County—

That was it, the wrong note from last night, even more dissonant this morning, out of tune with the triumphant chord Cuppy was playing.

It was the way O.C. had begun for them in the first place, the setup that had Lorena burning Roy Wax. Wax's explanation about the Korean factory and the business rival had always sounded like bullshit. Somebody had it in for him, and it had to have something to do with the rest of it. It was all too fluky otherwise.

Could that same enemy who sicced Lorena on Wax have also set him up for a double homicide?

Before Waldo could go back to his woods, he had to spend a morning trying to scratch that itch. But how?

Had Wax not intimidated Lorena and Waldo out of decoding the original peep-show scam, they'd have started by looking for Wax's Disneyland blonde. Waldo opened Lorena's surveillance photo collection and took another look. He still had a faint feeling he knew her. *Generic soap opera looks* rang again in his head but he didn't know why. For all the junk TV he watched, soaps had never tempted him.

If she was an actress, though, there had to be a way to find her. Maybe it was the déjà vu of another breakup with Lorena, but it came to him right away whom he could ask.

Jana Stiltner's casting office was still on Cahuenga, convenient to five studios and a little too convenient to the Sheraton Universal, where she and Waldo used to hook up during the quasi-managed mayhem of his early relationship with Lorena.

Three actors were waiting in her outer office, all tweedy, bespectacled professor types, and they eyed Waldo, fresh but perplexing competition. The boyish male assistant behind a desk pushed a sign-in sheet toward him. Waldo said he wasn't here to audition but was hoping to talk to Jana. The assistant, well trained, offered a shutdown smile and told him to leave his picture and résumé and he'd make sure that Ms. Stiltner got them.

"Tell her it's Charlie Waldo."

The assistant did a tiny double take at the name, said, "Of course, sorry," and scurried to a rear office. He came out half a minute later and said, "Come on back. Can I get you a water?"

Jana had been an actress; she once told Waldo she'd moved out from Illinois after getting every lead in high school and college only to learn that in Hollywood her wholesome midwestern looks played merely, as she put it, "best-friend cute." Back in their Sheraton days those looks played better than that for Waldo. At the time, Jana shared enough about her failing marriage for him to see a symmetry, that she and Waldo were each trying to find in afternoon debauchery a way to anesthetize the wounds of their snarled primary relationships. It was telling that Jana ended the affair with Waldo when she and her husband finally separated, not because she'd found somebody else.

Still, some of those afternoons had been indelible and there had never been a moment of unkindness. She greeted him now with a smile full of warmth and secret memory. "Didn't think I'd be seeing *you* again."

Waldo grinned. "I guess nobody did."

"So I've read. Alastair's a piece of work, huh." She seemed to know the key points of Waldo's recent history, so she caught him up on hers. She told him she'd cast an HBO limited series that won some awards and after that her business had taken off; she was even starting to cross over into producing. She was talking shop, but her eyes were all hotel room.

He said, "I've got a favor to ask."

"I can't even imagine what that might be."

"Take a look at a picture, tell me if you know her?" He showed Jana the hotel photo on his phone, blowing it up with his fingers to give her a better look at the blonde.

"That's Leila Massey, isn't it?"

"You tell me."

"I'm pretty sure that's who that is. Leila Massey."

"Why would I know her?"

"She was kind of hot for a while on *Days of Our Lives.*"

That would click with him thinking soap but wouldn't explain it. "Never watched it."

"She left because she booked one of those Adam Sandler movies and thought she was going to have a different career."

He shook his head; he wouldn't know her from a Sandler movie, either. Maybe he'd come across her in real life, maybe on a case? He couldn't place her. "She still working?"

Jana called up IMDb on her laptop. "Not recently, looks like. She might have left the business." Waldo came around behind Jana and looked over her shoulder, breathing her familiar perfume. He willed himself to focus on Leila Massey's short list of credits, presented in reverse chronology: at the top a handful of pilots and one-shots on cop shows, preceded by the Sandler comedy, the six years on *Days*, and before that a few starter gigs early in the 2000s. The vaguely familiar title at the very bottom, her first job, bumped him. "*Sea Legs*—what's that?"

"Piece of crap, is what it was. Don't quote me. Cop on a cruise ship, for some reason, I think she recurred as the guy's daughter—"

"Wait—Joel Rose."

Jana looked surprised. "Yeah. Pre–*Malibu Malice*."

Waldo closed his eyes, hoping the tumblers would click. There are no coincidences. Then again, actresses, producers, Hollywood, the constant shuffling of careers—everybody had to be just a degree of separation from everyone else, right?

Jana said, apologetic, "I do have a session starting."

"I'm sorry. Couple more quick things." He pointed to a line on Leila Massey's page that read, *Self*. "What's that?" Jana clicked on it. There were only a few credits, just some behind-the-scenes hype for the soap and the one movie . . . plus one season of *Celebrity Apprentice*.

Of course: *that's* how he knew her. She was one of those annual B-minus "celebrities" he'd never heard of, the one he'd pigeonholed at the time as looking like a perfectly generic soap star. He felt now like he'd seen a lot of her—it might even have been one of those deliciously grotesque Gary Busey seasons—but his only specific memory was her excruciating dismissal, in which, after some middle schoolish backstabbing by Christie Brinkley and the guy who used to be Pee-wee Herman, this *Days of Our Lives* blonde was reduced to tears in the faux boardroom by the now leader of the free world.

Waldo said, "I know you have the faculty of Princeton out in the waiting room"—Jana tittered and gave him those Sheraton eyes again—"but any chance you can help me find her?" The actress, a few more clicks revealed, didn't have a current agent. But Jana did know a guy at the Screen Actors Guild who had a thing for her, which, with one phone call, she was able to play into the address where SAG forwarded Leila Massey's residual checks.

Jana had been so accommodating, had taken so much time out of the work she was supposed to be doing, that it was no surprise to Waldo when she asked him, "Are you free tonight? I'd like to buy you dinner."

Lorena had no claim on him anymore, but it still didn't feel right. He said, "Maybe next time I'm in town," and tried to smile with some kind of indefinite promise.

She said, "I don't want to give you the wrong idea: I'm with somebody now. I'm actually engaged. Trying the death-do-us-part thing again, believe it or not."

"Really." He could have sworn she'd been flirting with him since he walked into the office. One more reminder of how long he'd been out of circulation.

"But there's something else I thought we could talk about. You know how I said I'm producing now? I was wondering: does anybody have your rights?"

TWENTY-EIGHT

Leila Massey's five-story building sat north of Hollywood in that no-man's-land that never gets better, west of the tourist scrub, east of the funky cool. The button for 3B read *McKenzie*, not *Massey*, but Waldo tried it anyway.

"*Yes?*"

"I'm looking for Leila Massey."

The woman said, "*She doesn't live here anymore.*" Waldo pressed all the apartment buttons in both rows and a moment later some other tenant's hostile buzz told him he could push open the security door.

The hallways were overdue for a paint job and the *B* next to Leila's brass *3* was just a shadow. Waldo knocked. He heard the scrape of the peephole disk. "Leila Massey?"

She said again, "She doesn't live here anymore."

He said, "I'm a friend of Paula Rose. My name's Charlie Waldo." The woman cracked open the door and looked at him through her security chain. He wasn't sure which of the names did the trick.

"What do you want?"

"I'm a private investigator. I was working for Paula at the time of her murder." He added, "I also know Roy Wax. Right now I think I'm the only one who knows how you're connected to both of them. If you help me, maybe I can keep it that way."

The door closed. Then it opened, without the chain.

It was like stepping into an East Coast autumn, drapery in deep reds and a half dozen candles breathing out a robust, woodsy scent. Leila had aged around her eyes in the way of early alcoholics or pretty girls L.A. had used hard.

Waldo said, "You knew Paula a long time," and that was all it took to get her to spill her whole story. She'd probably been telling it in her head since she read the news.

Back when Leila was a fresh ingenue in town, eighteen but usefully able to play fifteen, she got her first TV role, as a semiregular on *Sea Legs*. There she quickly hit it off with one of the youngest women on the crew, a production assistant named Paula Steinfeldt, who was beginning a glamorous, clandestine romance with Joel Rose, *Sea Legs'* handsome (and married) auteur. Unlike most production friendships, theirs survived beyond the show's cancellation.

Leila's subsequent run as a soap star was a blessing that proved to be an unexpected curse, leaving her less than famous enough to launch a full-on movie career, but—when the roles dried up and she couldn't meet her bills—a little too famous for a real-world job. Even when she tried a relatively anonymous gig like telemarketing, she'd be recognized by coworkers, who assumed she was only slumming toward research for an upcoming role; Leila would quit rather than have to explain her humiliating decline. She went home to Texas, where it was more of the same but worse. Abashed and helpless, she slid into depression and made her way back to Hollywood, where at least she could get through, say, a night at the laundromat, unapproached, mercifully unspecial alongside all the other has-beens and almost-was's.

How much better, Waldo thought, to be born just a bit less beautiful, like Jana Stiltner, and thus to have your dreams crushed in time to do something about it.

He asked Leila what happened to her friendship with Paula Rose during those years.

"We stayed in touch. It was harder for me when things weren't going well." She crossed to the kitchenette and started fussing with a pot of tea.

Waldo waited until her back was turned to him, giving her a touch of privacy before saying, "How much did she pay you to sleep with her brother-in-law?"

Leila stopped what she was doing. "Ten thousand dollars."

"And you had to give Paula the where and when?"

She turned and looked at him. "She made it really clear that it wasn't for blackmail. Paula said her brother-in-law was a terrible guy, that he knocked her sister around; she was afraid he'd end up killing her someday. But the woman was so cowed, she refused to see that her husband was running around on her, even though everyone around them knew. Paula said the only way she could save her sister was with hard proof.

"She knew I needed money." Leila put something together. "Wait—were you the private eye who was taking pictures of us?"

"No. I was helping Paula with another family matter, and then this all happened."

"I couldn't sleep a wink last night. Would you mind if I . . . ?" She took the lid off her cookie jar and took out a rolled joint. Waldo gestured *go ahead* and she lit up. He realized that the candles were to cover the smell.

Leila leaned against the counter. "That man killed her, didn't he? Roy Wax."

"I don't know."

"He didn't *seem* that bad. Goddamn." She took a deep drag and held it. "*Goddamn.* He killed her because of me." She held out the joint to Waldo.

"No, thanks."

"I should've just done porn." She took another hit. "I *could've*, you know."

"I had no idea," Joel said. "Paula didn't tell me about any of that." Waldo gave him a moment to chew on all his murdered wife had been up to. "It doesn't surprise me."

"Why not?"

Joel lifted and lowered a shoulder.

"Why wouldn't she tell you?"

"Because she knew I'd have stopped her."

They were in the Roses' living room, where he and Lorena had first sat with Paula and Joel. Waldo felt the shadows of both absent women. He said, "The sisters weren't close, though—that was true?"

"Not close at all."

"Would she have gone to those lengths to protect Brenda from Roy?"

"No," said Joel. "No fucking way."

"Then why'd she do it?"

"Because she hated Roy. That's all. I mean, she hated Brenda, too—but she *loathed* Roy."

"But why now? What changed?"

The answer was simple for Joel, obvious: "Trump."

Waldo didn't get it.

"She was wound up about Roy before, but the election put her over the top. She could barely sleep anymore. Paula—neither of us, but Paula especially—couldn't see how someone as competent as Hillary—proven, tested, *secretary of state*—I mean, even aside from the fact that she was a woman, and all that would mean for the country, and girls—here was the most qualified *person* ever to run for—"

"Okay," Waldo interrupted, "but how did this land on *Roy*?"

This, too, was obvious to Joel. "Brenda and Roy were the only people we knew who voted for him."

The Waxes were Them. That's what this was all about for Joel, the way it all cohered—Thanksgiving, and Stevie and Daron, and now Roy shooting Paula. He said, "You could see that's where this was all going to go."

Joel sat back on the sofa. A tic found his eye, his new reality hitting him again, his political rage crumbling back into personal grief.

Waldo said, "There was a call from this house to the Waxes', landline to landline, the day Paula was murdered."

"I don't know anything about that."

"It wasn't you."

"No. Must've been Paula."

"Or Stevie?"

Joel shook his head. "She never touches the landline."

"And you guys really had nothing to do with Roy and Brenda, except on Thanksgiving. Never even talked to them during the year."

Joel sighed and bobbed his head this way and that.

Waldo said, "What? Something you've been leaving out?"

"It's not important."

"It's *all* important. Something with the kids?" Joel shifted in his seat. "The drugs? Something more?" Waldo said again, "It's all important."

Joel surrendered, but covered the pain of the story with a half-bored air, like he was repeating some tired gossip about the neighbors. "The last couple years, Stevie and Paula have been fighting a lot. This one time it got really bad, and Stevie said something horrible, I don't even remember what. Paula confiscated her phone. And Paula—against my advice—decided she was going to look at everything on it, to find out what Stevie was saying about her to her friends. Stupid. Anyway, what she *found* . . . was that Stevie . . . and *Daron* . . . were sending each other pictures of themselves."

"Nude?"

"Daron. Stevie in a swimsuit."

"When was this?"

"Right after New Year's, I think. Stevie hadn't turned fifteen yet, I remember *that*. And Daron was twenty-one. Her *cousin*. Paula lost her shit. I mean, both of us did, but Paula was out of control. She talked to Brenda *then*, that's for sure."

"And Roy? Did you guys confront him, too? And Daron?"

"No, it was just Paula and Brenda—who blamed *Stevie*, which made it worse. And I remember Paula getting off the phone, and that's when she went at *Stevie*—remember, the two of them had been hammer and tongs already, Paula still had Stevie's phone—at which point Stevie announced to Paula that she was pregnant. And that Daron was the father."

Waldo pushed down the uncharitable thought that it sounded like the kind of thing that could have at least given Joel a season opener.

Joel said, "For a few days I was seriously worried about Paula. I thought she was going to have a stroke. I mean it: there wasn't enough Xanax in the world."

"What did you do?"

"I sat Stevie down and said that we had to start by taking her to the doctor. Which got Stevie to cop to the whole story being bullshit. She said Daron was into her but she wasn't going to actually do anything with her cousin; that was 'creepy.' But, shit, I'm sure she was leading him on. I mean, the swimsuit pictures? Probably so that he'd get her drugs. Swear to God, I don't know what that girl's thinking half the time. Anyway, she wasn't having sex with Daron; she wasn't pregnant; she just said all of it to pull Paula's chain."

Maybe even a two-parter, thought Waldo.

"Then there was a whole different incident a couple months ago, when Stevie disappeared for almost a week, and came back saying that she had been at Brenda and Roy's the whole time. That was another nasty phone call—Brenda completely denied it, and Paula never knew who to believe. But Paula just got more and more unhinged when it came to Brenda and Roy, because of all of that." He looked out at the pool, then added, "*And* Trump."

Joel had some questions about how his wife had managed to trick a pro like Lorena. Waldo had already sorted that all out on his bike ride over the hill from Leila Massey's and was able to walk Joel through it.

Paula, calling from a blocked line that Lorena couldn't identify, claimed she was calling from overseas, likely adding protection via voice-altering software, which had gotten fairly effective in the last few years. Lorena put "Brenda" through some vetting questions, but Paula knew plenty of her sister's real-life details and was convincing enough in her fear of Roy and his temper to engage Lorena's sympathy—no accident that Paula had picked a woman PI—and keep her from grilling too hard. An advance from PayPal closed the deal.

Waldo had even unraveled the original coincidence: Paula naturally learned of Lorena, a female PI specializing in marital work, from the Monica Pinch mess, every detail of which had been dominating all conversation around the Stoddard School. Pretending not to have heard of Waldo when he and Lorena first arrived at the Roses' was an oversell of her innocence, but slight enough not to give herself away at the time. Anyhow, Stevie, looking to spook Ouelette, would have heard about Lorena the same way.

Joel said, "So you think Roy figured out that Paula set him up? You think that's why he came up here and killed her?"

Waldo didn't know what to say. It was demoralizing to realize, but there were still some answers he didn't have, answers that would require one more trip south.

Anyway, Joel looked like he'd already lost interest in his own questions. His eye tic started up again. He looked so worn, a man with everything and nothing, and all the worst still ahead: a wife to bury, a home to rebuild, a wild daughter to raise alone. Waldo tried to read the pain on the man's rapidly aging face, wondering which of those grim prospects was at this moment torturing him to distraction.

Joel said, "He sent him money, you know."

"Who?"

"Roy. He sent that pussy-grabbing bigot *money.*" Joel shook his head. "I can't understand it. So much hate."

TWENTY-NINE

During the last leg of the trip to the Waxes' house, the burn between Waldo's middle and index fingers grew so much worse so quickly that he wondered whether the stitches had opened. He needed a painkiller but didn't want to dull himself, not until he finished up his business down here.

He was hoping he wouldn't get blocked at the gate again; the danger in the O.C. was gone with Tesoro and Roy Wax off the board, but there was no guarantee Brenda would talk to him. The gate guard greeted him with a knowing look. "Mr. Wax did it, didn't he?" Waldo turned his palms to the sky. The guard continued, embroidering the old nutty theory with an irresistible new thread: "I mean *Pinch*. I bet Mr. Wax killed the actor's wife, too. He was one of the investors in the network, and all this new business has something to do with that stuff. Am I right?"

Waldo saw an opportunity. "What's your name?"

The guard puffed up at the attention. "Schmitty."

"How'd you figure it out, Schmitty? How'd you crack it?"

They were peer to peer now. "Timing. Inductive reasoning. You were the link—why else would you be here?"

"And you were only a cop three years?" Waldo marveled.

Schmitty shrugged, *what can you do?* "Layoffs."

"What a waste," said Waldo. "Can you keep a secret, Schmitty?"

"Of course."

Which probably meant, *I'll give it an hour before calling talk radio and giving them a fake name.* Waldo said, "You're right. I'm *sure* you're right. But nobody knows it yet—the connection between Pinch and Roy Wax."

"Really?"

"Really. Just us. But I'm one tire track short of the proof I need to take it public." He closed the deal with more conspiratorial gibberish: "We can crack this. If I can pull that track from the Waxes' driveway, we'll have it. I've got my kit in my backpack. I'll be in and out in five minutes."

"This tied in with the black kid, too?"

"I think it is. I'll explain it all later. Can you let me in?" He meant, without calling Brenda Wax and giving her the chance to freeze him out. Schmitty hit a button, lifting the gate, and gave Waldo a sly nod, a partner in crime fighting now. Waldo returned the salute and pedaled to the Waxes'.

As he waited in front of their house his hand began to throb so badly that he broke down and reached for the Percocet bottle. He fumbled out a pill one-handed and forced it down without water before Brenda opened the door.

She noticed the bandages right away. "What happened?"

"Your husband didn't want me in the neighborhood."

"He did that, too? I'm so, so sorry. Please, come in. Can I get you anything?" He asked for the water he could have used a minute ago.

In the same living room he sat on the blue-and-white rattan sofa, his back to the French doors and the docks. Nothing in the house had been changed, but the excision of its overbearing, abusive master had given it a new lightness. Brenda said, "I'm just starting to learn how many bad things Roy was up to. We didn't have the kind of marriage where he told me much about his business." Still birdlike but now freed from her cage, she couldn't sit still; she fluttered about the room making this adjustment and that, leveling a picture, resituating a knickknack. "I'm so, so sorry for all you've been through." She corrected: "What *Roy put* you through."

"I appreciate that, Mrs. Wax, but there are a couple of bits I can't quite answer for Joel—"

"Poor Joel," she sighed.

"—questions about choices Paula made. I was hoping you might be able to help me make sense of them."

"If I can."

"I'm wondering two things, really: why Paula called Roy at home in the middle of the day—there are phone records of that—and why she happened to tell him she'd bought the dog. He needed to know about that before he went up there."

"As a matter of fact, I can answer those. Paula wasn't calling for Roy; she called *me.*"

"Why?"

"To scold me about Daron bringing Stevie down here. She started going on about all the drama their family had been through lately, and she mentioned the dog and what happened with you."

"And you told Roy?"

"I was pretty shaken up when we got off the phone, so I called him. Believe me, I've been feeling guilty about it. She was still my sister." She plucked a tissue from a discreetly hidden cozy and dabbed at her eyes. "Roy always had a violent side. I just never thought he'd act out, outside the immediate family."

Waldo said, "Actually, it's the other murder that has me confused. The schoolteacher, Mr. Ouelette."

"The detective said Roy and the teacher were involved with some kind of drug business. I didn't know that about Roy, either."

"I'm not sure I'm buying that. The teacher never had any kind of record. According to Stevie, he never even drank. And they didn't find anything else in his apartment—only one tiny packet of an expensive designer drug. I'm thinking the person who killed him planted it there."

"Roy."

"I do believe it was someone from Orange County. This drug's very expensive. It's getting popular down here, but it hasn't taken hold yet in L.A."

"Roy," she said again, like that cinched it.

"Maybe. Roy does have the connections for it. But he doesn't *need* the drug business, and with so much to lose, he seems like someone who'd be smart enough to steer clear of it. To go to those people and ask them to give him some drug to plant on Ouelette, and such an *unusual* drug . . ." He was being open about his doubts, hoping to elicit from her some tidbit about their white-shoe world that would help him make sense of the jumble. But the morsel she offered was the last he would have expected.

"I know where he got the drugs," she told him. "They're mine."

The stress and the Percocet and the aqueous shimmer through the French doors behind him suddenly conspired to give the room an unreal quality. He regretted surrendering to the pain earlier. He scrunched up his eyes.

She took it as a cue to elaborate. "I have an abusive husband.

I've been on antidepressants for years and I drink too much. At some point even all that wasn't enough."

"And Roy knew about it?"

"I didn't think so. But he must have found them in the bathroom; he was probably rooting around to pilfer an Ambien from me. Anyhow, my . . . little stash? It went missing sometime last week. I've been afraid to confront him." She picked up a photo of Roy and teenage Daron from the mantel, wiped some dust with her sleeve and put it back. "I'm sure it was Roy, Mr. Waldo. If you'd like, I'd be willing to share this information with the authorities, and I'm willing to accept my own consequences, possession charges or what have you."

Waldo threw her an easy curve. "The drug, seventy-eight—it's so rare. How did you even get it?"

"A girlfriend. Like you said, seventy-eight's catching on down here. Our kind of people are the ones who can afford it."

Seventy-eight, seventy-nine—so it wasn't hers. But why would she lie so desperately? She had no need for Roy to fall for *both* murders, when either one would put him away.

Unless.

Unless she needed Roy to fall instead of the *real* murderer, whom she was trying to protect.

Of course.

Daron wasn't just "into" his underage cousin; he was hooked on her. That apartment, that overpriced pony stall—it didn't look like a place that was seeing a cavalcade of girls coming through. And Stevie would have used Ouelette to taunt him, the same way she flirted with Amador. Only it worked too well, and Daron came up to the Valley and killed Ouelette, then picked Stevie up and brought her down to O.C. She didn't even know the teacher was dead until she was back up at Clara Lambert's; when she heard, she put together the timing, suspected Daron and worried about her own involvement, and went underground.

The *amount* of seventy-nine sealed it. You don't get to be Roy Wax–rich by leaving thirty thousand dollars lying around when you know five or ten will do. And a Marwin Amador sure wouldn't leave that kind of package lying around, either; any hired gun would have siphoned off most of it. No, it had to be someone who had no idea what the drug was worth . . . or someone who had no idea what *money* was worth.

Waldo was so muddled that he couldn't tell when he'd started thinking aloud, but he heard himself muttering, "Someone who never had to pull himself up by his bootstraps."

He saw Brenda's nostrils flare, then heard a *whoosh* behind him and turned to see what it was.

A pair of Brendas were in the room with him now, one above the other. Looking stricken, they both spoke, albeit with a single voice. "I'm so, so sorry."

"You say that a lot," Waldo managed to croak.

His brain wouldn't stop screaming. He was on the sofa, on his side, his hands pinned by what felt like duct tape. He could feel blood trickling past his eye. He focused on the leg of a coffee table and willed his vision back into singleness. There was a hooked fireplace poker nearby on the carpet and presumably a matching dent in his forehead. No doubt he was concussed.

Daron entered the room from behind his mother and walked over to Waldo, a fluffy bedroom pillow in his hands.

Brenda said to him, "Wait."

"Dad's a piece of shit. We know he killed Aunt Paula. Why not let him take the hit for the other one too?"

Brenda looked at Waldo, hesitating.

"Come on," said Daron. "You *said* we could."

"I know I did, but . . ."

Waldo said, "But now you'd have another body to have to explain."

"Not a problem," said Daron, turning to his mother to finish the sale. "Nobody has to find him. I'll take him out in the boat tonight, dump him in the ocean."

Waldo said, "I'll be missing. The gate guard knows I came to see your mother. You going to kill him, too?"

Daron shook his head, dismissing the concern. "Come on—nobody'll believe that my mother is a murderer." He knelt beside Waldo, ready to suffocate him.

Waldo said, "They should: she killed your aunt Paula."

Daron froze.

Waldo said, "You know what Stevie said to me the last time I was with her?" Daron lowered the pillow at the mention of his cousin-lover and listened. "That everybody lies to her, that they tell her they won't repeat things but they do, and end up getting killed. I couldn't get her to explain what she was saying—she was in one of her Stevie moods—but I figured she meant she told Paula about something she knew Roy was into down here, and Paula repeated it to Roy."

Daron said, "So?"

"But that wasn't it. The thing Stevie told her mother was that you killed Victor Ouelette, and Paula called and told *you* that"—here he looked at Brenda—"and threatened to go to the police. So you borrowed the same gun from Roy's closet, drove up to L.A., picked up some antifreeze for the dog on the way and shot your sister. To protect your son. Just like when you lied to me about the drugs now—to protect Daron. For that matter, just like when Roy had me maimed by a pimp to scare me out of O.C.—to protect Daron.

"Of course, Stevie could still claim Daron did it. But you knew no one would believe her. Hell, even Stevie's own father thought she killed Paula. She'd never have anyone take her side again."

Daron said, "My mother couldn't murder anybody. Look at her."

Brenda sat stock-still.

Waldo said to Daron, "Your aunt Paula was killed by two shots at close range, no struggle, with a third bullet in the wall. That was strange, too. How does that happen? Probably somebody who wasn't used to firing a gun."

"My father didn't have a lot of experience, either."

"If Roy was up in L.A. killing Paula at the same time I was kidnapped by the pimp, why didn't he just have the pimp kill me too? Wouldn't make sense."

Daron shifted toward his mother, looking for an explanation, then seemed to decide he didn't want it. He said, "That's enough," and turned back to Waldo.

Waldo tried to suck in all the air he could before the pillow came down and cut it off. He thrashed to make it harder for Daron but then felt Daron's weight pressing on his midsection; the kid must have climbed atop him, crushing his arms, now squeezed underneath him, the bite wound suddenly more agonizing than his hand but it didn't matter anymore, his entire body was rebelling at the lack of oxygen and he was helpless and he started to panic but there were no more moves left, his heart quickened and the pressure tore at his lungs and he tried to let go a little air to relieve it but he couldn't even do that and then his head started feeling lighter and this was going to be the end and it was strange because it wasn't all that bad, he could just go to sleep, that would make it all go away, even the agony of his hand and his arm, just let the sleep come, and he started to let go and as he did he heard, from miles and miles and miles away . . .

A banging.

Daron let up the pressure and like a miracle the bruising air was released and Daron must have climbed off and the pillow was still over Waldo's face but loose enough that he could draw a new breath. It seared his lungs and drove a fresh spike through his head. He focused on shallowing his intake and staying motionless. He could see nothing. The drugs and the trauma had put a double whammy on him and he could feel himself drifting off again.

Someone said, "Have you seen Charlie Waldo?"

Brenda said, "No."

"He came down this way." Schmitty. "He told me he'd only be a few minutes but he never came back." He was probably at the French doors; on the sofa Waldo would be hidden from him.

"Are you sure?" said Daron, his voice receding as his footsteps carried him to the door. He'd be counting on Waldo being dead, or close to it; all he and his mother had to do was keep Schmitty outside and shake him off.

Waldo found just enough strength to roll off the sofa. At the thud, Schmitty stepped past Brenda and into the room; from his spot on the floor Waldo could see him now. Schmitty asked him, "What's going on?"

Waldo pulled a breath and it tore his chest so badly that he knew he only had three or four words in him. He said to Schmitty, "Daron killed Monica Pinch."

Schmitty said, "I knew it!" and pulled a revolver Waldo hadn't even realized he carried.

THIRTY

When the teacher called on Dulci Apodaca to come up and take her turn introducing her friend, Waldo did not immediately recognize it as his moment, too. He had been thinking of her, foolishly, as Dulci Q. Together they ran through the questions and answers they'd rehearsed. The teacher led the class and parents in applause and Dulci hugged Waldo around the waist.

At the little outdoor celebration that followed, Don Q's graceful wife, Zuli, appeared to have already found a rhythm with the other second-grade moms, but Q himself stood off to the side looking uncomfortable. He seemed glad to have Waldo to talk to. "Nobody told me private school meant *I* gotta come here every damn week. We been at this bitch a month, and this the fourth time I been here. Track and Field Day, Arts and Crafts Day . . . and every time you gotta stand around after, eatin' *cupcakes* with these people. Don't these muthafuckers *work?*" He looked over at the dozens of his fellow parents, incredulous. Waldo wondered what kind of professional obligations Don Q himself was forgoing this morning. "Last week I had to sit two hours on a damn bleacher, all the second grade did was sing one goddamn song about pollution. Plus, truth be told, I definitely got a problem with these cupcakes." He took a bite out of his second.

Waldo said, "You got a good kid there."

"She likes *you*, for some damn reason." Don Q wiped some icing from his mouth with a napkin. "I may hit you up again, she wants you for anything else. 'Cause you still owe me."

"For what?"

"O.C., man." Waldo could have answered that the information Q had provided was, in the end, only a small element of solving the case, but he let it go.

Besides, he could see the pleasure the dealer was taking in the moment, watching his daughter on the playground, deep in a giggle-inducing handclap game with a redheaded classmate. It was hard to reconcile this loving daddy with the vicious criminal who'd only months ago introduced himself to Waldo by dumping a murder victim in front of his cabin and then having his goon beat Waldo senseless.

But maybe it wasn't all that complicated. Dulci was how Don Q made sense of his fucked-up life, in the same way Waldo found his rules and his Hundred Things to make sense of his own. So it didn't matter that Q felt out of place here: his daughter belonged, and for all the complaining, he'd show up for her every time he was asked.

On his way out, Waldo followed the voices of older boys and girls and came upon the Stoddard high school and what looked like the beginning of lunch break. He scanned the outdoor tables and spotted Koy Lem and Dionne Shapiro but not Stevie. Then she slipped her arm through Waldo's and squeezed his biceps. "Looking for me?"

"I was—but I didn't think I'd find you."

"I know. My dad wanted me to stay home at least a week, but it's, like, *so* depressing there."

"How about here? Is it awkward?"

"Why?"

"Well . . . Mr. Ouelette . . . ?"

"God. That was, like, so long ago." It had been a week and a half.

His last time with her, she'd said that the secret she'd asked him to keep about Conor was a test that he'd failed. But with Stevie, everything was a test: every declaration you could only pass by disbelieving, every seduction you could only pass by resisting. Hanging on his arm, the show of affection—what sort of test was this? But as they stood there together, watching life carry on, tragedy and chaos giving way to the everyday high school business of flirting and cruelty, awkwardness and heartbreak, it occurred to Waldo that he wasn't even the one being tested right now, that he was only a prop in a new bit of Stevie stagecraft designed for some poor teenage boy trying to act like he wasn't watching them, tearing himself apart while he tried to figure out how he was supposed to react to his new flame or almost-flame pressing her face into the shoulder of some older man.

Stevie said, "Can I ask you something, Waldo? What's it like when you get old?" He'd never thought about that word applying but maybe it was time to start. She said, "I hope I never have to be your age."

"No?"

"All the adults I've ever met are, like, total psychos. Every single one."

Stevie Rose let go of his arm and headed toward a crowded table. Dionne Shapiro squeezed against the girl next to her to open up a space for her bestie. All sorts of things happened, like, so long ago.

And just like that, Waldo found himself untethered from L.A.

Unriddling another case, doing what he did best, was deeply satisfying, but the solitude of his life in the woods was calling to him in a way it hadn't in weeks. He crossed the campus toward his bike already dreaming of its heavenly, ataractic features: his chickens, his vegetable garden, his long walks and his pond and his floating lounge chair. Dreaming of the quiet. The beautiful, never-ending quiet.

This wasn't like the end of the Pinch case, which had left him feeling larger, open, full of promise. This one had the opposite effect: it closed him down, reminded him how dark and dysfunctional society was, family by family, county by county. Better to escape it again, and the sooner the better.

There was only one remaining obligation before he was fully free of the world: he needed to let Lorena know how everything had shaken out. He'd do that carefully, without engaging. He didn't have the stomach for any more tension. He'd wait until tonight, when he was safely back in Idyllwild, and even then he'd do it in writing.

But there was so much to tell. The things he'd figured out about Brenda and Daron Wax alone would be heavy freight for an email, to say nothing of the actual confrontation with Brenda and the fireplace poker and the pillow. Plus she'd want to know about Cuppy's inventively expletive-laden reaction upon learning that he'd managed to arrest the only Wax who hadn't murdered any-one. She'd want to know about Brenda's spectacularly nervy re-quest that Waldo make an introduction to Fontella Davis, the "horrible woman," as Brenda put it, "who's always on television getting some even more horrible person acquitted"—a request Waldo granted in exchange for Brenda's voluntary surrender, along with Daron, to the Orange County Sheriff's Department. And she'd definitely want to know about Waldo's priceless phone conversation with Fontella Davis on the Waxes' behalf, in which Davis twisted herself in knots trying to rationalize the highly lu-crative representation of the murderer of one of her other clients.

Hell, he decided as he reached his bike, he'd just do it on the phone and do it now, get the conversation out of the way and put Los Angeles completely behind him before he even boarded the Greyhound to Banning.

But as soon as he heard Lorena's voice, he found himself say-ing, "You free for lunch?"

Her trip was much shorter—not to mention, by car—yet she still managed to arrive twenty minutes late. It was going to put time pressure on their lunch; he only had two hours before the last bus. Even then he spied her taking a leisurely stroll in the opposite direction, studying a display case full of English toffee, or pre-tending to. When she finally looked over her shoulder, she knew exactly where Waldo was standing, but now the playfulness and flirtation didn't delight or beguile him. Now he was looking at a woman who'd killed a man in cold blood, thinking about her sweet tooth.

She sauntered over. They didn't touch. She said, "Did you eat?"

"I was waiting for you."

"Go get your rabbit food. I'll meet you near the oyster bar."

Waldo had suggested the Farmers Market because he'd been having such success here finding fresh ingredients to bring home to her place, not only first-rate produce but fish and poultry that met even his exacting standards of low-footprint transportation. Now he shopped for his dessert first, perusing the many fruit selections at two different stands before settling on a magnificent Fuji apple. Then he headed for the fine-looking salad bar, which he had often eyed but never had call to patronize, as he and Lorena had never stayed on premises for a meal.

The kiosk, though, hit him with an unanticipated challenge: the only way to assemble a salad, it turned out, was in a hard foam container. What were these people thinking? He asked why they didn't provide the option of reusable plates, but neither the employees nor the customers waiting behind him had patience for that discussion, let alone one about biodegradability or the sins of the Dow Chemical Company. Worse, he'd taken so much time choosing his apple that Lorena would have already found a table where she'd be waiting for him with her own lunch, and he still had a bus to make. Waldo gave up on the salad. The Fuji that started as dessert had become his entire meal.

He found her where she said she'd be, sitting behind a loaded chili cheeseburger the size of her head, doing her best to drown a huge plate of fries in ketchup. "Where's your lunch?"

"Wasn't hungry."

"Uh-huh," she said, in a way that made clear she knew better. She edged her fries toward him rhetorically.

You'd think she'd want to talk about what she'd done—share misgivings, ask how he felt about it, *something*—but there was none of that. She started in on her burger, wholly untroubled. More at this moment than ever, she was a mystery to him.

The big question came floating back, the question of whether one could live a damage-free life while trying to sustain a relationship. He still had no answer. It was harder with a partner, for sure, but it might be that with a different woman it wouldn't be *this* much harder. Maybe, though, if the two of them had it all to do over again, if they hadn't gotten pulled under by Stevie and everything else, if Tesoro had never happened, maybe he could have found a way to let go, at least a little—not of his principles, but of his perpetual disappointment with Lorena for not even valuing them. Maybe he could have tried harder to make peace with her eating what she ate, wearing what she wore, driving what she drove. Maybe he could have convinced himself that no one can know what anyone else really needs, just like no one can really know anyone else's pain.

Waldo walked her through the denouement of the case and the aftermath with Big Jim Cuppy and Fontella Davis. Lorena devoured the burger while she listened, following each heedless chomp with a careful napkin across her mouth, rapacious with one hand and dainty with the other in fetching combination. Even the way she ate was Lorena and only Lorena. For all of their frustration with each other, for all of the madness of these weeks and the darkness of what she'd done in the end, he'd miss her.

She put down her burger and looked at him. "Are we going to talk about it, or are we just going to go on with our lives and pretend it didn't happen?"

He sighed and bobbed his head, relieved that she'd finally brought it up.

She said, "I believe a thank-you is in order."

He was surprised she'd frame it like that, but in a twisted way he could see where that would be what she was expecting. "Yeah," he said, "I guess it is."

Lorena held his eye while she wiped her fingers one by one, studying him for something—what? Sufficient gratitude? Finally she said, "So, thank you."

"For what?" He was befuddled; he assumed she'd been talking about killing Tesoro.

She lowered her voice and said, "For killing Tesoro."

He leaned back, even more befuddled, and said, "Wait—I thought *you* did it."

She cackled. "*Me?* Why *me?*"

"Because of that thing you said about us being square, after Santa Ana. I figured you meant this," meaning his bandaged hand. "I fixed your problem with Don Q, and you did Tesoro because he did this to me, and we were square."

"That's crazy. He cut you; he didn't kill you."

He said, "So . . . why were you thanking *me?* You thought *I* did it?" She nodded. "How would that make us square?"

"Because I saved you from the dog. So you saved me from Tesoro. Square."

"Oh. *Oh.*" The notion was so unnerving that he ate one of her greasy fries without realizing it until it landed in his stomach like an unexploded grenade.

She said, "Have as many as you want."

He gently pushed the plate away.

"So, what," she said, "it wasn't you?"

But it was a hell of a coincidence and Waldo didn't believe in those.

Then, in a flash, he understood the thing Don Q had told him over cupcakes.

What was it Q had said in Laguna when he first told him

about Tesoro? That somebody should one-eight-seven him, if they had half a reason. The chance Tesoro might make Waldo miss Dulci's show-and-tell—could something that small qualify? Then again, it could be that when your life is all about a little girl, you see everything about a Tesoro differently. Could be you only need a quarter of a reason, or even less.

He'd spell all that out for Lorena later. Right now she was saying, "I do have to give you props for Stevie. It sucks about her mom, but she'd have been up shit creek if you hadn't been in her corner."

"Thanks for that."

She offered her fries again. He demurred and bit into his apple.

They ate together without talking. He thought about all the fucked-up relationships they'd been around for the last two weeks, and the fucked-up women. He tried to imagine what it would be like to be with anyone like any of them, under any circumstance—a Paula, a Brenda, even a grown-up Stevie—and tried to imagine how it would be for *them*, trying to be with *him*. Every variant was unthinkable, really. Maybe he wasn't made to be with anyone, not anymore. Well, at least he had the right cabin for it.

Lorena polished off the last of the burger. She took a fistful of fresh napkins—Lord Almighty, the woman wasted a shitload of them—and gave every inch of her face a good wipe. When she took the napkins away, she was chuckling.

Waldo said, "What?"

"I thought you killed a man for me, and you thought I killed him for you."

He chuckled, too. "Yeah."

She rested her chin on a palm. "Kinda romantic, Waldo, if you think about it."

They held each other's gaze for a long, sweet time.

She twinkled and said, "Too bad the sex wasn't any good."

Even when she was looking at the damn toffees she'd known exactly where this was going to end up. Fucking Lorena.

His woods could wait.

ACKNOWLEDGMENTS

Thanks once again to Glenn Gers, Susan Dickes and Tony Quinn for the friendship, encouragement and incisive reads.

And to Jay Mandel, Jared Levine, Ailleen Gorospe and David McIlvain for minding the store.

Thanks always to Andrew Lazar, Christina Lurie and Steve Shainberg for their initial contributions and support.

When I was writing the *Last Looks* acknowledgments, I'd met almost no one at Dutton or Penguin Random House, but in the year since, I've been perpetually delighted by a team whose talent, dedication and thoughtfulness is unsurpassed in my working life. So thank you, Maria Whelan, Kayleigh George, Marya Pasciuto, John Parsley, Karen Dziekonski, Nicole Morano, Tony Hudz and Kaitlin Kall.

And especially Jess Renheim, who deserves her own paragraph.

I want to thank Harlan Coben, William Kent Krueger, Meg Gardiner, Gregg Hurwitz and Nick Petrie for standing up for my first novel; it won't be forgotten. Also the readers who've taken the time to share their enthusiasm for *Last Looks* on social media.

A special thank-you to my great friend John Michael Higgins, who's blessed my work with his own so many times over so many years, for this latest and most unexpected collaboration.

Another shout-out to everybody at Peet's.

If you're still reading this and haven't already checked out the Story of Stuff Project, please do.

The Waldo books would not exist without everything I've learned and keep learning from Amanda, Milo and Gary Gould.

My deepest gratitude, always, is for Terri Gould, for her patience and her kindness and her faith, and for, as a bonus, being the toughest and finest reader any writer could want.

ABOUT THE AUTHOR

Howard Michael Gould began his career on Madison Avenue before moving to Los Angeles, where he has worked as a screenwriter and playwright as well as an executive producer and head writer of a number of network television series. *Below the Line* is his second novel, following the introduction of detective Charlie Waldo in *Last Looks*.